THE BUTCH AND THE BEAUTIFUL

QUEERS OF LA VISTA

KRIS RIPPER

RIPTIDE
PUBLISHING

CHAPTER 1

I wasn't hiding behind the topiary. People in suits this expensive don't *hide*.

I was trying to dodge Liz's brother for the third time. He hadn't caught me yet, but he eventually would, and I wanted to put that moment off as long as possible on this, the happiest day of Liz's life. Or whatever.

It probably would be the happiest day of her life. Liz had a sentimental streak the size of the Pacific. And she and Marla were deeply in love. Since Marla was only a little bit crazy, I was genuinely pleased for them, but that didn't mean I wanted to be buddy-buddy with my co–best man all afternoon. He was going to ask me to fix everything he'd screwed up, while eyeing my breasts—just wait for it.

If your ex ever shows up on your doorstep one brisk autumn evening, plies you with wine, and says, "We're getting married, you're the best man, and we're doing everything ourselves," run like hell. Obviously. Do not, whatever else you do, slosh more wine into your glasses and say something totally absurd like, "That is going to be *amazing*. How can I help?"

My co–best man was actually supposed to be helping, at the moment. Oh god. What if he *had* screwed something up? I had visions of Bobby surrounded by torn tissue paper and massacred crafts. Fucking lesbian weddings. I had no idea why people were so into DIY. I'd hated arts and crafts in school, and adulthood made everything worse.

"Jaq?" he called, edging into view. "I know you're hiding!"

Liz and I had dated off and on for five years. I should probably feel at least a little bit guilty about leaving wee Bobby in the lurch.

I was on the verge of coming out of my, uh, lingering place, when a woman I'd never seen before walked up to him. In a stunning, intense, ocean-depths-blue dress that draped off her curves and flowed around her.

"You're Bobby, right? Liz said I should find you. I'm Hannah."

That was the *other* ex? I'd heard a lot about Marla's ex, who was serving as maid of honor, but apparently everyone forgot to mention she was gorgeous. I ducked more completely out of sight and caught my breath. Then, utilizing skills learned over the course of watching many James Bond movies, I edged around the sculpted bush to see better. Did Hannah have a sculpted bush? I told my brain to take a break. By all accounts, Hannah was batshit, histrionic, and in the middle of a nasty divorce. She probably *did* have a sculpted bush, though. She was from LA. I think it was go sculpted or wax off down there, no exceptions.

Bobby, clearly unsettled in the face of a hot woman, stumbled over his words. "Um, I'm not actually in charge—the person you should talk to is Jaq—"

"Any idea where I can find her? Unless—if you don't need help, I can just head back to my room."

I couldn't let that happen, now, could I? All hands on deck.

I strolled out into the open, you know, like you do when you have in no way been hiding from your former almost-brother-in-law.

"Oh, hi, Bobby." My voice, so very casual. I turned to the perfect stranger, whose name I didn't know since I hadn't been eavesdropping, and held out my hand. "Hi. I'm Jaq."

"Hannah." Handshake: firm. Palms: dry. Nails: short, squared-off, French manicure.

Batshit, histrionic, nasty divorce. Do not assess.

"Good to finally meet you," I said.

"Jaq!" Bobby shifted restlessly from foot to foot. "I've been looking for you—"

"Sorry, Bobby. Took a walk. What's up?" I gave Hannah a pointed last look before turning to Bobby.

"It's the paper-bag things! There aren't enough of them to reach all the way to the altar thing."

"There're two hundred of them. I mean, it's not that far."

Even at twenty-five he still looked like a sixteen-year-old wearing a suit too big for him. "We tried!"

Who was "we"? Cousins? Nieces and nephews?

"I'll be over in a few minutes," I told him, hoping he'd take the hint and skedaddle.

"Fine, but it's almost four—"

Screw hints. I lightly shoved him. "Go on, baby brother. I'll take care of it."

He sighed. "Why didn't they hire someone to do all this?"

"Hey, you're preaching to the choir." Another shove.

"Yeah, okay. Fine." He turned away, then looked back. "That suit looks really good on you, Jaq."

The eye-flick downward was only a second long. I shoved him a third time. Harder.

"Get to work."

He grunted and took off.

"I thought he was Liz's brother," Hannah said.

"Well, they *are* both Asian." I paused to see if she could take the ribbing.

"I literally just thought that. Then I was like, shit, he could have been adopted or something. Or you could have. So should I shut my big mouth, or—"

I have a few ideas for things you could be doing with your mouth. "He's totally Liz's brother. I'm just her ex."

"And I'm Marla's ex." Hannah offered a charming half smirk. "You know this means we have to have sex, right?"

Damn. And yes. But damn.

"Did I shock you? Sorry. I really should stop talking altogether. You'll tell everyone I'm mute, right? Unless that's totally ableist, which it probably is."

"I didn't say I objected to sex." Okay, obviously I *should*, but come on. Like, look at her. "Before we get there, though, we have to survive the wedding, and at the rate we're going, I'm gonna have them recite their vows sitting in the car so they can drive away real fast. And that's if I can find their car keys, and Bobby's the last person who saw those."

"That bad, huh?"

"Shambles might be an improvement." I gestured to her dress. "Do you want to help, or—"

"Or I'll sit in my room rewriting my entire life. Lead me to the work." The smirk reappeared. "I'm glad he's not your brother. Or that look he shot at you would have been wildly inappropriate."

"What can I say? We met when he was a teenager. I think I ruined him for femme girls."

Her laugh was higher pitched than her voice and didn't seem to fit anything else about her. She had the exhausted eyes of a wary fortysomething and the laugh of a teenager. She was probably in her midthirties, like me, and Liz, and Marla. It was kind of a miracle we hadn't met before, but she and Marla had hooked up in college—or so I'd heard from Liz, who'd repeated *histrionic* three times during our conversation, as if I'd never been known to go in for a drama queen before.

We took the direct route back to the "venue," which, let's be very clear, was a hillside. A hillside. With a flat area where the couple stood to get married, and another flat area where chairs were set out for everyone else. Folding chairs. Is it really a "venue" when you can set it up and take it down in less than an hour?

I tried not to pay too much attention to the flashes of leg I was getting from Hannah as she walked beside me. Cheers to comfortable dresses that allowed for urgent wedding-catastrophe-related walks up hillsides.

"I gotta get to the gym," she muttered. "And stop smoking. God."

Damn it. Smokers. I hated kissing smokers.

"I quit, you know. For six years. *Six years.*" She looked over, so I nodded, because it seemed like she needed some kind of validation about having quit—for six years. "I'm quitting again," Hannah continued, as if I'd challenged her. "The second this divorce is final, I'm quitting again."

"How long were you married?"

"Seven years." She smiled wryly. "She's the one who talked me into quitting in the first place, and believe me, I'm aware how idiotic it is that some part of my brain thinks I'm actually getting back at her by smoking again. It's just . . . so fucking hard to stop."

"I've had some girlfriends like that. Bad for me and hard to quit."

"Exactly."

We finally reached the folding chairs, and it became clear that either we didn't have all the paper bags for the luminarias, or we'd been shorted. And I didn't think for a second we'd been shorted.

"Oh damn."

Bobby looked up from where he was trying to adjust the spacing of the bags he had. "See?"

Hannah shook her head. "What on god's green earth are those?"

"Luminarias," I said. "Each one has rice and a glow stick in the bottom. Some of them have quotes printed on the outside."

"Quotes?"

"A mix of Maya Angelou, the Indigo Girls, and k.d. lang."

Hannah covered her mouth, but a small giggle escaped. "You are *kidding me.*"

I pointed to my face. "Not my joke face."

"They are such fucking lesbians. Really, they should write a handbook."

"Lesbian wedding of the decade. They're also giving away plants."

"They *are not.*"

I nodded solemnly. "If they had more money, maybe they'd be giving away Subarus. I could get behind that. Because who needs a plant in a jar that's probably going to be dead in three days anyway?" I grinned at Bobby's pained look. "Sorry, bud, but you know your sister's the poster child for the enlightened dyke."

"Jaq . . ."

"Fine. I'll behave. Listen, are you sure you unloaded everything from my truck? You're missing a box of luminarias."

"I'm pretty sure. I think. I mean, there was a lot of stuff—"

He meant *Your truck is pretty much trashed, so it's possible I missed something,* but I wanted Hannah to get the idea that he meant wedding stuff, so I interrupted. "I'll go check it out. How bad is the reception area right now?"

"Well. I kind of have the cousins on it."

"Kind of?"

"They weren't all that focused when I last checked on them."

"Bobby, you have to—" But he wouldn't. Liz got all the *do as I say* in that family. I turned to Hannah. "So, you feel like whipping a bunch of teenagers into shape?"

She laughed. "That'll keep me from drowning my sorrows in nicotine."

"Unless it makes you smoke more. Anyway, follow Bobby. The hotel provided tablecloths, but we need to get the table with the plants set up, as well as a table for gifts, the receiving table with the book they want people to sign, and probably a bunch of other stuff I'm forgetting."

"And the wedding starts in two hours," Bobby added.

Hannah glanced around, eyebrows raised. "But where's the coffee? You skipped a step."

I surveyed her dress. Definitely no pockets. And she wasn't carrying a bag. I pulled out my money clip and handed Bobby a ten. "Get the pretty lady who's about to save your ass whatever she wants, and me a large coffee. If there's money left over, get yourself something too."

"Okay, Jaq."

Hannah inclined her head toward mine and murmured, "So obedient."

I shuddered. "That's sick. And thanks for helping. Welcome to the family."

She laughed again. "I hope you make good on that welcome a little more personally later, Jaq."

I would have come up with something really clever to say in response if she hadn't already been walking away. Because you can't call out your clever comeback at the top of your lungs—that'd be weird. Plus, I had a job to do. An important one. Glow-stick luminarias were at stake. The entire wedding hinged on my finding the missing glow-stick luminarias. What if they'd been printed with life-changing quotes by bell hooks, or maybe Maggie Nelson? What if their absence changed the course of history because the exact person who was supposed to see that exact quote at that exact moment . . . didn't?

Or I could stand on the hillside all day rationalizing my lack of clever comeback.

I trudged down the hill, trying to remember the sequence of loading bins into the truck. I might have shifted things out of the way enough for one of them to get trapped under the seats. Possibly.

That dress, though. And Hannah's hair, pulled back in a braid, looked like it'd be wild and untamed if it wasn't quite so controlled. I have kind of a thing for wild and untamed.

Batshit, histrionic, nasty divorce, smoker, I chanted. *Do not feed the animals, Jaq. Keep all arms, legs, and other body parts inside the vehicle at all times.*

CHAPTER 2

The wedding came together. Doesn't that always happen? Every wedding I've ever been a part of has had some moment of preceremony crisis when it seemed like it simply wasn't going to go as planned, and every damn one of them turned out fine. Like there's some kind of slightly sadistic wedding god who gets off on fucking with people but can't bring himself to actually ruin weddings.

I can tell when I've had too much wedding: I start coming up with deities and their tragic backstories. Wedding fever is a little contagious, and you don't have to be interested in having one to catch it.

The found luminarias, once distributed, lined the path to the altar. I set the cousins on breaking every single glow stick. Two hundred. Two *hundred*. Thank goodness Liz and Bobby had a lot of cousins. Hannah had organized the plant table and given me a *look* when I came down to see it. I wasn't exactly positive, but I think the look translated to something like: *Oh my god, lesbians./Who the fuck does this?/Actually, they're pretty cute, shut up.* But don't quote me on that. It was just a look.

We were damn hot together. The photographer couldn't get enough of us, especially after the picture where Hannah squeezed my ass and I jumped. My shirt was a complementary shade of blue to her dress, and we had no problem stepping right up to each other.

"If I'd been thinking more clearly," she said through her smile as the photog snapped away, "I would have gotten two room keys so I could seductively slide one in your back pocket right now."

"I'd've probably thought you were trying to steal my wallet and dropped you with my jujitsu moves."

She laughed. That was gonna be a good picture too.

The ceremony itself was sweet and touching and, um— Okay, I didn't actually listen. But I was there for the rehearsal, and I can confirm it was both sweet and touching. And thankfully not too long because Hannah was barely holding back shivers. You wouldn't think May would be quite this chilly, but the second the sun set, it got *cold*. And yes, you're damn right I offered her my jacket. I'm a gentlewoman. I'm fucking *dashing*.

I wouldn't have put it over a puddle or anything, because it was extravagantly expensive, but sure, I offered the hottie in the blue dress my jacket. And settled it over her shoulders, too.

I tried to tell myself that getting involved with Hannah was a bad idea, but I was already committed to having sex with her. And in my defense, sex with batshit women is often worth having, as long as you go into it knowing that's all it is. I know that's some horrible cliché, but . . . grain of truth. Grain of truth.

"Baby! It's amazing, isn't it? *Amazing*! Listen, listen, Jaq, listen—" Liz had been mediating her nerves with wine, clearly.

I made my voice soothing. "Yeah, kid? You good?"

"I am *soooo* good. You know—you know, Jaq—" She hiccuped, and leaned over until she was half in my lap. "Jaq! You know—you know that I love you, but you and I—you and I never would have worked out." Hiccup. "You and I—we were good, but we—we didn't— You know, once I found Marla, it's like everything *happened*, like everything fell into place for me, you know?"

If no one's ever written a book about how to escape the bride at her own wedding when she's slobbering all over you, someone should.

"Honey—baby—you are going to spend the night, aren't you? I mean, for fun—just for fun—"

"School night, Lizzie. That's what you get for having a Sunday wedding."

Her face turned down comically and she opened her mouth to say something else, when an angel appeared at our side. An angel in blue.

"Liz, can I steal your best man? She owes me a dance."

Liz immediately beamed up at Hannah. Make that . . . pot as well as booze. Booze made Liz chatty; pot made it so she switched moods in an instant. "Yes! Steal her away! Jaq so needs to be swept off her feet, you don't know—"

That was more than enough of that. I wrapped my arm around her shoulders. "Okay, doll, time for you to go see your wife."

"Jaq! Don't call me that! You know I hate—"

"I know you do. Go tell Marla what a horrible person I am." I made eyes at Marla that I hoped she was sober enough to interpret as *Do something before she climbs into someone else's lap.* She was just saying to her new bride, "And how are *you*, hmm?" when Hannah took my hand and tugged.

I went willingly. So, so willingly. "Thank you, thank you, thank you a thousand times over."

"Did you call Liz 'doll'?" Hannah's lips curved up in a slightly wicked smile. "I can't believe you did that."

"I can't believe she didn't give the whole fetishization-of-Asian-women lecture. I mean, I've heard her give that one to a professor, after an all-nighter, with nothing in her veins but coffee. *And* get a standing ovation." I mimed smoking. "Somebody's been into the good antianxiety meds tonight."

"Somebody should have shared." She took me in her arms, sending a fierce shot of arousal through me. I flushed. All over. "So, Jaq. Do you need to get swept off your feet?"

Flirting. I knew how to flirt. I could even be good at it, sometimes, when I tried. "Why? You think you could pull that off?"

"I've done some sweeping of women off their feet in my time."

And god, she led. I was in my suit, dapper as hell, and the woman with the dress and the severe braid was *leading* as we danced.

When I didn't say anything, she kept talking. "Do you know everyone here? I can't get over how everyone seems to know each other. It's creepy. La Vista is not small enough for everyone to have fucked everyone else. And I grew up here, but I flew south before I tarted it up."

"Queer La Vista's pretty small. And I haven't fucked *everyone* here."

"Only most?" she teased.

I glanced around, like I was taking stock. "Oh yeah, definitely most."

"Slut."

"Jealous."

She huffed a laugh, shaking her head. "I am. Seven years is a long time to be married. We were still in college when we got serious."

"I had a serious girlfriend in college."

"How'd that work out for you?"

"Walked in on her, drunk, kissing my roommate."

"Oh, ouch." She spun me. When I came back to her arms, feeling winded—not from the exertion—she said, "Your roommate, though. What a bitch."

"He really was."

She grimaced. "Double ouch."

"No, no. She was an out-and-proud bisexual. So was he, actually. They were a better couple than she and I were, anyway."

"Still, must have hurt."

I shrugged and turned us until she was facing the bar. "Woman on the end, tall, black, mohawk." Mmm, and damn, Jess looked good in an ankle-length orange dress. Not everyone could pull off orange, but it looked great on Jess.

"Yeah?"

"She's the one I caught kissing my roommate." I watched her eyes narrow as she took in Jess. "But, like, look at her."

"She still swing?"

I hit her arm. "She's still bisexual. Or pansexual. Or omnisexual. I don't know what she's calling herself. But I do know your dance card is full, doll." I switched up my grip and after half a beat she followed, letting me lead.

"Should I give you the lecture about calling people 'doll'?"

"Only works if you're pissed, Chinese, and five feet tall."

"You're prejudiced against people over five feet tall."

"True. I like my women like I like my pool game—short and sweet."

Hannah shifted. "I bet you don't like your women sweet at all, Jaq. When's the earliest you think we can get out of here?"

For a split second my better angel argued with the horny devil on my shoulder. But come on, everyone knows how that cage match ends. "Gonna have to be soon. I need to get up to teach angry high schoolers tomorrow."

"Oh, a teacher, huh? I don't know how you do it. I barely went to class when I was forced to be there by law."

"Well, now they pay me, so it works out."

"Good point. If they'd paid me to attend school, I might have been more invested. So. Your room or mine?"

"Yours." I calculated quickly. I hadn't planned to stay at the hotel overnight, so everything was still in my bag, barely touched. "You should be able to sleep in in the morning even if I have to get up."

Hannah raised her eyebrow. "Oh, are we spending the night? Here I thought we were just hooking up."

"Shit, sorry, I—" *I am an idiot. Good god, Jaq, get it together.*

"Hey, I'm not complaining." She moved in until we were swaying more than dancing, lips brushing my ear. "It's been way too long since I spent the night with a beautiful woman. Let's go."

The certainty that we were hooking up should have made me feel more confident, but instead I was weirdly off-footed. I wanted desperately to recapture how in control I'd felt hours ago, before we met. Before I realized how irresistible she was.

Her hand, warm, remained in mine as we left the dance floor. We might have looked like we were walking side by side, but it was Hannah leading and me keeping up.

I snagged my best friend from forever out of a knot of people (not all exes, damn it, I'm only kind of a slut). "Zane, Hannah. Hannah, Zane. I'm taking off, so hold down the fort."

Zane rolled her eyes at me while shaking hands with Hannah. "Please. Do I look dumb enough to have signed up for wedding duty? Plus, Jess is here, and she might be single, and I'm here and definitely single, so—"

"Spare me the gory details." I kissed her cheek. "See you tomorrow afternoon."

"When we'll work off all the cake. Good to meet you, Hannah."

"You too."

Halfway down the hall she said, "Another ex?"

"We grew up together. First kiss, at eleven, but decidedly *not* an ex. Total failure of a first kiss. I mean, it was like kissing my sister."

"Please don't tell me there was tongue."

I shuddered. "We'd just found out what a French kiss was! We didn't even really know it had to do with sex. We thought it was how French people kissed, and French people were cool, so we tried it."

"French people are cool." She hit the up arrow of the elevator, then reeled me in, one hand on my hip, the other running over my shirt. In the lobby. In front of the main elevators. "Want to give it another shot?"

"I've kissed people since then with better results." We were almost exactly the same height, though I consoled myself with the thought that she was in heels. "You want me to show you how it's done?"

"Teach me, master."

I squared off, resting both of my hands on her back, holding her tightly. She probably expected me to go all-in, leaned like she was ready to take my face off the second our lips touched, but I didn't let her. I kissed the corner of her mouth, decorously, and she missed me by a mile.

"Bitch."

I grinned.

She squeezed my ass.

"Now, now. We're in public!"

She took a long breath, still close enough for me to feel it. "I need this so badly right now."

"Me too."

But somehow, no matter how hot the sex would be, I thought we were talking about very different things.

Oh well. You win some, you lose some, and if the sex is good, you don't keep score.

I hate to be clichéd, but the sex was *really* good.

I like being butch. It works for me. It's always worked for me. Ever since I saw Queen Latifah in that movie where she and her girlfriend rob banks, I knew that's what I was. It's not just clothes; it's a presence, a way of handling yourself. Being a butch dyke isn't like a religion or something, but it's also not a style, or a hobby, or a phase.

And when you're butch, some things happen kind of a lot. One of them is that the women you date seem to assume you're dominant, or that you come on strong, that you're toppy. I don't mind being a little bit toppy. That's hot. But when it's every single time—when it's the only way someone sees me—it gets exhausting. I blame *Fifty Shades of Grey*. Do I look like a billionaire businessman? No. I may look good in a tie, but I'm not a dominant force, okay?

Hannah did not need me to be toppy.

"You look so fucking sexy in your suit," she purred against my ear, pressing me into the wall, the door, the doorjamb to the bathroom, kissing me all the way. "I could eat you, Jaq."

"Go ahead."

She laughed. "Not yet."

I could feel her breasts through the fabric of her dress and my shirt, but I needed a hell of a lot more than that. It took seconds to push my jacket off her and find the zipper at the top of the dress. "May I?"

"Such a gentleman. And fuck yes."

The sound of the zipper seemed to turn her on; she threw her head back and sucked in air, which I took as an invitation to kiss all that skin, working my way down her throat. I didn't want to move too quickly, even if this was a wedding fling, so instead of immediately stripping off her dress, I let my hands wander, slipping along her back as I kissed her, dipping lower to her ass. Hannah wasn't skinny. She wore her body just like everything else: with attitude, unapologetic, and sexy as fuck.

"You're a tease, Jaq." She coaxed my lips back to hers. "Don't you want me naked? You're still in your suit and I could writhe against you."

I ran my hands along her hips, over the dress. "This feels more torturous for you. A bit stifled there?"

As if to prove she wasn't, she shifted until she could bring her thigh up between my legs. I laughed.

"So that's a no, huh?"

"I'm never stifled." She pinned my hands to the wall on either side, holding me in place so she could kiss me and do even more suggestive things with her leg. "Pussy want to get off?"

"Tell me you're not a cat person."

"No cats, no dogs, no kids. I'm selfish." Teeth grazed my jaw. "Very selfish."

I stopped straining for more kisses and watched for a minute. Up close her lips were thinner, widened with liner, and her skin lightly dotted with scars here and there. Old pimples picked too long, maybe. I always expected people who lived in LA to have vaguely tanned skin, whether from a salon or the sun, but Hannah was pale, her complexion slightly uneven.

And the hair. I was desperate to get my hands in it. "Need my limbs back."

She released me immediately, dragging her fingers down my shirt. "I want to make a mess of your suit. It's so crisp. My first thought when we met was 'I wonder if I can fuck her in that suit.'"

"That was damn near my first thought when we met too." The clasp at the back of her elaborate braid felt straightforward, but I failed at smooth while trying to get it off.

"Do you want me to—"

I didn't, but if I couldn't get it to work, I was going to have to give up. "Is this the Fort Knox of hair clips?"

Her fingers carded up the back of my head, where my hair was shortest. "Not something you deal with a lot, I guess." No impatience.

Got it. The clasp came loose, and oh god, yeah, that was fantastic. Auburn hair I could tell immediately was curly, trying to bust free from the high-security braid and clip combo.

"Mmm, that feels good." Her thigh pressed a bit more insistently against me as I carefully unwound the braid.

"So it turns you on when someone plays with your hair? I'll make a note of that."

"You could say that." She untucked my shirt. A second later she shrugged out of her straps until the dress gathered around her waist, and pressed back against me in only a sleek demi-cup bra (also blue, a few shades darker than the dress). "Oh yeah. That's good. Let's move things to the bed, but let me undress you slowly as we go, okay?"

She didn't seem like a masculinity fetishist, so I elected to believe she just really liked my suit. As well she should, because I looked fucking hot in it.

When we stepped away from each other, she shoved the dress off her hips, and oh, hello, blue thong. I licked my lips and stepped forward, walking her back to the bed.

"Like the blue," I murmured.

"I don't do lace, but I still like to feel sexy. My favorite thing to wear to business meetings is a conservative suit and fuck-me lingerie underneath."

"Hot."

"Oh, I really am."

Fuck, it was such a turn-on when I was with someone who knew they looked good. I know, I know, culture/patriarchy/insecurities whatever, but Hannah stretched out for me like she couldn't give a rat's ass about any of it.

She spread her legs, and I took the invitation, pressing down against her, aligning our bodies, not even a little surprised when she pulled me in with her legs.

"How lovely it is to meet you," she whispered.

"Back at you." Now that I had access to all of her skin, I took advantage, kissing a pale shoulder, letting my fingers play along the edges of her bra. She retaliated by sliding one hand down the back of my pants, locking her legs around mine even more so I couldn't move.

"Did you go commando?"

"I always go commando."

She thrust up, one finger dipping into my crack. "Oh fuck. That's just wrong. Or right. I can't decide."

There's such a thing as moving too slowly. At least, when I'm not the one in charge.

I kept sucking on her neck, my nose practically in her hair, while I finally pushed her bra up. One of those sculpted, half-padding affairs, revealing delicious little breasts with hard-as-pebbles nips that begged to be rolled, and licked, and lightly pinched until she moaned.

Hannah writhed, holding me pressed against her with that single finger still teasing my crack. "More, damn it!"

More worked for me. I got a bit rougher and nibbled at her earlobe, making her gasp. Her movements were becoming a little frantic, and I ground down against her as much as I could with her legs wrapped around me like a damn octopus.

"Oh fuck— Yes— More—"

I added a twist to my move, and she arched off the bed.

"I'm coming, Jaq! Coming—"

A woman saying my name while she comes does something terrible to me. Makes me feel stupidly warm and vulnerable. I hid my face in her neck and kept kissing her while she came down again, sternly counseling myself that this was a fucking fling, and none of it meant anything beyond tonight. Because batshit.

"Sorry about the suit," she said.

"Are you smirking right now? That's unladylike."

"Well, we certainly wouldn't want *that*." She released my legs and rolled me, already working on my buttons. "Now that's done, I can concentrate. I've been picturing this moment for hours."

I do all right, dating-wise, but that's not to say I take it for granted when a gorgeous woman has been thinking about having sex with me all day.

Since I was clearly not necessary, I let her work, unbuttoning, untucking, spreading my shirt open so she could look at me.

"Ooh, a binder. Will you take it off?"

"Sure. Of course."

"Some people seem to treat their binder as a second skin, so I never know."

I shook my head, and she gave me enough room to sit up. Taking off a binder—even a relatively old one—is not something to fuck around with. I contorted my arms and shoulders and head in the right way and pulled it over.

"Oh my god." Her hands were on my breasts before I'd even managed to drop the binder.

"I only wear that if I think it makes the shirt look better."

"If I had breasts like yours, I'd never wear a bra at all." She leaned in to kiss me, pushing me back down again. "Lord."

She played with my breasts, sucking my nipples, and all the time she kept my hands pinned above my head. "You pro– or anti–ass play?"

The question, coming at the end of a torturous few minutes of teasing my nipples until it was everything I could do not to fuck my breasts into her mouth, surprised me.

"Um. Pro, I guess? It's not something that's come up a whole lot."

Hannah laughed. Wickedly. "Oh, I'm an ass girl. And a pussy girl. And a tit girl." Then she abandoned my breasts and let go of my wrists in order to push down my trousers, at last. Before I could so much as spread wantonly and beg for her tongue, she added, "Don't come until I tell you."

Damn.

Torture was another theme. I made a mental note. Not that we'd ever have sex again, probably, but I always liked to take good notes, even if something wasn't going to be on the test.

Her lips, her tongue, her fingers. I rode the line of *too much* and she kept me there, three fingers deep, sucking my clit, taking breaks to use her tongue like a precision drill directly on the nerves that most wanted an orgasm.

I couldn't help pleading. I didn't even know I was doing it until I heard my own voice panting, "Please, please, please."

"Since you asked so sweetly." She looked up at me, licking her lips as I shuddered. "Hold that knee back, sugar. Yeah, like that."

I registered her fingers withdrawing, but only vaguely. Until I felt them again. At my ass.

I'm not a total novice, but what I'd done before was more "sexy fingertip" not so much "finger pushed in to the hilt." Or "finger fucking in to the hilt, then out, then in, then out, then two fingers." That was a little new.

And her eyes held mine, watching as I took it in. I breathed and relaxed as much as I could, caught between her gaze and her fingers. Any brief burn was lost in the rest of the sensations, and I couldn't stop myself from bucking into her hands.

She lowered her head while the thumb of her other hand began flicking my clit. It was far too much, and it was glorious, all the sexual circuits in my body connecting and lighting up like Times Square at Christmas. I couldn't control the way I was trembling as her lips sucked in my labia and her fingers relentlessly fucked my ass, urging my body higher and higher.

She pulled away just long enough to say, "You can come now," then got right back to it. Burying her face in my pussy, her tongue finally where I needed it, impaling me, thumb playing my clit in quick little circles.

Some orgasms are localized; this one was a full-body affair. I held myself open for her, nails digging into the skin behind my knees, and every muscle in my body went rigid while she continued to fuck me. I shook like a live wire, and Hannah held me down, held me up, held me and fucked me until I was nothing but a fucking twitching mass of nerves.

Then she climbed over me, got in my face, and frigged herself to another orgasm while I watched. One hand went behind her, the other to her clit, and oh god, was she fucking her own ass right now?

"Oh, ooh, fuck yes, *fuck yes*—"

I managed to get my hands to her thighs in time to feel the orgasm rip through her, all that muscle going hard under my palms, but that was it.

"Good god, woman. You could have shared. Maybe I wanted a piece of that."

She grinned down at me, hair falling all over the fucking place. "I thought for sure I'd fucked you unconscious."

"Not quite. Almost, but not quite." I stroked her sides. "Let me guess—you don't cuddle."

"Harsh. I cuddle. But only after I wash up. Bring you a cloth?"

"Definitely. I could—"

"No, no, I'll get it."

Hotels are great. In a hotel, no one's ever going to fault you for tossing your dirty washcloth on the ground so you can sooner get to spooning the woman who nearly came in your face.

My phone alarm, set early that morning, would go off at five thirty. A glance at the clock informed me it was a little after midnight.

"That was good," she murmured, settling in, pushing herself back against me. "I guess you're considering this a one-off?"

Yes. The answer is yes. Because batshit and histrionic and nasty divorce.

"I thought *you* were considering it a one-off," I said, to stall.

She sighed, tugging my arm tighter. "I could be. I probably should be. But sex that good isn't something I take lightly."

"Me neither." That was probably revealing more than I wanted to be, but it was true. Good sex was putting it mildly. Good sex meant I was physically satisfied; tonight had an edge of something a lot deeper than that.

"If we don't do phone numbers before you leave, you can get mine from the happy brides." She yawned. "I can't believe you have school in the morning. Ha."

"But they pay me now, don't forget."

"There's not enough money in the world to get me back in a classroom." She yawned again. "Good night, dapper Jaq."

I didn't have a clever endearment, so I brushed her hair out of the way and kissed the back of her neck. "Good night."

She shivered.

Sleeping with someone and having excellent sex with them are two totally different things. I tried not to take it as some kind of sign that Hannah and I did both very well.

CHAPTER 3

The five smartasses in my first period Journalism class greeted me the way they'd been doing for the last three weeks, since I had a lapse in judgment and showed them the Carol Burnett bits of *Annie* on YouTube.

"Good morning, Miss Cummings!"

Then they cracked up. Everyone else was asleep or indifferent.

"Seriously, Ms. C, were you out drinking last night?" Sammy—classic "grew too tall too fast" lanky teenage white boy—gestured to his face. "You got some bags under your eyes there."

"Maybe you should give her a makeover," Merin suggested. Merin was one of those kids—the kids who were super smart, lacked all motivation, and only existed to give the other kids a hard time. She wasn't actually homophobic; she ascribed to the *South Park* rules of insulting everyone equally.

"Cram it, both of you." Actually, I looked damn good—for someone who rolled out of a Berkeley hotel room an hour ago and somehow got showered, dressed, and all the way to La Vista High in that time. Barely.

I may have hit snooze once. Or twice.

"Oooh," a couple of my kids said.

"Homework? Anyone?"

"I got your homework right here." Dana grabbed her crotch. She was still growing into her insubordination, and I didn't think crotch-grabbing was really going to fit the bill. But hey, it was a good effort.

"That would have been a lot more effective if you hadn't been sitting in a desk when you did it. Hand your papers forward, then get to work."

Monday's in-class journalism assignment was always the same: troll through the bins of donated newspapers until you find something interesting, then share with the class. It was pretty informal. The kids mostly got up to pick through the papers, and the two or three still seated, like Merin, waited regally for their classmates to sit down before snagging sections from them.

Grading can't actually be accomplished in class—or at least I never worked out how to do it. But I could spend that time sorting the papers into two groups: "can be graded in five minutes" and "didn't anyone ever teach you to use capital letters at the beginnings of your sentences?"

The homework had been "Describe yourself as if you were a witness to a crime, and about to be quoted in the paper." Merin had written—handwritten, as in scribbled—"White bitch, 17, with scraggly hair and a perpetual sneer." I laughed out loud.

"Merin. Get up here."

She unfolded herself lazily. "What, Ms. C?"

I waited until she had come all the way up to the front before gesturing to her paper. "I believe it's customary to use the name of the witness."

"Huh-uh. I'm a minor. They better not use my name." She pointed at the paper. "Seventeen, see?" Then, with a palpable sense of triumph, she turned and ambled back to her desk.

I saluted her. "One point to Merin. Who's got something interesting to show us?"

The newspaper exercise wasn't really about finding something interesting or absorbing some kind of journalistic ethos through newsprint. It was more about holding the paper in their hands, getting a feel for how it was laid out, for the rhythm of the pages. It was probably all for naught, judging by the big papers going out of business, but I figured it didn't hurt to expose them to other forms of media than they were used to, even if none of them imagined going to work on an actual paper someday.

Almost none of them.

LaTasha Moore had plans. She was usually the only person who found something genuinely interesting in the paper. She looked up at me and said, "Is a drag performer the same as a drag queen?"

"What?"

"Yeah," Sammy said, still flipping through his own section. "It's a guy who gets done up like a woman and does a show. Like RuPaul."

"But this isn't a guy. It's a woman."

Sammy raised his eyebrows. "Wait, the paper's covering drag? Let me see that."

Before he could grab it, LaTasha snatched it away.

"Sammy, back in your seat. LaTasha, what's the article?"

"This lady died. They're calling her a drag performer."

Damn. I knew what she was talking about. La Vista's not that big, and like I told Hannah, the queer community's even smaller. "Is this from a couple months ago?"

She checked the date. "Yeah."

"She was a drag king," I said.

Sammy turned all the way to me like I was a breathing encyclopedia of gay. "It's a hate crime, then, right?"

"It's not a hate crime if it's just some chick being killed," Merin said.

Dana waved one arm over her head and started talking at the same time. "I don't get that stuff. If you get killed, someone hated you, right? Why isn't every crime a hate crime?"

I clapped my hands before we could go too far down the rabbit hole. "Put a pin in the hate-crime conversation. LaTasha, share your article."

"This drag performer woman was attacked when she was still in her drag costume, and beaten to death. They found her body in an alley off Steerage Street."

A couple of the kids snorted. Steerage was La Vista's one-block Castro, where the gay club, Club Fred's, and the two queer-friendly bars were.

"Do you think they figured out who killed her, Ms. C?"

Nope. I doubt they looked that hard.

"I'm not sure. Do you want to look into it? I'll give you points to do that instead of the homework."

"Aw, no fair." Dana pouted dramatically. "I don't want to do homework, either!"

"Okay. Everyone who wants to investigate a murder instead of their homework, turn in whatever you find out."

Merin made a vague effort at raising her hand and didn't wait to be called on. "So that means any kind of research, right? Not just"—she waved the Sports section around—"newspaper?"

"Any kind of research, providing it would be acceptable in a Works Cited. So no Wikipedia unless you want to hunt down the original sources. Who's next?"

Merin shot LaTasha sideways glances for the rest of class while LaTasha not so covertly messed around on her phone. She was probably, knowing her, actually doing research.

I dismissed them when the bell rang and started mentally preparing for the rest of my classes. Teaching high school English and history to teenagers, who routinely failed to use capital letters and whose notion of the past was calling Nirvana an "oldies band," left a lot to be desired, but there were always a few students here and there who made suffering through the rest of them worth it.

I called Liz while grading papers later that day, with a bottle of cream soda and a bag of chips.

"What is that horrible noise?" she demanded.

I moved the phone, on speaker, to the other side of my kitchen table. "Sorry. Um. Late lunch."

"If it's Doritos, Jaq, stop eating right now and get yourself some real food."

"It's the day after your wedding, don't you have better things to do than lecture me about my lousy food choices?"

"Not really. And you were right, by the way. Wedding, work week, honeymoon is a stupid organization of events."

"Ha, told you so." *Be subtle, Jaq. Be casual.* "So hey, any chance you have Hannah's phone number?"

"No."

"What? I just wanted to—"

"Don't bullshit a bullshitter."

I took a fortifying sip of cream soda. "Shut it, Lizbet."

"Don't do this. I don't even want to tell you about this divorce. They would have fit right in on a reality TV show, it was that ridiculous."

"I don't even want to hear about her divorce. And it's irrelevant." Kind of.

"Hannah is the definition of a hookup."

"Listen, I'm not proposing to her. The sex was good, and I wouldn't mind having . . . more. Good sex. With her."

"Oh my god, I told you she was batshit. Of course the sex was good! Hell, I gotta go, babe. Listen, don't do this. Hannah's a hot mess. Enter at your own risk."

"Duly noted, can I get her phone number now?"

"I'll text you."

I was in the middle of calling her a big fat liar when she hung up.

The text never came. But that was fine. I finished the stack of never-ending grading, sucked down my soda, and texted Marla.

Marla sent Hannah's phone number, a note that she'd flown back to LA "for more divorce crap," and an all caps "GOOD LUCK WITH THAT."

With friends like these. Jeez.

I probably wouldn't call her. The absolute last thing I needed was drama. My last semiserious relationship had ended when my then-girlfriend accused me of having an affair with a barista I'd smiled at too long.

No. I could not do more drama-queen energy. Not again.

And anyway, if Hannah was in LA, there wasn't any reason to call her. Plus, I only had to kill a few more hours before meeting Zane at the gym, where I'd work off all the wedding cake—and, if I was lucky, distract my brain from how damn sexy Hannah looked when she laughed.

Zane and I worked out three times a week. She worked out because aerobic exercise was good for her moods, and she wanted a strong heart, and blah health reasons. I worked out so I could have an extra piece of cake at weddings without having to buy new clothes.

"You bitch." She dialed down the incline on her treadmill. "How can you be in better shape than I am? It makes no sense. We work out the same, I eat way better than you do—" She growled in the general direction of the digital readout. "Screw you, Life Fitness. Bite me."

I laughed. At least, it would have been a laugh if I wasn't huffing and puffing so hard. "Just lucky, I guess."

"Speaking of lucky, tell me all about Batshit."

"Liz has a fucking big mouth."

"No— Well, yeah, she totally does. We actually had to meet up for work downtown. New commercial venture, excellent business opportunity, whatever. You'd think I wouldn't have to pretend to care if I was meeting with a friend, but no, still faked it." She leered at me, or came as close as she could while dripping sweat and panting. "I hear you didn't have to fake it."

"Who even says something like that?"

"It was hot, right? I mean, with that body—mmm."

"Hell yes, she was hot. It was hot. We were hot. I'm not getting attached, but damn."

"Sure, sure." She pumped up the incline again. "I hate you so much right now."

"You love me."

We stopped talking for the rest of the workout, which was grueling. I forced her to stretch after, even though she whined pretty much the whole time.

"You are so buying the first round." She did a few little jumps before we headed for the locker room.

"Please tell me you're talking about Club Fred's and not that disaster smoothie bar next door."

"The first round at Fred's will be cheaper than smoothies."

Smoothies meant we were being healthy. Fred's meant something else. I knocked into her shoulder. "Negative?"

"You keeping track of my cycle now?"

"Ew." I held the door for her. "And no, but that's usually when you push for postworkout liquor."

"Yeah. Big fuckin' negative. Got my period two days ago."

I tried to see if she looked especially depressed, but I couldn't tell. Which meant it'd hit her so hard she was actively hiding it.

"Well, shit. Sorry, kid."

"Yeah, well, whatever. Let's drink."

Ouch. Sympathy rebuffed.

Club Fred's belonged to one of the women I kind of wanted to be when I grew up. Fredi was this butch leather dyke who stalked around behind the bar like if you raised your voice to her, she might literally have bent you over and given you a few swats until you learned your manners. (And . . . yes. Please. Anytime, Fredi.) She had a little mullet. And chin whiskers.

And for some reason Zane was under the impression Fredi hated her. Because when we were twenty, we snuck in one time and she booted our asses out so fast we barely had the chance to smell beer before we were slinking to Blockbuster to rent something to take our minds off our astounding humiliation. So we rented *Reality Bites* and *How to Make an American Quilt*. And yes, one of us had a Winona Ryder thing, but I'll never tell which one.

"Watch, she's gonna ignore us. Fredi! Yo! Fredi!"

I sighed. "Maybe if you sounded slightly less like a frat boy, we'd get served faster." I caught the other bartender's eye. "Hey, Tom, do you think we could get a beer and a soda?"

"Sure thing. You guys go to the gym again?"

I flexed for him. "What, you can't tell?"

Tom was tall, cut, and blond, and his dimples were permanent fixtures on his face. "Oh, honey. You always look good to me. Mozzarella sticks tonight?"

Zane moaned. "Tom, you always know the right things to say."

"God, like we need more crap after yesterday." I glanced down toward the kitchen. "I hope they come fast, I'm starving."

He leaned over the counter. "How was it? Tell me there was a screaming match."

"Absolutely not!" I said. "Actually, it was great. They looked gorgeous, both sets of parents weren't douchey—" he laughed "—and somehow we managed to set the whole thing up without anyone dying or anything going undone." I sketched a bow, which he returned with a nod. "But the next time someone says they want to plan their own wedding, leave me out of it."

Zane pitched forward with a *thump*. And stayed there while Tom laughed and petted her head.

I appealed to Tom. "What'd I say?"

"I'll let Zane tell you. But keep your calendar open for a winter wedding, Jaq." He winked and went off to help customers.

"Oh my god, are Tom and Carlos getting married?"

"Yes. Isn't it *lovely*?"

I grinned and poked her. "Ha. You agreed to plan it for them, didn't you?"

"I did not! I said I'd help out. They took me to dinner. I may have taken some notes about the things they were interested in—"

"You totally agreed to plan it. You're a glutton for punishment, babe."

"I was only trying to keep track of their ideas! And, okay, I may have started a few lists."

I could picture it. She'd have been on her phone, plugging everything into a bunch of searchable documents in Evernote, probably coming up with a whole taxonomy on the fly, tagging with things like *cake*, *reception*, *color scheme*, *decorations*, *venues*. I couldn't help giggling. "God, where were you at the time? Tell me it was somewhere fancy."

"San Marcos Grill," she mumbled.

"Oh, nice!" The Grill was one of those joints on the new side of the Harbor District where you could sit at the windows and look out at the Bay. Not that it was such a great view—from La Vista, the Bay was mostly grimy and gray, brushed metal with a layer of road dirt kicked onto it—but it was definitely fancy.

"Shut your stupid face. And where are my mozzarella sticks?"

"Hold your horses, Jaffe," Fredi snapped.

Zane sat up straight. "Sorry, Fredi." When Fredi didn't scold her again, she turned back to me. "So go on. Tell me all about her."

"There isn't a 'her.' We just had a nice time."

"That's your story and you're sticking to it, huh? Well, okay. But—" She sipped her beer. "We're getting old, Jaqs. Old. Very old."

"We're thirty-four."

"Old." She stared into her pint.

"How many cycles has it been now?" If I couldn't remember when she started trying to get pregnant, would that make me a bad friend?

"Just five. *Only* five. If I were consistently boinking a cis man, I wouldn't even technically be infertile yet."

I put a hand on her arm. "Wait. Do you think you—"

"No. No, I'm not saying that. It's just hard to spend so fucking much money every cycle and get . . . nothing back from it. It'll happen. Probably. And you know, adoption's an option— Fuck, sorry, I didn't mean it like adoption's less valid, but it wasn't my plan." She sighed. "It's not like it's the end of the world if I can't conceive. I just . . . have a list, you know?"

I knew. I knew way more about human reproduction than any queer girl who didn't want kids should ever know. And I'd known Zane's list since she'd come up with it at the end of college: graduate, get a decent job, buy a car, establish an IRA, buy a condo, pay off the car, have a kid. She'd done all of that but the last one.

"Tell me about Tom and Carlos," I said, hoping the change in subject was welcomed and not insulting.

"Tom's easy." She raised her voice. "Carlos is gonna be a problem, though."

Tom's laughter sounded from the sink where he was washing dishes, and was joined by that of a few of his customers. A voice I knew very well rose above the din.

"Excuse me, *Suzanne?*"

"Oh fuck. Carlos?" Zane spun in time to catch Carlos walking up. The crowd always parted around Carlos a little, even though people went out of their way not to actually stare at the little person. "Oh, hey, didn't see you waaaaay down there."

"Did you just make a fucking dwarf joke at me?"

"Did you just 'Suzanne' me?"

He grinned. "Bitch. Hey, Jaq."

"Hey, boy." I leaned over to kiss his cheek when he took the stool beside mine. "So you're finally letting him chain you down, huh?"

"You know the only one with the chains in our household is me, baby."

Sure, I knew that. If you spent any time at Pleasure Principle, a tiny little excuse for a kink club in seedy East La Vista, you'd know too. The boys liked to get out. And Carlos liked sporting his custom equipment and bowing his much-taller boyfriend. Fiancé, I guess, these days.

"Congratulations," I told him. And meant it. No one had a real easy ride of it around here, but being gay and a little person and in La Vista seemed unduly harsh. Not that anyone *deserved* happiness, really, but if they did, Carlos and Tom would.

"Merci, chère. Anyway, it was only a matter of time now that the law is on our side. Right, lover?"

Tom glanced down the bar, then leaned over for a quick kiss. "You can make me your husband any day."

"You're disgusting." I may have sounded a little raw with longing. Damn it. *Subject change again.* "So my queer kids decided they're going to continue meeting at the Harbor District Sobrantes shop during the summer."

"Really?" Carlos nodded. "That's very good. And no one has a problem with that?"

"They're mostly on their own during the summer anyway, and all of them are working at least part-time. And I talked to Kim, who's managing over there, and she said we can have the back room for free as long as we clear out before AA needs it."

"Let me know if they want a donation or something," Zane said. "I can swing one if that would help."

"I think we're good."

Carlos's face lit. "Oh, that reminds me—both of you should hear this. Let's get a table, okay?"

It was still early enough to place an order of fries with Tom before we left the bar and snagged a booth.

Carlos let Zane slide in first so he'd be on the outside of the bench. "Last week I sat on an interview panel with this kid Josh. Real clean-cut, maybe twenty-three, doing mock interviews for the little business undergrads. We're talking in between interviews, and he mentions this vat of bile"—he gestured around—"and I mention Steerage Street, and pretty soon we can tell we know some of the same people, so he pitches me on this nonprofit idea he's working on with his 'partner.'"

I curled my fingers into air quotes. "'Partner' how?"

"Business and *other things*, if I'm catching his drift. Not that it matters. Listen to what they're doing."

We both bent our heads toward Carlos.

"They want to start a drop-in center for queer youth downtown. Soup kitchen component, contract with the health services bus to be there on consistent days and times, some jobs counseling, donation center for decent clothes and unused toiletries, meeting rooms for groups, lockers, the whole nine."

"For homeless kids?" Zane asked.

"The age group for the center would be fourteen to twenty-five, with obvious safeguards in place, yada yada, but they'd have some specific stuff targeting homeless kids. Drug and alcohol counseling, networking with shelters, that kind of thing." Carlos shook his head. "They've got a location picked out and he swears they're gonna pull it off."

"That sounds amazing," I said. "Why are you dubious?"

"Oh, I'm not. I feel like a fool for believing any dumb kid who thinks he's gonna change the world, but this kid was believable. Shook my hand at the end of the day and told me he'd give me a call so I could come down to the open house when they get it done. And even though he's a punk twenty-three-year-old kid, I bet you anything he and this partner of his will be showing me around the place before the end of summer." He sat back, grinning like he'd started the whole thing himself. "I love good-looking young men who know exactly what they're about."

Zane rolled her eyes. "You love good-looking young men regardless. Do they need donations right now?"

"It sounds like they need investors right now more than donors. Though he told me the website will be up and running anytime now."

She nodded. "Will you give me his information? Maybe I can help with something."

"Take a picture." Carlos withdrew a business card from his wallet and set it on the table so Zane could plug a picture of it into her little database of notes and tags and other random information.

"What're you tagging it?" I asked.

"*Business, queer youth,* and *hope for the future.*"

I pulled her over so I could kiss her cheek. "Hope for the future, babe."

"I'll drink to that." Carlos raised his glass.

We raised ours as well.

"Hope for the future!" we chorused, like jackasses.

Carlos was getting married. Zane was planning for a kid. I couldn't help but feel like I was the odd man out, toasting the future.

CHAPTER 4

There are two St. Agneses. St. Agnes of Assisi is known for being the younger sister of St. Clare (of Poor Clares fame), and St. Agnes of Rome is known for rejecting all matrimonial suitors because she promised herself to Jesus. The latter is the patron saint of rape survivors.

Sometimes I learn things and I don't even know what to do with them. What do you do with the concept of a patron saint for rape survivors? Let alone that the church thought a thirteen-year-old girl who was dragged naked into a brothel and miraculously escaped unscathed was the best prospect for the job?

In La Vista, there are two Catholic churches, but only one St. Agnes, and I've been attending mass there since I was baptized. My parents got married there a scant seven months before my sister June was born. We held Mom's funeral there when I was seven.

I'm the only one of the four of us kids who still lives in La Vista, which means I'm the only one who goes with Dad to mass every Sunday.

Zane and I did first communion together when we were little, and her older sister and my older brother did it together a few years before us, but she stopped going to church when we started college. I kept going. After Mom died, it felt like church was the last safe place. Sometimes it seemed like I could still feel her with us when we were sitting there, like if Mom was going to visit us anywhere, she'd pick the smooth brown wood of the pews and the shafts of light colored by stained glass.

Even after all these years, I feel that way in church. Obviously I'm supposed to be there for the Jesus of it all, but I really show up because it feels like visiting my mother. She'd been devout, not in a pushy or sentimental way, but in a genuine way. She'd believed in helping people, in taking care of your neighbor, and that if you did all that, you'd be taken care of too.

My mom had believed that it was St. Agnes of Assisi we should be honoring, because she'd been totally overshadowed by her older sister when she was alive, and she was completely overshadowed by St. Agnes of Rome after she died. Poor St. Agnes—literally. Those girls took their vows of poverty *seriously*.

I sat in my pew next to Dad on Sunday morning, half tuning out the sermon (the new parish priest was Italian and I could barely understand him), watching the way light filtered in through the windows. We weren't a huge parish, or a wealthy one, but we did okay. And even if the church was still pretty screwy in a lot of ways, the new pope seemed like a pretty great guy.

That's what I was thinking when I saw her: *The new pope is a pretty great guy. I wonder how long I'll be thinking of him as "the new pope." I mean, you do that with a president for like six months or something. I think the last pope was gone before I'd even stopped thinking of him as "the new pope."*

I knew that hair. That tight braid. I knew the curve of her jaw, her neck.

What the hell was Hannah doing at St. Agnes?

I would have expected a shot of arousal, but what hit me instead was a shot of . . . yearning. I wanted to run my fingers through her hair again. I wanted to kiss the divot of her clavicle.

Danger, danger. Arousal, of course, was a basic biological thing. Wanting to unpin someone's hair and gloriously release it from its braid . . . was something else.

I didn't bother redirecting my gaze. Proof that not everyone has a sixth sense when they're being watched: I stared at Hannah for the rest of the service and she never even turned her head.

"Distracted?" Dad murmured as we shuffled into line for communion.

"No." *Yes.* She was ahead of us, in a different line.

"Oh really?"

I wanted to poke him, but that would probably be seen as irreverent. "Hush."

"Tell me later." The woman in front of him looked back, and he made the awkwardness into a moment, grasping her hand. "And how are you, dear?"

After the service I made my excuses to Dad and one of his cronies with the express purpose of catching her before she took off.

"Of all the churches in all the world," I said. Not the most original line, I realize, but it did the trick. Hannah turned and raised both eyebrows.

"I had to walk into yours. Well damn." We exchanged cheek kisses that broadcasted nothing of the few hours we'd spent together in a hotel room last week. "I like your Sunday best, Jaq."

"Same to you." Conservative black slacks, dark-blue sweater. Still, the swell of hip and belly made me think dirty thoughts. "I'm a little surprised to see you here."

"I should probably be less surprised to see you. Marla pointed me in this direction. She said I'd like it better than St. Pat's."

"St. Patrick's is bigger, but we like to think we have more character." I gestured, not quite sure what I wanted to say, or ask. I was the last person who could express shock that someone was going to church. "So . . . you're Catholic?"

Hannah's eyes widened. "Wait, this is a Catholic church? Are you sure?"

"Okay, okay, stupid question."

"Only a little, sugar." She glanced up at the cross with St. Agnes below it. "I guess I'm a bit of a lost lamb, technically, but it seems . . . worth trying. Hell, I don't know. I'm willing to try almost anything."

Sunlight gleamed off her skin, momentarily highlighting the dark circles beneath her eyes even though she'd covered them with makeup. "Well, what's your goal? I mean, with trying things?"

"Oh, that's easy." She held up a hand to her forehead to shield the sun. "I'm just trying to get by. If it makes you uncomfortable I'm here, I can go back to—"

"No, no, that's not—" I touched her arm. "Not at all."

"Glad to hear it." Her smile flickered to something deeper, warmer, then blinked back to the smile I'd seen earlier. "Hello," she said to the space behind my shoulder.

"Hello there."

Dad. I half turned. "Dad, this is Hannah. I met her at Liz's wedding last week. Hannah, my dad, Richard."

"How nice to meet you, dear."

They shook hands.

"Nice to meet you too, Richard."

"You new to the flock around here?"

"Just relocated."

I pointedly didn't goggle at this bit of news. Relocated? As in permanently?

"Oh, from where?"

"The City of Angels." Hannah offered that surface smile again. "Though don't hold your breath on the angel front."

"I haven't been that far south in years. When Jaq and the kids were young, I used to travel for work."

"Oh, what'd you do?"

Dad waved a hand. "Sales. Computers, back when the only people buying were universities."

It hadn't been quite that long ago, but this was how he liked to tell the story, so I didn't object.

"Well, that must have been a fascinating thing, Richard. Listen, can I buy you two a coffee? I've got an appointment to look at one of those nice little condos down the street—the newer building, on the waterfront—but I have a little time to kill before then."

Dad laughed and clasped her hand. "That's a lovely offer, but I'm afraid I have to decline. You ladies should go out." He waggled his eyebrows at us.

"Dad! Behave!"

"My behavior is fine, Jaqueline." He kissed my cheek. "Have a good day, sweetheart. Very nice to meet you, Hannah."

"You too." She watched him walk away before shooting a dazzling smile at me. "Coffee?"

"Sure. There's a Sobrantes up the street and over."

"Sounds great."

Early May and the weather was just about perfect: warm in the sun, the breeze was cool, and I wasn't sweating too much by the time we got to the coffee shop. I opened the door for her, and she swept inside, stepping back to survey the menu.

I ordered my usual medium mocha, with whip, and Hannah got herself—after some conversation with the kid behind the counter—a small soy latte with a shot of caramel syrup and an add shot.

We took our drinks to the sidewalk and sat at a little table in the sun.

"Thank you." I lifted my drink.

"You're welcome." She waved a lazy hand. "Too bad you had to jump up and leave that morning. We could have enjoyed ourselves a little longer."

"No reason we couldn't do it again, if you're going to be around."

"Or plenty of reasons. I'm no one's idea of a catch."

"I'm not much of a fisher. Plus, if you score an apartment in that building, I'll just be banging you for the view." That's right: keep it casual. No feelings need apply.

She laughed, looking a little surprised. "Well, I'm bargaining on the house in LA selling in a reasonable amount of time, which it probably won't, because my ex refuses to lower the price even though our real estate agent has practically begged us."

Yikes. "Sounds tricky."

"I tell myself if I could afford to buy her out, I would, but that might not be the best thing, either." She stretched her legs out, crossing booted feet. "Divorce is a funny thing. It's a long, drawn-out death knell for a life you once thought you'd live. As hard to let go as any other beloved artifact, I guess."

"I've never really gotten that far into a relationship. I mean, I've had girlfriends, but none I seriously considered marrying."

"I think I envy you. Commitment is such a bitter pill. Sorry, the last thing you want to be doing is sitting here listening to me bitch about my past. Tell me about you, Jaq. Your dad seems nice."

I gave a few stock lines about my family (Dad's great, Mom's dead, two sisters, one brother, and my dad still has the family dog, Ducky, who's nineteen and mostly incontinent). She gave me a few about hers (parents divorced and happily remarried to other people, no siblings, no pets). We covered jobs (I was a teacher, which meant I was constantly scraping for spare change; she was in contract law, which I assumed meant she had a lot of fucking money and no real worries). And only after all that did I ask her why she was moving back to La Vista.

She brushed back her hair. "I started sending out feelers for jobs in the Bay Area about three years ago, and for a long time, no one was interested. My marriage dissolved, my life twisted until it was unrecognizable, and suddenly I got a phone call asking me if I'm still interested in relocating."

"Good timing." *Everyone said it and there it is. She's flighty! She moved across the state because of a phone call! Time to cut ties, Jaq.* But sitting there, watching the wry turn of her lips, the way her self-deprecation glossed over some deeper wound, I only wanted to talk to her more. Not less. No matter what my inner angel said.

"Or spectacularly bad. If they'd called sooner, maybe I'd still be married. We would have done all right if we didn't have to share a house, I think." She grimaced. "Okay, I take it back. It was good timing. I am definitely not interested in still being married."

I risked saying lightly, "Was she that bad?"

"God, I'd love to blame her for all of it. But no clusterfuck that big could have really been only one person's fault." A glint of teeth in my direction. "I'm sure you've already heard that I'm crazy. Well. That's no lie."

I shrugged. "I don't need to hear stories. I'm sitting right here, you bought me coffee, and I like the way you cross your ankles." Keep it casual, that was the ticket.

Another flash of the real smile, the one that made me want to unravel her and kiss her back together. Which, yes, was stupid, and reckless, and probably a side effect of mass making me feel happy with humanity.

"You like the way I cross my ankles." Damn, her voice was sexy.

"Maybe."

She held out her hand. "Well, Jaq, I've heard a lot of pretty things in my time, but that's gotta be one of the most sincere."

"I do my best." We shook hands, formally, both of us smiling.

"I should get to my meeting. Thank you for coming to coffee with me."

"Thanks for buying. I'll . . . see you around." I almost told her I'd call her, but the return of her more public face made me stop.

"You certainly will."

Both of us stood and exchanged cheek kisses.

"Good luck with the apartment."

"You too! Oh, god, that's ridiculous, I meant: have a good day!"

I waved and watched her walk away. Man. She knew I was watching, judging by the swing in her hips. But hell, of course I was watching.

When she turned the corner, I headed to the closest bus stop, catching sight of St. Agnes in the distance. Okay, clearly this would not be a relationship. But I was an adult. I could draw a line between "boinking Marla's hot ex, who just so happens to be moving to La Vista and has the body of a forties pinup girl" and "having a serious relationship with someone who doesn't deny being crazy in relationships."

Decision made. *Dear Jesus, thank you for bringing me back together with my one-night stand of last week. Should we get it on again, it will be all about you. Not in a creepy way. Love, Jaq.*

CHAPTER

I waited five days before calling. When Hannah didn't return my call, I figured I'd see her at church on Sunday. I didn't.

I told myself this was better than the alternative. Better to be done with the whole idea now than drag it out, no matter how good the sex was. Whatever connection I thought I'd felt was probably fabricated based on some dumb desire to feel something. It didn't matter. She was sharp and sexy, and recently out of a relationship. No way she was interested in more than a hookup.

Life continued. An ex-girlfriend had a baby. I sent flowers and a stuffed elephant. I helped my dad plant strawberries. My classes were gearing up for the end of the school year, my handful of seniors in Journalism and Creative Writing were gearing up for graduation, and my queer kids were gearing up to survive spending a lot more time at home during the summer.

All of them were at least a little caught up in the end-of-the-year excitement, sometimes despite themselves, but the real thing they had to process this close to the last day of school was their home lives. Only Sammy was out to his family. "Out" in a tentative, quiet way. "Out" as long as he never brought a boy around and promised he'd try to "do better," as if being gay were something he could fix if he worked hard enough at it.

The GSA met every Friday at lunch in my classroom. When it first started five years ago, the rest of the school had avoided my hall during lunch as if they might catch something. The kids said occasionally they'd get harassed coming in or out, but the hall itself was a coffin during our weekly meeting. These days apparently the shine had worn off jeering the queers, at least on Friday lunchtimes, so when Merin showed up, it was at least possible she didn't know we were there.

Then again, it was possible she did.

She slid in the door, eyes wary, interrupting Callie, who would probably be calling herself Calvin or Corey in a couple of years, when she had the ability to present the way she felt. Since Callie didn't speak much, I was irritated, and called to Merin that we were having a meeting and to catch me at some other time.

"It'll only take a second," she said, still standing there, right inside the door, no trace of the aggressive sneer she usually wore like armor.

That alone was enough to intrigue me.

"I'll be right back," I told them, making eye contact with Callie especially.

Merin slid back out into the hallway half a step ahead of me and shocked me, to my guts, by leading with, "Sorry."

For a full minute I just blinked at her. Kids like Merin didn't apologize. And when they did, it was—intense.

"What do you need?" I asked, dashing the minilecture I'd planned to give her.

"It's about LaTasha."

"LaTasha?"

She shifted, her big floppy sneakers squeaking on the floor. This close up, her hair appeared damaged where the elastic bit into it every day and she looked damn tired. She probably had a job—at seventeen, most of them did something—but she hadn't looked this tired before.

"Merin, what about LaTasha?"

"She's freaked out by this murder thing. Keeps talking about it." She glanced up, eyes skating across mine, not catching. Her tone was a little defensive. "We're kind of neighbors."

I didn't know if I should take that in the "I spy on her from my bedroom with binoculars" sense, or the "I see her around even though we aren't friends" sense.

"Okay. The murder she found in the paper?"

A languid shrug that belied the tension coming off her in waves. "Guess so."

"How can I help?" I needed to get back to my room, and I had no idea what we were actually talking about, except that Merin wasn't telling me everything.

"Can you talk to her or something? Tell her it's not a big deal?"

"Well. I can ask her about it."

"Thanks, Ms. C." Without even looking up, she turned on her squeaky soles and took off down the hall, loping toward the far doors.

"You're welcome," I mumbled.

Merin. LaTasha. Merin was a junior, but LaTasha was graduating this year. She'd been on my internal list of "kids who're gonna be fine," but I flagged her name and returned to the GSA in progress.

Sometimes the ones I thought were holding it all together were really the ones I should worry about. And Merin wouldn't reach out unless she thought something was wrong. Damn.

Callie was laughing at some hijink of Sammy's when I returned to the meeting, so at least that was good. Laughing freely was one of the greatest gifts the GSA could give my little queer kids. Crying freely too.

Zane and I caught a workout early, and when she asked if I wanted to go out, I said no. I wasn't in the mood. And to be more specific, I was a little worried I'd see Hannah if we went to any of the usual places. I didn't want to see her out there grinding on some other woman. I figured I'd give myself one more weekend to feel sad that my brief fantasy of seeing her again (okay, getting it on with her again) didn't work out before I forced myself back into dating-potential spaces.

I always wished I were one of those people who didn't have any desire to date. I could have partied and screwed and enjoyed myself forever if it wasn't for this irritating half-assed desire for a steady relationship. So inconvenient.

Three episodes into *Brooklyn Nine-Nine*, I'd managed to get a good, solid chunk of grading done for my normal English classes, as well as sight-proofing the last newspaper of the year. Sounds lazy, I know, but at this point—after the articles were plugged into the layout, when our in-class copyeditor had been over them, when I've edited each of them at least once, and the section editors have been over them as well—I just couldn't read them again. So I scanned them. And it wasn't as bad as it sounded; you could catch a surprising number of basic punctuation errors at a glance. Plus, the most important thing was to go over the captions. This group had thought they were pretty clever in the fall and had snuck a bunch of roughly coded dirty jokes in the captions, which I'd privately found hilarious and publicly castigated them over.

They'd been tricky. Swapped letters to hide curse words, coded language to refer to, uh, things that should not be referred to in a high school newspaper. The only saving grace was that I had caught on before the administration did and had already punished them when my vice-principal "dropped in" to gently break it to me that my class was "taking advantage" of my "trusting nature." Fortunately they'd only noticed one joke in one paper, and not the more subtle jokes in the rest of that issue and the two before it. Really, I was a little proud of the class. Obviously I didn't let *them* know that.

I celebrated the first part of my weekend work with a fancy cream soda and was standing at my freezer when my phone rang. Hannah.

No. Not gonna answer.

I carefully put the phone on the counter.

No good could come of answering that phone. Maybe it was a wrong number. She was calling a Jamie or a Julie and she slipped and dialed me instead. Or maybe she had a question about St. Agnes. She might have forgotten what time mass was, which would account for her absence on Sunday.

All right, obviously that was totally ridiculous. No one calls on a Friday night to ask what time church is.

People only call on Friday nights for one reason. Right?

The phone stopped ringing. *Missed Call from Hannah.* Good. Let it be missed. She wouldn't leave a message. She'd find someone else to entertain her.

I made a big show of not caring, using the freezer door to propel cold air at my flushed skin, assuring myself that I was flushed because of the heat, not because of Hannah's name on my phone. Or all the possible promises it could hold.

Missed calls could be ignored. Or returned. I reluctantly closed the freezer (Dad would have said, "You think electricity's free, missy?"). I even more reluctantly picked up my phone and went back to grading.

It buzzed in my hand. *New Voicemail Message.*

She'd left a message.

The bitch of it was that I liked the *idea* of having a steady lady in my life, the kind of friend who could call, casually, on a Friday night and propose we do Friday-night-things. Like dance. And kiss. And have sex. It was such a great idea. But when I'd put it into practice in the past, it had always devolved into tears and hurt feelings and the sensation that I'd stumbled into *The Lesbian Twilight Zone*, a dimension of sight, sound, and emotional processing the likes of which the world has never seen.

Damn that blinking light on my phone.

I gave in and played the message.

"Babe! Tell me you're available to come out with me! I've had nothing but fucking horrible meetings all week and I need to get very, very drunk." A pause. The line filled with white noise for a second. "I'm smoking my last cigarette, Jaq! Last one! I'm done with all that! I'm also standing outside Oakland Airport and I need both hands to keep my dress from indecently exposing me, so I gotta go. Call me back if you want to get together!"

Click.

I'd left her a message a week ago. Which she hadn't returned. Now she wanted to go out and get drunk with me, because of course she hadn't even noticed that I don't drink.

Everything about it was a bad idea. Except the part where if I called her back, I'd get laid. And it wasn't a school night. I'd already decided not to get emotionally involved. One time. One night. Sex. Sex would be so much better than grading papers.

What the hell was I thinking? I could not go out and watch Hannah get sloppy. *No more babysitting drunks* was a rule I'd made after the last time I'd babysat a drunk and called it "dating." We'd lasted long enough for Zane to sketch a diagram of the relationship in chili cheese fries one night at Club Fred's. When your best friend makes a food sculpture to demonstrate how badly matched you and the person you're banging are, it's probably time to end it.

When you're already thinking about that and it hasn't even started yet . . . that was probably also a sign.

I sank into my chair and tried to focus on— I had no idea what I was even grading anymore. I glanced at the last three papers and had no recollection of even reading them.

Damn it. I pulled out my phone again and stared at it, as if it were an oracle. As if it could give me an answer. Maybe some kind of rating system. Is there an app for that? You say, "I'm thinking about calling Hannah back and going out with her because I'm bored and lonely and she's hot and the sex is good." And your phone flashes *Good call* or *Are you fucking serious right now?*

Someone should invent that.

Screw it. I downed the last of my cream soda and dialed.

"Jaq! I'm so glad you called. I just got into the hotel, but I haven't checked in yet. Where are you?"

"Home. Grading papers."

She laughed. Damn, she had a good laugh. "Listen, come out drinking with me and I'll make it worth your while. I promise."

"I don't drink."

"How do you stay hydrated?"

"I don't drink booze," I clarified. "Not in years."

"Do you not go to bars?"

"I go to bars."

"Then come out with me, Jaq. I mean, unless you can't be around it or something—"

"I can be around it."

"Tell me where we should go, and let's go there. I was a good little girl and didn't drink a drop on the plane, but now Mama's gotta relax."

I cracked a smile despite myself. "Mama?"

She giggled. Grown women don't usually giggle, but her laughter bubbled up like a hot spring. "I am *in need*, Jaq."

I knew I should resist. But damn, come on, she was *in need*. "You been to Club Fred's?"

"Is that like Club Med?"

"Okay, that was the original idea, but it was like twenty years ago, so now it's a mash-up of Club Med and twenty years of drunks and club kids."

"Sounds dreadful."

"It has its charms. You want to meet there? It's on the corner of San Pablo and Steerage, and the parking's terrible."

"I will meet you there, gorgeous. But wait—"

"Yes?"

"Listen, Jaq, I like you, but—"

Oh my god.

"—I am going to be disgusting tonight, so you have to promise not to hold it against me. Tomorrow I will be a brand-new girl, all right?"

It took me a minute to recover. "So why are you inviting me along, then?"

"Honey, I'll be drunk and slightly pathetic, not stupid. Plus, a good fuck is the perfect thing to get my mind off this week." That giggle again. "Not that I'm calling you easy."

I really am. I made my voice stern, like I was lecturing my kids. "I hope you aren't going to be too drunk to perform. I'm considering that a verbal contract, counselor."

"Oh, it is. I'll change out of my responsible clothes and meet up with you in . . . an hour?"

"I'll see you there."

"Wonderful."

Even as I hung up, I thought she might not show. As I got changed, I texted Zane to shut the fuck up if she should happen to see us (and ignored her mocking replies). I tried not to drive when I didn't have to because street parking was always a bitch at my apartment, but tonight I took the truck. I'd want the quick getaway, and I'd definitely want to be able to ferry Hannah off into the night if she decided to come home with me.

A good fuck. Yeah. I could definitely manage that. I lectured myself on not getting emotionally involved all the way to Fred's.

Hannah was easy to spot in the crowd. She wore a garnet-colored blouse and black slacks that seemed to bell out slightly at the bottom. Her hair was pulled back again, this time secured with a small black bow.

Not that I was staring at her as I walked across the floor to her. Until she laughed, tilting her head back, at which point everyone in the vicinity who had any inclination toward women looked at her.

"Hey there." I moved in a little closer than I'd normally stand.

She reached out and this time she kissed me lightly on the mouth. *We are not at church anymore, Toto.* "Jaq, I'm so glad you're here. I was just talking to—" Delicate pause.

I turned to the woman she'd been talking to, all flowing braids and wild skirt. "Alisha. Hey, girl."

"I can't believe you're out on a school night!" Alisha called over the music, brushing back her mane of wild dark hair.

"It's Friday!"

"What?"

"Friday! Not a school night!"

"It's Friday?"

Hannah laughed again. "It better be. Because I am *not* flying back to Los Angeles. Not gonna do it."

"Oh, Los Angeles?" Alisha's face brightened. "Why were you there?"

I leaned back against the wall while Hannah explained that she was between homes at the moment, and that she used to live there. Alisha, face set on cat-with-laser-pointer (at least she wasn't set on dog-humping-couch-leg), leaned in closer to hear. After exhausting LA as a topic, Hannah asked Alisha about herself.

"I'm so boring compared to you! Someday I'm going on an adventure, though, I swear."

"Is that right? What kind of adventure?"

I couldn't gauge Hannah's tone completely, but I didn't think I'd have to worry about her taking Alisha home with her tonight. She caught my eye and flashed a smile.

"I don't know!" A slightly manic gleam lit Alisha's eyes. "I don't even know! Maybe I'll ride my bike across Europe. Or maybe I'll hike the Appalachian Trail. Or go to some remote jungle where no one ever goes and just . . . be there, you know? Just be there, in space, like no big deal."

"Sounds incredible!" Hannah hooked my arm. "I owe this lady a drink, Alisha, but it was really nice meeting you!"

"Oh, you too!" In seconds she'd turned away and was talking to the two guys behind her.

"Wasn't she adorable?" Hannah said into my ear as we made our way to the bar. "A little light on smarts, though."

"I don't think it's that. I think it's more that she's—heavy on dreaming. Always was. I think she was a big drama kid in high school."

"Good god, you remember her from high school?" She shook her head. "My folks sent me to St. Patrick's, which I was pissed about at the time, but now I think it might have been a blessing. I don't have all those memories of everyone and their brother. My graduating class had twenty-four people in it, and as far as I know, I'm the only queer."

"I definitely remember everyone and their brother." I gestured to the couple at the jukebox. "The redhead's brother was my second kiss, I'll have you know. We were twelve."

"Ooh la la. Tell me more about that. Is he also a redhead?"

I touched my hair like I was nervous. "Why? You got a redhead thing?"

"I like all kinds of hair." Then she reached up to touch my hair too, and I shivered. "Wish you had a tie on, though, princess."

"You did not call me 'princess.'"

She grinned and leaned in close, lips brushing my ear. "Would you rather I called you my prince? As long as you know I'm the queen."

So unfair the way her words unsettled me. They were just a joke. She was being playful. But damn.

I heard Zane's laughter before I saw her, and I couldn't decide if I was relieved or annoyed at the interruption.

"Hey, slacker!" She hugged me from behind.

"Shut up. Hannah, you remember Zane?"

"Of course. Nice to see you again."

"I'm glad someone thinks so. Jaq's shooting daggers."

I glared at her. But not *daggers*. "Seriously?"

Cue Zane's impish grin. "You love me so much right now. I can tell. Did you tell Hannah about the *Queers of La Vista*?"

"Oh, what's *that*?"

"Nothing," I said. "Only Zane's bizarre fixation on making everyone around her into a soap opera."

"It's not everyone! It's just everyone at Club Fred's. Like over there we have the quiet, contained gay guy. It's not just an act, it's a lifestyle, and it looks like he's on Facebook—but I bet you he's reading a book on his phone. He considers sitting here reading more social than sitting at home, but no one's quite sure how to break into his shell."

Hannah's gaze tracked Zane's. "He looks like a nice guy. Maybe a little serial killer with that turtleneck, but otherwise."

"He's lovely, really. Owns the local independent theater downtown. Anyway, Hannah, are you here-here, or still doing the back and forth?"

"Oh, the back and forth, trying to sell my house."

I groaned. "Don't tell Zane about—"

"Selling your house?" Zane insinuated herself between us at the bar. "Tell me more. What's the market like down there? For a hot minute it was a buyer's market here, but right now we're seeing a lot of folks take their places off the market in order to update them. When they hit again, the prices will be through the roof."

I sighed. Heavily. "Do we really have to talk housing market?"

Hannah shot me a grin and leaned closer to Zane. "Tell me all about it! The house has been on the market for six months and we've gotten two bites—*two*—but my ex refuses to lower the asking price. Does that even make sense?"

I gave up. Plus, Zane managed to get a lot more out of Hannah about her ex than I had, probably by merit of not being all that interested.

"You know how some people have a kid to save their marriage? Sandy and I bought a house that"—elegant fingers crooked in the air—"'needed a little TLC.'"

Zane winced. "Famous last words. What shape is it in now?"

"Oh, perfect, but we ended up spending so much on the remodel that she's lost all perspective when it comes to pricing it."

"Yeah, improvements always have more value to sellers than they do to buyers. That's inconvenient for you, though."

Hannah nodded, sipping her gin and tonic. "All I want is to sell it, split the money, and start over. But until that happens, I feel like part of me is constantly waiting."

"I sympathize. I have seen that happen and it's ugly." Zane shook her head. "Is your agent going nuts?"

"You have no idea. She used to try to get me to intercede, but I think she realized that any time I made a suggestion, Sandy refused out of spite. Now she goes straight to the source."

"She can't afford to buy you out?" Zane asked. "Seems like that would be the easiest thing."

Hannah's eyes cut away and she shrugged. "I guess not. Anyway, Zane, when I'm a little more free with my finances, you'll definitely be hearing from me to buy up here."

"In La Vista? Or in the Bay Area at large?"

"I guess it all depends exactly how free I am with my finances, right?"

Zane, with a move I knew she'd practiced because I'd seen her, flipped a business card to land on the bar in front of Hannah. "I'm so interested. I've shown a few of those places, but the Harbor District is still a tough sell to a lot of people. And I mostly do commercial, though I'd definitely make an exception to get an in there."

They talked for a while longer (something something real estate something). Hannah finished her first G&T and excused us to Zane. This time she said, "I owe this lady a dance."

"Or three," Zane said. "Enjoy yourselves, girls!"

"Oh, we will." Hannah winked at me.

I let her go first, thinking I should have dressed up a little more. Not that a tight white shirt with a black vest over it didn't make me look good, but something about Hannah leading me through the crowd toward the dance floor made me wish I'd upped my game. Like with a tie.

Man, I liked settling my hands on her hips and leaving them there.

This was raunchier, sweatier, sexier dancing—not that a formal keep-your-distance dance couldn't be sexy, just that it got its sexy from a different place. On the floor at Club Fred's, the sexy came from pressure, slide, *grind*, and Hannah was right there with me. I'd expected her to drink more and dance less, but I definitely wasn't complaining.

"Naughty, naughty!" she called after I held her pressed against me for a prolonged minute of "dancing." She hooked one leg around my ass, letting me take her weight, and we ground against each other mercilessly until I almost lost balance and crashed us to the floor.

We separated for a few breaths, laughing amid all the bodies pulsing and sweating around us.

"Damn!" She tugged me to her. "Rain check on that. More horizontal next time!"

"Hell yes!"

We got back to dancing and took turns performing silly moves, spins, turns, always ending up with arms locked around bodies, breathing hard against skin. I could have skipped working out entirely; dancing in Fred's with Hannah kept my heart rate up, and more than that, kept me interested. We challenged each other—to be goofy, to be sexy, to be ridiculous.

After one such (poorly judged) move, in which I landed in a slide not at all like Tom Cruise, she tugged me close. "Come back to the hotel with me."

It was the moment I'd been waiting for since I heard her message, but now that it was here, I faltered. "Thought you were getting drunk?"

"That was the plan, but plans change." She tipped her forehead against mine. "Can you be my distraction, Jaq?"

Yes, and *no*, and *I don't think that's really what I want, but I guess if it's the only thing I can get* . . . I made my voice low and playfully seductive to cover my confusion. "I think I might be able to handle that."

She laughed and led me away, off the floor, past the bar, my hand securely in hers. It was a move I usually found eye-rolling, but like most eye-rolling moves, when I was inside it, I didn't have any objection. This might end up being a bad idea, but right now it was hot.

I'm going off to get fucked by a beautiful woman. Eat your hearts out, Queers of La Vista.

Not that anyone paid attention or cared in the least, obviously, but for a moment I let myself become a character in a romcom, triumphantly following my date out the door.

CHAPTER  6

Hannah was staying in one of the nicer chain hotels in La Vista. Not that anything in La Vista is particularly nice, but this was about as fancy as it got, as in the doors face an interior hallway, not the street.

"There's a hot tub," she purred in my ear. "It's too late to use it, technically, but I'm sure my key still works."

"I don't have a bathing suit."

"Neither do I. We'll have to be creative." Her face did a . . . thing.

"Did you just waggle your eyebrows at me?"

"Are you feeling the power of my eyebrows? They can be very seductive."

I laughed and pushed her lightly. "Stop it. Open the damn door."

"You're right. And I'd rather not get arrested, so I suppose skinny-dipping is a bad idea. All I have is this slip." She trailed her fingers over her stomach. "I think white satin probably goes translucent in hot water, don't you?"

White satin. I swallowed. "You know, on second thought—"

Hannah held up her room card. "Lost your chance, Jaq. Next time you shouldn't thumb your nose at my seductive eyebrows."

"My bad."

Nice room, clean bathroom, welcoming-looking bed.

"Stand still, sugar. I'm gonna open you up like a gift."

I turned toward her and held my hands out to my sides. "I look wrapped to you?"

"Oh yes. Wrapped all sweetly with a missing bow." Her fingers traced my collar. "If I had a tie in my luggage, I'd put it on you just to take it off again. I might lead you around by it first."

"Kinky." I tried not to betray how breathless she made me.

"Mmm. Stay still."

I could do that. I could stand in the middle of the hotel room while Hannah turned on a lamp and turned off the ceiling light, casting everything in shadow. Last time we'd been in an anonymous room like this, we'd barely stopped for breath. This time she made me wait, and the waiting was good, too. It gave me time to notice that she was a bit of a slob, that even though she'd only checked in a few hours before, she'd made her mark on the room. Shoes here and there, suitcase unzipped only partway so that clothes spilled out as if escaping. A larger purse than the one she'd had at Club Fred's sat on the desk with at least half its contents surrounding it, as if she'd had to pick through to pull out whatever she wanted to bring with her.

An e-reader poked out from within the bag. *So she reads.* I know it's judgey of me, and I know not everyone gets their storytelling rocks off with the written word, but I always feel so much better when I'm kissing someone who reads. It's an automatic common ground, a sign I'll never have to explain my bookshelves, or the stack beside my bed.

"See something you like, baby?"

I shook my head at her. "Really? And yeah, that doesn't look like a Kindle."

"Kobo Glo." She walked over to grab it, fluffing her hair out as she went.

I totally did not go slack-jawed at the idea of running my hands through her hair.

"Here, look." She handed me the Kobo. "I didn't mind my Kindle, but this is a little more sleek to my eye."

"I only have an incredibly old Kindle, so for all I know the new ones are practically iPads now, but this is definitely more finished-feeling than my Touch." I ran my fingers around its edges. "But does it get the same battery? I never think to charge my Touch."

"More or less. I think it probably gets the same as the Kindle with the light, but not quite as good as your Touch." She grinned. "I could use a little of your touch right now, if you can put my book down."

"But it's so *sexy*." I lewdly ran my fingertips down the sides.

"I'm so sexy, you brat."

"That's true." I tucked her thing back into the purse and turned, but she backed my ass into the desk before I could go anywhere. "Hello."

"Hello." A leg slid between my thighs, and she slowly raised her arms to fluff out her hair. "Now do you see something you like?"

"Next time let me do that. I, uh, like your hair."

"Mmm. If you're a good girl, maybe."

Then again, the way her breasts pushed against her blouse when she had her arms up wasn't exactly a hardship to bear. I reached out, but she tsked.

"Don't move."

I leaned back on the desk and enjoyed the sight of a woman trying to turn me on.

"Now, Jaq." She raised an eyebrow. "Have you been naughty or nice this year?"

"Are you going for Santa? You do know it's May."

She tipped my chin up with a finger. "Naughty or nice?"

Damn. "Naughty. Very, very naughty."

"I thought so." Her fingers dragged down my throat and started working on my buttons. "I think I'm going to sit on your face and get off tonight."

Fuck yes. I made my voice coy. "Is that my punishment?" A second later she took my nipple in some kind of inhuman vise grip, and I gasped.

"Excuse me? Allowing you to taste me is a gift, sugar, don't you think?"

"Yes. Yes, I do." I sucked in a breath when she let go. "Oh my god."

"Too much?" She dragged her knuckles over my aching nipple.

"Not too much. Unexpected, though."

"I do my best." She went back to the rest of my buttons, then pushed the vest out of the way, and the shirt, so she could run her hands down my body. "God, the shape you're in. So fucking sexy. I don't have anything like the willpower to have your body."

"You get a lot of complaints?"

"I don't get any complaints. Ever. Now." Her fingers were cool as they dipped inside my slacks. "You're gonna taste so good."

I nodded, as if I were agreeing, when really I was just abjectly offering my approval of whatever was about to happen that included her unfastening my pants and then tasting me. Because *yes*.

"Nice." My slacks landed in a heap on the floor. "I do love a woman who doesn't bother with panties." She sank to her knees. "In the chair, and spread your legs for me."

"Hell yes." I abandoned dignity and jumped into the chair.

"Eager girl." She pressed my thighs apart and began a thorough investigation of my body. Starting at its center. No seduction, no finesse.

You know how they say the tongue is the strongest muscle in the human body? Hannah really reinforced that old lesson. And she had *control*, too. I was twitching and jerking and bucking up into her mouth and she was absolutely relentless, holding me down and fucking me. She flicked my clit over and over again with the tip of her tongue while she *looked* at me. I shuddered.

It was way too fucking intense, but I couldn't ask her to slow down. I couldn't lose face. She was trying to push me to the edge, I could feel it, and I'd be damned if I let her win. I gathered all of my dignity and absolutely refused to come in thirty seconds like a teenage boy, even if the things her mouth was doing were probably illegal in some parts of the country.

So I grinned, probably a little dementedly, and she slowed down.

Wait, was that my plan? Yes, right? Or no? Hold up, what was my goal?

I reached for a nipple and started playing with myself.

Of course she pulled far enough away to say, "No touching."

I sighed heavily and pouted.

I don't know how long she tortured me with her tongue and her lips, dragging them across my skin, sucking in bits of me that couldn't resist that kind of pressure, driving me a little insane. By the time she rose up to stand over me, I was tingling, and all I could do was stare up at her.

"Go lie down," she said. "You can take the rest of your clothes off."

Right, because I still technically had on my shirt. And vest.

Hannah giggled, surveying me. "Don't tell me I broke you. You didn't even come."

"Do you have any idea how impossible that was? I'm exhausted now." I slouched low in a mock swoon.

"That's how naughty little girls prove they're nice."

"Did I?"

"You did." She knelt over my legs, and the hotel chair creaked beneath us. "Now for your reward."

I inhaled the scent of her that close, that hot. "Your wish is my command, my queen."

"Oh honey." She took my lips, kissing me deeply, stealing my breath. She tasted like both of us, and it was heady as hell thinking that in a few minutes, so would I. "On the bed."

Because I thought she'd like it, I lowered my eyes. "Yes, my lady."

She growled. "Fuck yes."

I stretched out on my back while she stripped off her clothes and climbed over me. When she didn't scold me for resting my hands on her legs, I rubbed little circles with my fingertips. "Your skin's so fucking soft."

"That's fat, honey."

I lifted my head so I could lick a swirling design on her thigh. "Nope. No, definitely skin. Definitely soft."

"Mmm, I don't like being teased."

"Oh really?"

"Really."

I did it again, taking my time, curling my tongue into the tender skin of her inner thigh. "How do you feel about that?"

She shuddered. "Oh fuck."

I wanted her to come apart like she'd so easily taken me apart, so I kept playing with her skin, lazily, like it wasn't going anywhere, like we might be here all night. I wasn't about to rush. Even though she smelled so fucking good I could barely keep from drooling.

"Damn you, just—" She attempted to pull me in closer.

I refused. "Patience, your majesty."

"Smartass." But she let go of my head in order to grab the headboard and raise herself over me.

I could have stopped her, but fuck it. So much better to use my fingers on her waxed lips, use my thumb to spread some of her moisture all the way up to her clit, making her jump.

"You are my fucking tool, get to work."

"That's not a very nice way to talk to your prince." I inhaled deeply and leaned forward, thumbing her more open for my tongue.

She moaned, rocking into me, and I couldn't help smiling. She wanted it fast, I wanted it slow, so I concentrated a little too intensely with the tip of my tongue and, when she backed away, I punished her by ignoring her clit altogether.

It only took her a minute to catch on and dig her fingernails sharply into my scalp. "You trying to be cute?"

Yes. I brushed my cheeks against her, and she cried out, pressing me in harder. For a second I thought she might come right then, humping the side of my face, but she got herself under control and dragged one of my hands to her mouth.

My turn to writhe while she sucked my fingers, knowing she wanted me to watch, even though what I wanted to do was reach down and fuck myself while she fellated my fingers.

She released me and said, lips glistening, "My ass, okay? If you fuck me right now I'll come on your face."

And okay then. "Sounds good."

I'd never quite done this before, and it took a minute to find the right position. I could angle myself and reach in between her legs, which had its advantages.

"This is like school." She watched me, letting me slightly rearrange her so my left arm wrapped around her leg and my right arm slid between them.

"I get consistently excellent marks in this subject," I shot back, before applying my lips to her labia, playing, teasing, buying time to get my spit-slick fingers to her ass.

She started trembling before I'd even gotten inside, so I didn't push in immediately. I sucked a little at her skin and let my fingers pulse against her pucker, knowing she was desperate by the way her hips bucked, trying to fuck me on both sides.

"You little brat, damn you, give me what I need—"

So rude. I wished I had lube, but she'd probably spank me if I paused the festivities at the moment. Maybe literally.

Not that I was against that.

My middle finger pressed more insistently, and she sighed, pushing out, making it easier for me to get in. It had been a while since I'd played like this, and I'd forgotten how tight the ass could be, even when it was ready and willing. I crooked my finger, and she moaned again, so I backed off my oral attentions a little until I was laying sweet little stripes along her lips with my tongue.

Hannah shook above me, her weight mostly on the headboard. My neck was gonna fucking kill me after this. I made a mental note to demand a massage later.

"Oh god, oh god, do it— Jaq— More—"

I could have used both of my fingers, but they'd be going in pretty damn dry, and it wasn't really my style. Instead I fucked her good with one finger while—hey, convenient—crooking my thumb back to tease her slit.

"Ahhhhhhhgh—"

High marks, baby. I latched onto her clit and took her hard, everything moving at once, trying with my other arm to hold her in place while she bucked and cried out.

There was nothing like a woman coming in your mouth and around your fingers all at once. Her muscles went tight as she hit the peak and held it as long as she could, while I flattened my tongue against her and let her control the last few seconds of sensation.

"Oh fuck, oh fuck, yes, yes, Jaq, yes—"

I had no hand to spare for myself, so I squeezed my legs together and felt my own arousal throb there, not sated, but I was content enough to let it grow without release while Hannah pulsed through a second wave, pulling my face harder against her until she was completely wrung out.

"God, Jaq, that . . ." She shuddered and sighed and let go of my head. "You don't mind if I tie you to my bed and only let you loose for bathroom breaks, do you?"

I carefully withdrew my finger. "My boss might have a problem with that plan."

"Lord, girl, I can't even tell you how good that was." She slid down, still a little above me, but at my side now, pulling my face up for a kiss. "You taste like fucking."

"Damn straight."

"Oh, nothing was straight about what we just did." One of her hands drifted down my side. "Feeling frustrated?"

"Not in a bad way."

"That's no good."

"Are you pouting right now?"

She laughed, fingers slipping into my cleft. I let my legs fall open in a way I hoped landed on "sexy," not "desperately horny." Then again, they weren't mutually exclusive. Hannah didn't seem daunted. "Pussy wants a little love?"

"*Please.*" I thrust against her questing fingers.

"Poor pussy." She lowered her head to my chest so she could take a nipple in her teeth.

My body couldn't decide where it wanted more attention. Obviously my clit wanted her fingers to fucking get it together, but damn, her mouth felt so good.

Oh, oh, yes, fuck yes, she slid inside, and I reached down to press her in deeper. I got a sharp nip from her teeth in retaliation, but I didn't care. I kept trying to fuck myself on her fingers and her hand and my hand and anything at all that I could reach.

"Get yourself off, baby." She kissed across to my other breast. "Do it. Get yourself off while I fuck you."

Oh yeah, let's do this thing. I let her take over, good deep strokes into my cunt, while my own fingers shifted to my clit, and for a second the visual overwhelmed me: she was sucking my breast, but she'd turned herself so she could see our hands, both of us fucking me and watching me unravel.

It was too much. I let go of everything and closed my eyes, giving over to the orgasm, and how fucking hot it was that she was watching my fingers on my clit as I fucked myself over the edge.

I gasped and tried to ride the orgasm for as long as I could, but *just enough* became *way too much* faster than I liked and I flinched away from her fingers.

"You are so fucking hot." She lightly kissed my chest, directly over my sternum.

"You too. Also you owe me a neck rub."

"And a shower. Come on, prince."

She managed to get up without making any embarrassing noises. I wasn't quite as lucky.

"Ow. What the hell did you do to me, woman?" I groaned, stretching my arms above my head.

"Fucked you but good. You complaining?"

"Not even a little." Then, not quite sure if it was appropriate, I kissed her.

"Mmm." She kissed me back, but only for a moment before pulling away. "Shower."

Right.

"Fancy hotel shower." I walked ahead of her. "Little soaps and shampoos."

"Jaq."

I made sure my eyebrow was cocked irreverently before I turned back to her. "Yes?"

"Spend the night. Since you don't have to work in the morning. I'll buy you breakfast."

My heart did a little stumble, and I told it to get the hell out of my unemotional not-relationship. *This is no place for hearts.* "Sure. But I know you're just using me for my mad sex skills. You don't have to bribe me."

Her lips curled. "Now that you've figured out my plan I can never let you leave."

"You supply the hotel soaps and I'm yours." And I turned the fuck back toward the bathroom before she could see how true I wanted that to be.

"Don't tempt me."

I wanted to tempt her. I wanted to seduce her. I wanted to spend the night and eat breakfast in the morning. I wouldn't say no to being tied to her bed, either.

Batshit, I lectured myself as I turned on the water and waited for it to get hot.

Then she pressed against me and reached around to tweak a nipple.

I was in so much trouble.

CHAPTER 7

I didn't have to get up early for school, but I did have to get up at some point, after two slightly less athletic romps in the morning.

"But why are you leaving?" Hannah was draped upside down on the bed, limbs every which way.

"To be fair, it's noon."

She scrunched her nose, making me laugh.

"Roller derby bout."

"Roller derby bout. *That's* what you're getting out of bed to do?"

Yeah, I couldn't really picture her at a bout. "Uh-huh. Want to come?" The second I said it, I froze. Jesus, what if she said yes?

"What, now?"

I would have sat down, but I thought she might try to seduce me or something, so I dragged the chair over and propped my feet on the bed. "Yeah, doors open at four, bout starts at five, and it's a doubleheader, so it'll probably run until ten or so."

"Five *hours* of roller derby? Do they lock you in?" She rolled over and reached for one of my feet. Oh god. *Stay strong. Do not give in just because she's giving you a fucking unsolicited foot massage right now.*

"I like roller derby, so five hours is actually a good thing. You want to come?"

"Can't. I'm due at Marla and Liz's for dinner."

I let my jaw drop theatrically open. "Oh-h. Funnnn."

She switched to tickling in retaliation. "I didn't even really agree to it. They proposed dinner, I said I thought I was probably free, then I got an email from Marla's calendar telling me what time to arrive."

"From her *calendar?*"

"Yes. Like she's my boss and she scheduled me for something." The massage intensified. "Don't you want to stay here, with me, and irresponsibly dodge all of our commitments?"

"Hey, don't lump dinner with the charming brides in with roller derby. I'm actually looking forward to my thing."

"What, more than staying here with me and having a lot of sex? We could spend the whole day naked and call for room service, Jaq!"

I pulled my foot away. "You clearly haven't seen what public school teachers get paid in this state."

Hannah groaned and flopped onto her back. "That's really what you say when I propose a naked day in a hotel room?"

That's really what I say when I'm taking this way too seriously. "So beg off Marla and come with me to the bout. Have you ever watched roller derby?"

"My brain classifies it as 'football, but fewer pads, no ball, roller skates.'" She waved a lazy arm. "At least they're hot. Full contact in a violent way, not a sexy way."

"Hannah! You—you didn't . . ."

She slid farther down the bed so she could hang her head over, looking at me, still upside down. "I think that's the first time you've actually addressed me using my name. Now *that's* sexy."

I sputtered. There's no classier way to say it. I tried to respond, didn't know what to say, and sputtered.

Hannah, of course, laughed at me. "Oh, you're blushing! That's adorable as hell. Fine, you can leave me to watch women in tight clothes skate around in circles. I will go play nice with our exes while they try to tell me everything I'm doing wrong in my life."

"Have fun with that."

"Oh, your turn will come. Presumably they think I'm in more dire need of meddling, but I don't think you should assume you're off their list."

I rolled my eyes. "I've been dodging Liz all week, actually."

"Ha. There you go. You sure you don't want another orgasm or two before you leave me?"

"You're insatiable," I mumbled. I leaned down for a kiss, which was probably ridiculous, but fuck it. Kissing Hannah felt good. "Behave yourself with the newlyweds."

"I won't have an opportunity for anything else. And with the new puppy—"

"Don't get me started on the new puppy. Zane's calling it their love child."

She snorted. "Too damn true. Have fun watching the ladies skate."

"You know I will."

Hannah didn't rouse herself from the bed, but she did blow me a kiss as I left.

My friends were fucking trouble. Always had been. Zane and I had been in the same year at school; Carlos had been one year ahead of us. We hadn't met Tom until college, which probably explained why he was the nicest one.

"I can't *believe* you spent the night!" Zane called over the roar of the derby crowd cheering on the tiny jammer as she wove and slipped through her opponents, scoring five points in ten seconds while no one seemed able to catch her.

"What? What's the problem with that?" At least I managed to catch myself before saying *We already spent the night together last time*, which would have been so very stupid.

"I don't think Zane's saying there's a *problem* with it," Carlos said. "It's just not all that characteristic of you."

Zane shoved my shoulder. "I'm fucking proud of you! You've had kind of a dry spell lately!"

"Hey! I can spend the night with people!"

"You could, sure. But usually you come up with some dumb excuse to escape home, that's all." The jam ended and she grabbed my water bottle, since she'd already finished off her own. Yelling is thirsty work. "It's not a big deal, Jaqs. Only, we were beginning to think maybe you'd, y'know, never love again or something."

Carlos swooned, dropping his arm over his eyes. "Here lies Jaq, paralyzed by a broken heart, destined to become a spinster—"

"You assholes." I slugged both of them. "I'm not like that."

He straightened up, some of the manic gleam leaving his eyes. "Well, you *have* been a little gun-shy the past few years."

Zane coughed, "Decade."

"It has not been a decade! I've dated people in the last decade, Suzanne!"

"You have." Carlos patted my arm. "You have 'dated' in the last decade. We remember. There was 'Probably tried to steal your identity' girl. And 'So drunk she literally can't see straight and bumps into things' girl."

Zane laughed. "And don't forget 'Let me tell you about a personal tragedy every time I see you' girl!"

Tom choked on his beer and had a coughing fit. Eyes watering, he said, "I forgot about her! You were dating her when we met, weren't you?"

I winced. "Um. No. That was . . . a different girl."

Carlos laughed. "Our Jaq likes a tragic figure."

"Oh, bite me."

The jam heated up, with elbows being thrown all over the place and at least half the skaters in the penalty box, including the jammer, which meant no one could score until she was out.

Zane refocused. "Listen, I had an entire conversation with Hannah and she never once brought up a personal tragedy. Or this one time where she maybe applied for a credit card accidentally under her roommate's name but it's not like she was *trying* to break the law—"

I hit her again.

"Sorry, sorry, I'm just saying, I like Hannah. And I don't care what Liz says, maybe she's batshit, but she's got a career and money in the bank and she makes you smile, so that elevates her above pretty much everyone you've dated in a long damn time."

"Forever," Carlos added. I punched him too.

The jammer hit the track again, and Zane went into battle cry mode to cheer on the Berkeley girls against a San Francisco team. The rule goes like this: when La Vista's playing, root for La Vista; when the East Bay's playing, root for the East Bay; and when the Bay Area's playing, root for the Bay Area. Our local girls had never made it to the regional competitions, but we'd root for California after that, if there was some kind of national competition.

I had no idea if there was a national roller derby title, but it was way less dangerous to think about that than it was to think about

Hannah. Shouldn't my friends be warning me off her? Wasn't that the role of friends? So why were they encouraging me instead? It'd be so much easier if everyone agreed that this was a very bad idea.

Wasn't it?

I might have been a little distracted. Not by roller derby.

"That's not fair," I said ten minutes later, interrupting a deep conversation about craft beer and its emergence as a hobby.

"Here we go," Carlos said.

Zane patted my knee. "What's not fair, hon?"

"I don't come up with dumb reasons to avoid relationships. They're real reasons. I have classes in the mornings, and I grade papers on the weekend. I go to mass with Dad. I have, you know, actual obligations."

Carlos and Zane traded a look. Tom resolutely watched the bout, wincing when two blockers smashed the tiny jammer in between them.

"We know they aren't *fabricated* excuses," Carlos said. "But you do have an awful lot of them."

"And it doesn't matter what they are." Zane slung an unwanted arm over my shoulders. "You're a good egg, Jaqs. Someday you'll let some poor woman stick around long enough to notice."

What the hell did *that* mean?

The whistles blew for the end of the first bout, and Tom, probably mercifully, dragged me along for a snack run.

"Am I really that bad?" I muttered while we waited in an endless line at concessions. "I mean really."

"I don't think they're saying you're bad."

I endured the pause with great aplomb. Until I realized it wasn't a pause. "*And*? If they're not saying I'm bad, then what are they saying?"

"Oh. Well. I'm not sure. I think they're . . . teasing."

I socked him in the arm. "Yeah, thanks. I kind of caught onto that, nimrod."

He kissed my forehead, which is a thing you can do when you're nine feet tall. Or six foot three, but he felt taller because Carlos was so short. Some sleight of brain thing made me think Carlos and I were the same height and therefore Tom towered over both of us.

"They're happy you're happy."

"I'm not *happy*. It's just a . . . thing. That I'm doing. Like, at the moment. Okay? Jeez. Third degree all over the place."

"It's really not the third degree. But you are protesting kind of a lot, aren't you?"

Before I could pointedly not dignify that with a response (or protest), one of my many loves came rolling up.

"Prz!"

"Hey, hottie." Mz Prz—Priscilla to her mother—stood as tall as Tom in her skates. Her dark skin shone in contrast to a shock of bright white hair she'd clipped in for the bout and now pushed out of her eyes. "I had to come say hello."

I reached up to kiss her cheek. "You're up next, right? You aren't warming up?"

"Technically I *am* warming up, but I could see you from the track."

"Naughty girl. Get back out there. I won't be responsible for you pulling something because you improperly stretched."

She bent all the way over, her body compressing into two parallel lines as she folded neatly in half.

"Show off. And next time you do that, maybe I want the other view."

"Now who's naughty? Stick around for the after-party, would you?" She straightened and batted her eyelashes at me.

"Go win the bout and I'll see."

"That's an excellent incentive." With a final flick of her white extensions, she glided back to her team.

"The line is moving." Tom nudged me.

"Oh shut up."

He laughed.

Prz was a gorgeous, willing woman, and both of us were single. So why was I hesitating about planning to hook up with her later? I forced my mind into positions it didn't want to be in trying to come up with any reason but the obvious. Nothing. Couldn't make it work.

Hannah would be stuck at Liz and Marla's for hours yet, and I had no reason not to go to the after-party. Except for the totally bunk idea that Hannah might—just maybe—call me later. To come over to her hotel room again. Even though she almost certainly wouldn't do that, if she did, I wanted to be available for it. Which was . . . the worst, most ridiculous, so-not-casual thing I could possibly do.

I found an excuse to skip the party and went home. Alone. Like a damn fool.

Hannah didn't call.

CHAPTER 8

The end of the school year always reminded me of whatever soap had the hourglass. *Days of Our Lives*, right? The last two weeks before graduation, I felt like I was grasping for bits of sand and they were falling through my fingers.

Like LaTasha. I had yet to assess her mental state. I only had her for Journalism, and she seemed fine. She'd gotten all her work in, edited her section, finished layout on time, and offered to copyedit the rest of the paper. Business as usual.

I called in reinforcements.

"Dude," I said when I found the Only Other Queer Teacher At LVHS in the staff room.

Bill—aka Mr. Kent, everyone's favorite science teacher—looked up from his crossword puzzle. "Dude."

Bill was from Elsewhere. The world outside La Vista. He hadn't learned to drive in the parking lot at the ball field, and he had never taken a teenage crush to Sobrantes and then for a walk on the pier, pretending to be totally chill. That he hadn't done any of those things was part of his charm.

"'S up?" he asked, and grinned.

I slid in across the table from him, figuring I'd better take advantage of having him to myself. Bill was bisexual, which was apparently trendy enough again so that all the women at the school who weren't married wanted to date him. I felt bad for the bisexuals. It seemed like such a wholesome thing to be, but it was treated like a fucking designer accessory.

"Uh-oh. You have your serious face on."

"You have LaTasha Moore for science, right?"

He crooked his fingers into quotes. "Yes, Jaq, 'science.' She's in my Physics class, why?"

"You notice anything weird lately?"

"No." He paused, leaning back in his chair. "Not that I can think of. I guess she might be a little quiet these days, but that class is all seniors, so it's hard to tell what's a graduation-related deviation from the norm and what's . . . something else. Why?"

"Someone told me she was—" Actually, I didn't know what Merin thought. She hadn't given specifics. "One of her classmates is worried about her, but she seems fine to me."

"She's been carrying around a black notebook. Have you seen that? It's always in her hand, not her bag."

I tried to draw up a mental image of LaTasha in class. "I think I've seen her writing in it. Maybe. That's new?"

"She didn't have it a few months ago, or at least she wasn't carrying it around like it was her diary and she wanted it in her hands at all times." A few other teachers came in and Bill leaned toward me, keeping his voice down. "What's up?"

"I really don't know. Probably nothing. Keep an eye on her, though, would you?"

"Sure thing. Sammy invited me to join the GSA over the summer, by the way."

"He did not."

Bill nodded, maybe blushing faintly. "I take it he's been getting his nerve up for days."

"I bet he has. You're welcome, of course. I would have called you about it. Eventually. Probably when summer was half over."

"You don't think it's a bad idea?"

"To be queer in public?" I conspicuously did not lower my voice. "No, Bill. I think it's pretty much living life. But your situation's different than mine."

He narrowed his eyes. "You mean because if I'm not too loud about it, I can pass?"

Ouch. I almost defended myself, except for the fact he was right.

"Sorry. I didn't realize that's what I meant, but I guess it is. Also, you're a guy, which changes things. I'm less of a threat to the universe.

Still, you should come. If Sammy got up the guts to ask you, it must mean a lot to him."

"I'll think about it."

I could use the help. Not that the kids were a handful, but it was hard being the only one there to catch their anxiety, to soothe their fears. Especially when it was still so valid to be afraid. I couldn't tell them everything would be all right now that we could get married, because that wasn't really the root of the problem, and never had been.

"You should come," I repeated. "For me. I didn't want to pressure you about it before, but now that Sammy broke the ice, consider yourself pressured. Pressured, pressured, pressured."

"Thanks, Jaq."

"You feeling loved? I'm trying to make you feel loved."

"Oh is *that* what you're doing?"

"Hush." I got up. "Anyway, talk to you later. And watch out for my girl, okay?"

"Sure thing."

I offered a generic wave to my fellow teachers on the way out the door. Four of us had started teaching around the same time and had remained kind of close, Bill and I being two of them, but pretty much everyone who had been around longer and everyone who'd been around shorter stuck to their own.

LaTasha had a notebook. Maybe it was a diary. Maybe it was fanfiction of her classmates. Or teachers. *Shudder.* Maybe it was physics formulas. (Does physics have formulas? Is the plural formulae?) Maybe it was a list of pros and cons of different colleges, though I was pretty sure she was on her way to San Francisco State.

It didn't matter. Unless it did. I wished like hell Merin had given me more information.

Wednesday. Two weeks and two days until graduation. Two weeks and two days until the lock-in of Grad Nite, which most of us would be chaperoning. Two weeks and three days until summer. I pictured the stacks of papers I had to grade and the final exams I still had to give, and sighed.

Days passed in a blur. LaTasha seemed fine, if a little reticent, maybe. Merin seemed preoccupied by LaTasha. Sammy had picked up a better job than dishwashing for the summer, and would be waiting tables at one of the cute little bistros on the revamped side of the Harbor District. Hannah texted to say she'd be moving into her new place (relatively close to Sammy's bistro, actually) on June fifth and asked if I wanted to help her move. Followed by two winking emoticons.

Eventually I couldn't dodge Liz anymore, and she forced me to agree to come to dinner on the third. I wanted to claim that I'd have way better things to do on a Friday night, but I'd have to invent something better to do, and personal sloth outweighed my desire to avoid Liz. When the woman set her mind on something, she always followed through. It was really obnoxious.

I called Hannah for moral support when I was on my way to dinner.

"Good luck, sweetheart." Nothing about her tone was supportive.

"What's that supposed to mean? Are you making fun of me somehow?"

That giggle again. It was irresistible.

"No, but let's say they got more out of me than I planned to reveal. Oh, look, gotta go, Jaq! Packing, you know."

"What packing? You did all your packing—your stuff is all in storage—you don't have to pack—"

"Ta!"

Did she just say "ta"? Did she just hang up on me?

Damn her.

I texted her *What did you say to them? We should have our stories straight!* But she didn't reply.

It was with deep suspicion that I rang the bell at their neat three-bed, two-bath house in suburban La Vista. I couldn't really imagine settling down like that in a little lesbian love nest in the 'burbs. I mean, marriage is cool, but does everyone have to go full-on American dream? Not that there was anything wrong with it, but Liz used to be one of those radfem horror shows who took a decade to come around on the whole "trans people exist" idea. It was hard to accept that now she had a wine cabinet and a creepy/ironic gnome statue in her front yard.

Though the wine cabinet was actually pretty nice, I decided as I sipped a chilled ginger beer in their living room.

"I can't believe you drink that. It's like pure sugar."

Marla waved a hand. "Plus ginger. Even worse than pure sugar."

"I like both ginger and sugar." I gestured grandly around. "So how's married life?"

"It's bliss," Liz said, making disgusting googly eyes at her bride.

I pretended to gag. "Don't make me puke all over you."

"Aim for Liz if you must, but that rug cost a fortune."

"Oh, thanks a lot, wifey!"

"Call me 'wifey' again—"

"I will!"

I wandered out to the back patio where they'd set up appetizers, waving a jaunty hello at the little brown-and-white puppy, who was locked in the fenced-in pool area. "I'd pet you, but I'm eating," I explained, sampling the chips and salsa. Excellent salsa, not the store-bought kind. The chips were pretty high class too.

"These are fancy!" I called. "You guys trying to impress me?"

"This is the general standard of living around here," Marla called from the kitchen. "We eat good salsa *all the time.*"

I shook my head. "You filthy married people. Flaunting your fancy salsa in my face like you're better than I am."

She laughed, emerging with a bowl of guacamole. "Sit, hon. Tell me everything."

"What everything?"

"Oh, *you* know. Everything."

Since I knew she was asking about Hannah, I told her about my classes, and my queer kids, and we talked about Dred's baby for a few minutes.

It was always a little weird when one of my exes procreated. Which was probably why I hadn't visited Dred and her kid.

"I can't believe you." Liz took the chair beside Marla's. "Didn't you tell me you were huge into her?"

"I was. Ten years ago. Shit, longer now."

"To Mildred." Marla raised her glass.

"To Mildred." Liz shuddered. "And to not having a baby ourselves."

"Amen." I clinked my glass against theirs. "Really, girls. How's it going?"

"It's going fantastic. We haven't been married long enough to start bullshitting about that yet, right Liz?"

Liz put her left hand over her breast, which wasn't an appropriate swearing to any deity I could think of. "I promise, someday I will bad-mouth you to all of my friends behind your back to prove that I love you."

"Damn right you will."

They kissed.

"You sicken me." That wasn't a figure of speech. They really were disgusting.

The puppy yapped something that its mothers apparently took as a demand for dinner, which for some unknown reason required both of them. I contemplated reading my book during the ensuing chaos, but settled for being happy I didn't have a puppy.

Unfortunately, when they came back the fun and games were over.

"So, hon." Marla smiled, and I knew exactly what she was going to say. "Tell us about Hannah."

I played dumb. "I heard she's just signed a lease for an apartment in one of those new places down in the Harbor District."

"Oh, you *heard*, did you? Listen to that, Liz, she *heard* somewhere that Hannah got an apartment."

Liz blinked in mock confusion. "I wonder from whom? Does Hannah have any friends around here that you know of? Unless you told her, Marl?"

"Oh, I didn't tell her. Did you?"

"I definitely didn't."

I groaned. "Fucking hell. Shut up. Both of you."

"Are we to understand that, in fact, you heard all this from Hannah herself?" Liz raised her eyebrows theatrically. "Did you hear that, Marl? I think Jaq and Hannah might have exchanged, um, phone numbers."

"Phone numbers, you say?"

They were awful. I considered actually gagging, but rejected the idea because it'd be gross. "Okay, the two of you have to stop. You'll go back to normal eventually, right? This is some kind of wedding hangover and you'll be separate individuals at some point soon?"

"Well, Marl, I don't know—"

I threw a chip at Liz and got her in the chin.

"I hope you were aiming at my mouth."

"Don't get dirty with your wife sitting next to you."

She sighed, shook her head, and sat back, a series of small motions that did not exactly reassure me. "Look, babe. You know I don't want to get in the middle of your business—"

"Then don't."

"But you don't even—"

"It's my business." Yes, that was the right way to go. They couldn't argue with that. "Do I look like I need a babysitter to you? Something about me look fragile?"

They glanced at each other. *I fucking hate couples.*

"I love Hannah," Marla said. "You know that. She's smarter than most people I've ever met, she's funny, and she genuinely cares about people. At least sometimes."

"Well, if I was looking for references, I'd take that into consideration."

"Look, I'm not trying to talk shit," Liz said. "But Hannah's a little edgy at the moment. You know? There's the divorce, and the house, and she's crazy."

"And Sandra Dee already found herself a new lover."

"A boy."

"Boy?" I asked.

"He's twenty."

"And he's not a *boy*, Lizzie. I mean she. She's a young woman."

"With a dick."

See what I mean? Liz is kind of a bitch. I was glad this poor trans woman Hannah's ex was dating would never have any reason to be around her.

Marla sighed. "Dick, pussy, I don't care. The point is that Hannah got burned bad by Sandra Dee, who left her for someone half her age."

I might not have known everything there was to know about Hannah's past, but I knew basic arithmetic. "Twenty is not half of thirty-six. And is her name really Sandra Dee?"

Marla shrugged. "Sandra Deostino, actually, but who's paying attention to the details, right? The point is that Hannah may not be exactly . . . stable right now."

"She's batshit." Liz narrowed her eyes at me. "And she's a drama queen. That's not a good combination."

Marla cleared her throat. "I love Hannah like a . . . like a woman I was once in love with and who's now more like a—a close cousin— I mean, you know, a second cousin maybe, but we've known each other a long time—"

Liz busted up.

"Oh be quiet. I'm just saying I know her and she's great, but this isn't exactly the best moment for her to be getting involved with anyone. She's, well, not delicate, or anything, but you know this isn't exactly the first time she's been hurt."

"It wasn't your fault," Liz said.

"Well, it wasn't *not* my fault either."

I settled for raising my eyebrows. Illustratively.

"It wasn't that big a deal, I guess, but things kind of ended badly between us. I mean, it's all fine now, obviously."

"Things like that happen." Not that I had any idea what "that" was, but I didn't want to know Marla and Hannah's whole relationship history.

"I guess I— You know, this is her new start after her marriage was a disaster, and I don't want her to jump right into anything."

"I don't know what you guys are imagining is going on here, but no one's that serious. We're just having a good time."

Another look passed between them.

"Well, be careful," Liz said. "We told her to be careful too."

"Wow, hi, you know, none of this is your business. I'm not your responsibility, and neither of you get a vote in what we do. Cripes."

"We're not trying to have a vote, Jaq—"

"So what's for dinner?" I might have raised my voice. A little.

The diversion worked. We ate in peace for the rest of the evening.

CHAPTER  9

I followed Hannah back to the hotel after mass on Sunday. She hadn't been joking when she'd asked for help with the move. The truck was down the street, already full.

"Wait. You already loaded the truck?"

"Well, I had to pick it up yesterday because they're closed today, so I figured I might as well not waste my money by parking it here and ignoring it. Plus, Marla wanted to help, so I made her a truck loader."

I surveyed her belongings, arranged haphazardly in the back of a small U-Haul. "I wouldn't hire her again, if I were you. This is unregulation loading technique here."

"Probably my fault. Anyway, we gotta stop for coffee and fattening pastries."

"Oh we do, huh?"

"You don't expect us to work on empty stomachs, do you?" She stepped a little closer to me, like she wasn't exactly thinking about working at the moment. Or pastries.

Redirect, damn it. "We can drive over to the new place and park, then take a walk down to the Sobrantes we went to a few weeks ago."

"Perfect. A walk. That puts off the actual moving even longer, though I insist we take our pastries back to the new place."

I crooked an eyebrow at her in what was meant to be a sexy interrogative expression. Given the way her lips curled up, then tightened, as if she was trying not to grin, I assumed "sexy interrogator" somewhat failed. I soldiered on. "You, me, and pastries, all alone in the new place. Intriguing."

"It's tradition. I like to break bread before I move in. It feels like a good omen. Doubly because you're here."

"I'm a good omen, huh?"

"Well, you have already insulted my moving truck organization, so I don't know . . ."

I wanted to kiss her, but instead I punched her in the arm. "Let's go grab whatever's in the hotel room and start working."

"Yes, ma'am. And I'm changing my clothes."

Good point. My church suit wasn't really cut out for moving. "Can we stop by my place for a minute?"

"Sure."

Hannah's hotel room looked a lot more lived-in since the last time I saw it. It was trashed.

"Are you staying here alone? Or are you crashing with a boy band on the cusp of obscurity trying to generate a final scandal to hold on to their publicity for a few more weeks?"

"Aw, did you come up with that in your head right now? I've always been this way. My mother used to despair of me when I was a kid and shared a room with my sister. We fought constantly over the state of it. Monica argued that she couldn't find anything if it wasn't put away, and I argued that I couldn't find anything if it wasn't on the floor where I could see it."

I grinned. "Both compelling points. Let me guess: your mom sided with your sister?"

"Actually, she refused to take sides and told us to work it out."

"How'd that go?"

"Both of us still have scars—emotional *and* physical. Anyway, what you see is what you get." She waved an arm at the room and bowed. "I'm not sure I left out any good moving clothes, actually. I kept out, you know, impress-the-real-estate-agent clothes, and fly-home-to-sign-papers clothes. Not home now, I guess, though it'll be a while before I get used to calling La Vista home again."

"Your folks around here?"

"My mom is. It's just the three of us. My dad moved to New Mexico with his wife about fifteen years ago, so at most I see him if I fly out there for Thanksgiving." She picked up a peach blouse off the floor. "Not really good for our purposes. Do you mind if we stop somewhere else?"

"Let's do it."

"Great." She started shoving—literally shoving—clothes into her suitcases. Nice clothes. Dry-clean-only clothes.

I tried to let her do it, but my palms were itchy with the desire to take the job away from her. "Jeez, Hannah, you're really— I don't think you should crumple that bra like that—"

She grinned at me, all teeth. "Aw. Are you freaking out right now, sugar?"

I pushed her out of the way and rescued the slip balled up in her other hand. "I can't watch you do this to your beautiful clothes. Let me do it."

"Let you pack my dirty clothes into my suitcase? Okay." She arranged herself on the bed in my peripheral vision, and for a couple of minutes I was too busy straightening out the mess she'd already made. When I raised my head, ready to be triumphant, she was lying on her stomach with her breasts pushed together and her chin in one hand, one leg lazily bent up behind her. Looking right at me.

"Maybe you should take notes," I suggested, making my voice something that wasn't "so turned on I no longer care about the state of Hannah's suitcase."

"Maybe I am."

It was a silly thing to say, but she said it in this deep, seductive voice. I couldn't even muster an eye roll, and my mouth was dry. "What you need is one of those cigarettes on the long holder. Also, you should be naked except for red high heels."

"And red lipstick. I like the picture you're painting, Jaq. Anytime you want me to wear heels and watch you clean, you let me know." One of her hands drifted to her breasts, resettling them. Or teasing me. Or both.

I will not lick my lips like I want to taste her. I'm an evolved woman. Not a raw, desperate animal.

She mimed blowing smoke in my face. "Darling, do hurry up. I'd like to move in sometime today."

"Don't make me gag you."

More fake smoke blown in my direction. "You wouldn't. You like the way my lips move when I speak."

"Who says that? What does that even— Never mind." I turned away, diligently back to my task, but now all I could think about were her lips.

I managed to pack Hannah's clothes in a way guaranteed not to damage them, but I let her get everything else. In retaliation for the tease, I grabbed her e-reader and started poking around in it, but she didn't seem to mind, blowing my evil plan.

True crime. Lots and lots of true crime. Huh. That was unexpected. Her collection was mostly nonfiction. I always felt a little awkward around people who read primarily nonfiction, as if their reading habits put my detective stories and romance novels to shame, even though intellectually I didn't think that was true. I taught high school English and I've gone head-to-head with some diehard "real books" crusaders, who thought the only books worth reading were written prior to fifty years ago, but I let the kids read anything they wanted.

"You're not annoyed that I'm basically looking at your entire personal library right now?" I called. She was in the bathroom doing . . . I had no idea. Packing, ostensibly, though I couldn't imagine what she had in there that was taking so long.

"Back when we all had shelves and paperbacks, books were on display. This is pretty much the same thing."

Which was true. Though I was far more willing to pick up a romance novel if it was digital. I contemplated that as I paged through her collection. "I think I suffer book shame."

She stuck her head out. "Book shame? The English teacher has book shame?"

"Yeah, that's kind of the problem. I don't like a lot of the things English teachers are supposed to like."

"You'll have to show me later, Jaq."

"No way."

"Tsk, tsk. I showed you mine." Gone again. "I'm almost done in here!"

"I hope so," I mumbled. "You've been in there forever."

"I heard that!"

I smiled and opened a random Mary Roach book. "Don't know what you're talking about! Now be quiet, I'm reading."

She laughed.

We went to Walmart for moving clothes. Hannah led me directly to the men's section.

"Work clothes are always better, and usually cheaper, if they're meant for men. Now let's see. I can get khaki, or black, or khaki, or blue, or khaki, or camouflage."

"Those are tough choices." I wandered along the wall. "Oh no. Hannah."

"Hmm?"

I held up a dark-blue jumpsuit. "I will buy you dinner if you wear this to move."

She narrowed her eyes. "Do I have to wear it to dinner?"

"No. Only for moving."

"Interesting." She walked close enough to brush against the jumpsuit. "I'll buy you dessert if you get one too."

"Deal."

"We should get hats. We aren't proper movers without hats."

We loaded up with jumpsuits and hats before stopping at Sobrantes for pastries.

"You think we're getting enough?" I asked, when we emerged with two paper bags.

"This body takes a lot of calories to maintain. You don't get this way on accident." She ran a hand over one hip and down her thigh.

"Oh god. Stop. I can't think about sex while we're standing here. It's wrong."

"Is it, though? You know, we should have parked at the building and walked up here."

I shrugged and took the bag she'd tucked under her arm and her coffee. "I'm just glad you're the one driving."

She got us awkwardly into one of the designated loading/unloading spots and we went upstairs, where she unlocked the door and gestured me in first.

"Oh my god."

"I know."

"The Bay view costs more, but there's a charm to the East Bay view, don't you think?"

"It's spectacular." I walked up to the wildly expansive front windows. I could see St. Agnes, and the winding street where Zane had grown up, and the roof of the high school. To say nothing of the hills beyond.

"If you're gonna live in La Vista, you should always see it like this. The agent for the condos tried to downplay that it's on the 'bad' side of the building."

"There's a bad side of the building?"

"Apparently. Bad in the sense that you can see boarded-up shop windows and For Lease signs everywhere."

"Huh." I looked in the opposite direction as far as I could. "Oh, you mean as opposed to all the bright colors and chrome they're doing with the 'new' Harbor District?"

"Even the sidewalks are cleaner on that side. It's surreal more than anything, though I guess that kind of thing appeals to people."

"It's so impersonal, though." I glanced at all the familiar landmarks, parsing what made La Vista specific, instead of what made it just another "reclaimed" urban area with bold splashes of color and an overall impression of being hosed down at the end of the day.

"I'd prefer to be on this side, where you can still see the awning for the tea shoppe—with two *p*'s and an *e*—even though they went out of business when I was in middle school."

"Ha. I didn't notice that. Why do you think they got the top of the awning branded, anyway? They were hoping a helicopter would fly over and randomly decide to stop for tea?"

"The world will never know." She came up behind me until I could see both of our reflections, then reached around to unbutton my shirt.

"Kind of into exhibitionism, are you?" I asked. (Was Sammy at work yet? I could definitely see the bistro from here.)

"Not really." She turned me and went back to my buttons. "I'm on the fifth floor and this is the tallest building down here. You wouldn't be recognizable. But that's not my kink anyway. I just like you less dressed."

"Oh yeah?"

"Uh-huh."

"But we're not going to have sex on the carpet, right?"

She nuzzled in to kiss my neck. "Not if you don't want to."

She bent her head lower and pushed my shirt out of the way. I bit back a moan. "Um— Hannah—"

"I'm just teasing you. I plan to tease you all day until you're going a little bit mad, and then, when you're desperate for me—" She took a nipple into her mouth and nipped at it with her teeth.

I sucked in a breath. "You're a horrible person."

"And proud of it." She reached around to my butt and squeezed. "Thanks for helping me move."

"You're repaying me in sexual favors, right?"

"Bet your cute ass I am." She took a step back, leaving me turned on and bereft. "God, you look good. Mm. I gotta pace myself today. Now, where the hell is my vegan apple fritter?"

"How can you even think of apple fritters right now?" I muttered, rebuttoning my shirt.

"Oh look, a delicious still-warm bear claw."

I snatched the bag out of her hands. "Gimme that."

"Where did you put our coffee?"

"Kitchen."

We sat on a patch of carpet in front of Hannah's stunning floor-to-ceiling windows and had a little picnic of coffee and pastries.

"This is going to be a good move." She stared into the distance. "I think."

"I think so too."

When she turned to me, her moment of contemplation had clearly passed. Now she just looked slightly evil. "Time to get into our uniforms. I'm legitimately excited about our coveralls, Jaq."

"You're kind of sick, aren't you?"

She grinned.

Which is how we came to be two women in blue jumpsuits (with matching ball caps) moving her into her apartment.

"It's actually a *condo*," she whispered on trip seven, the futon trip. Thank goodness Hannah didn't have much in the way of furniture.

"I thought you weren't going to buy yet."

"Figured what the hell. Once the house sells, I'll have more than enough money, and I can get by with the payments until then. They actually have a few rental units in this building, but I don't want to make it easy for myself to—" She broke off to nod to someone coming down the hall as we awkwardly shifted to the side, but the man didn't even look over. "These uniforms are as good as disguises." She kept her voice low.

"We should wear them to Club Fred's next Friday. Wait, no, the Friday after."

"Are we going to Club Fred's two Fridays from now?"

"Oh, um." Crap, what did I do? In the heat of the moment—or the heat of moving the damn futon—I'd slipped up and acted like we'd be going to Fred's. Together.

Sweat poured down my back as I lifted my side of the futon. Play it off. No big deal. "It's Come As You Are night. Fredi's trying to broaden inclusivity or something and started up these theme nights." There. That was casual. I wasn't proposing we like *go* together. I was just saying it'd be funny if we both showed up in blue jumpsuits. I was presenting us another opportunity to wear them. Sure.

"Sounds fun." She grunted, shoving her side up high enough to make the corner. "Though I'm not sure this is really how we *are*."

"Yeah, that's why it'd be funny." Whew. Crisis averted. Though now that I had this idea of Hannah and me arm in arm at Club Fred's again, I kind of— No. Avert. "Okay, this angle's going to screw us."

We somehow managed to swing the futon around and kind of edge it inside slowly, inching forward, sliding it along the wall of the hallway, inching more, sliding more, until we finally got it into the wide-open space that made up most of the condo. The bedroom and bath were off to the right, and the kitchen at the far back, open to the living area.

She lifted her end. "Stop gawking and get back to work."

"Man, though. This view."

We picked up the futon again and shifted it against the wall and out of the way. I flopped down, but Hannah didn't. She stood over me with her hands on her hips.

"We should keep going. Not that there's anything all that important in any of those boxes, but 'new' Harbor District or not, I'd rather get them inside. Though I'm not in any hurry to get you out of your coveralls, Jaq."

"Try to control yourself. I heard the lady we're moving in is a real beast."

"I heard she likes to take advantage of her workers."

"That's inappropriate!"

She tugged my hat down over my eyes. "Let's go say really effusive hellos to my new neighbors and make everyone uncomfortable."

"Sounds fun."

The dinner she'd earned by wearing the jumpsuit was gourmet pizza, with artichoke hearts, garlic, and kalamata olives. The dessert I'd earned by wearing the jumpsuit was coconut cream, strawberries, and shaved bits of dark chocolate. In Hannah's kitchen. Delivered to me by her fingertips. It was astoundingly, alarmingly sexy.

"You like my cream?" She smirked, lifting a bright-red spatula to her lips so she could lick it.

"In all contexts." I swirled another strawberry through the bowl and sprinkled it with chocolate. "Where did you learn this? It's amazing."

"Oh, Marla didn't lead with the whole 'Chef Sandra Dee' bit?"

"I did hear about Sandra Dee. But not her job."

"Well." Her eyebrows arched. "Then you must have heard about the kid she left me for. I guess that's the new interesting thing about her."

I shrugged. Sexy dessert was quickly becoming less sexy. "We don't have to talk about it."

"You know, everyone thinks I'm all wrapped up in this drama about how she left me for this twenty-year-old transgender kid who looks a hell of a lot better in a slinky dress than I do, but that's not—" She paused, picking an errant chunk of chocolate off the cutting board and savoring it before she continued. "I admit, the age thing is a thing. When someone leaves you and hooks up with someone who's not legal to drink yet, that makes you wonder why they were with you in the first place. I don't *think* she was trying to save me, but how would I know?"

"Do you need saving?" I tried to make it a cheeky question, but her slight smile was tired.

"Maybe I do. But I wasn't looking for that with her. The cooking was nice. Have you ever been with someone who cooked, effortlessly, constantly feeding you?"

"Never. Sounds kind of awesome."

"It was. It made me feel cared for. Of course, that's a whole other cliché, but I can't help it. Food isn't always love, but it can be." She picked up a slice of strawberry and sprinkled it with chocolate before offering it to me.

I took it, letting my lips graze her fingertips, inhaling the tanginess and the underlying sweetness. "I think it's only fair that I tell you I can't really cook."

"Me neither, baby. Probably why I was so hot for her in the beginning. She'd go into the kitchen and poof, food would emerge. You think it's possible that's genetic? Some of us can't cook and others can't stop cooking."

"I think there's a lot of math and science and art involved, so if any of those things can be genetically passed on, some combination of them might make for a line of decent cooks. Though I think my mom could cook, so maybe it skips a generation."

"What about your dad?"

"I guess I assume she was the better cook between them. He always tells stories that begin with 'Your mother loved to make' and then whatever it is—turkey at Thanksgiving, or ham at Christmas. Corned beef with cabbage." I shuddered. "I'm 100% Irish-American, but don't get me near corned beef with cabbage. The taste for that definitely skipped me."

"I like corned beef. Not with cabbage, though."

"Ugh. People eat it in other forms? There's no justice in the world." I scooped up a little cream with my finger and sucked it off. "Anyway, I didn't mean to start a whole thing. But I wouldn't have ever thought to whip my own cream, even without coconut. Or grate chocolate."

"No imagination at all. It's the vanilla that makes the cream work. Well, and the sugar."

"But you hardly put any in and it's still . . ." I tasted it again, you know, to better describe it. "It's delicious."

"Yeah." She reached out, not for the cream but for me. Her fingers ran through my hair. "This cut is perfect for you. It's a pixie with a bit of flair."

"I have flair?"

"Don't act like you don't style your hair. This is, what, a good five- to seven-minute job here." Which she took no great pains to keep the way I'd styled it, fingertips doing lovely things to my scalp, practically making me purr. "It's a school night."

"I know." Past bedtime on a school night, actually. Nearly midnight.

"I won't ask you to stay. This time. Let me walk you out, Ms. Cummings."

"I could— I mean—"

She slid one final slice of strawberry, all by itself, between my lips.

"You could. But let's not. Plus, now that you've seen my view, you won't be able to stay away, remember?"

"So true. This view is something else." Even more beautiful at night, all twinkling lights and a ribbon of cars on the freeway in the distance. "Also, now I know you offer dessert, which changes everything."

"Technically I *bargain* for dessert, so don't go taking it for granted."

"Never." I didn't want to leave. She hadn't specifically asked me to stay. If I asked, she'd say yes. If she asked, I'd probably say no. Damn puzzles of human interaction. Give me a crossword any day.

Plus, I had class in the morning. I didn't know the commute from here. Unless I was going to wear my new jumpsuit, I'd have to head home first. I could, obviously, but a walk of shame was a hell of a way to start a week.

"I should go," I finally said, hating myself a little for it.

"I'll walk you out."

So responsible and tame. For a second, I was almost tempted to call in sick to work, go back to the kitchen, propose we find alternate uses for the last of the cream (and chocolate). But no. That would be foolish. I never called in sick. And this was supposed to be casual. Wasn't it?

"Thanks for having me over." I kissed her on her doorstep, like a proper date. A proper good-bye.

"Thanks for helping me move."

I wanted her to put her hands in my hair again and pull me to her, but she didn't. She smiled, kissed me again, and stepped back. "We have a date for Friday at Club Fred's, right?"

"Not this Friday. This Friday is Grad Nite, and I will be locked in the high school gym with the entire senior class until 6 a.m."

She giggled. "What did you do wrong in a past life that made this your fate?"

"Clearly something awful."

"Can I buy you breakfast Saturday morning, then?"

"You gonna be awake at 6 a.m.? Because I do not plan to stay awake much longer than that."

"I'll set an alarm. See you then, Ms. Cummings."

I gave a jaunty little salute. "Good night, Hannah."

"Good night."

She'd dropped me at my truck earlier so I could drive it closer, which was a whole lot better than the bus, but it was still damn cold when I got in. If I took my shower as soon as I got home, I could be in bed by twelve thirty and set my alarm for a little later for the morning.

But it sure would have been nice to be curled in bed with Hannah instead.

CHAPTER 10

The Journalism class delivered its last stacks of newspapers Monday morning the final week of school, which took most of them out of the classroom for the first half of the period. Enough of them so that Merin apparently felt comfortable beckoning me to her desk and asking if I'd done my job.

"My job?"

She raised her chin in the direction of LaTasha's empty desk. "Yeah."

Of the three other kids too apathetic to deliver papers, two had headphones on and the third was asleep. I sat backward on the desk in front of hers. "It'd help if I knew what was actually going on. She seems fine to me."

"Of course she *seems* fine. She always seems fine. It's her biggest life skill."

"So? What're you worried about?"

She rolled her eyes. "What, I gotta do all the work around here?"

"Yeah, I've had you in class all year, kid; I don't expect you to do *any* of the work."

"Harsh, Ms. C." She glanced around, eyes resting on each of her classmates in turn before coming back to me. "Sammy said your little club thing is meeting up over the summer?"

"The GSA? Yeah." I bit off an accusatory *Why?* There were kids who'd target the GSA, but Merin wasn't the type, and if she were, she certainly wouldn't be asking me about it.

"You allowed to meet like that? Unsupervised? Not on school property?"

I narrowed my eyes. "Are you threatening to turn us in?"

"No. I'm saying you should shut Sammy's stupid mouth or he's gonna get you in trouble."

"Thanks for the unsolicited advice. Can I help you with something, Merin?"

Her eyes dropped again, giving me a slightly better chance to assess the bags beneath them, the torn bits on the parka she wore every day, all day, year-round. Maybe she was drawing my attention to LaTasha because she needed help herself. I flashed to that drop-in center Carlos had been talking about. Merin wouldn't ask for help, but she might be able to justify dropping in if a place had snacks, or even lockers.

"We'll be at the Harbor District Sobrantes on Fridays at five thirty," I said. "Since I know you'll miss me horribly over the summer, you should think about coming by."

"Miss you, my fat ass."

"Keep it clean, Merin."

She grunted. "Yeah, well, anyway, I got a friend who maybe would go. So thanks."

Asking for a friend was the oldest trick in the book. I couldn't decide if she was serious, but she definitely seemed to want me to take her seriously.

"We don't bite, and you're both welcome," I said as the door opened. I stood up. "How was it?" I called to Sammy as he and Dana walked in: "Did you get sentimental over your final deliveries? Did you shed a tear?"

"Final delivery until next year, you mean," Sammy shot back. "Mr. Kent told us he'll be sad going back to only reading the *Times-Record* for the next few months."

"He's so gay," Dana muttered. "Like *so* gay."

"Actually, he's bi." Sammy snapped back and forth, as if to illustrate the point.

"Same difference."

"It's really not."

I clapped my hands. "Thank you both for playing 'Name that Absent Person's Sexuality' with us today. You can do whatever you want for the rest of class."

Dana pulled a face. "Like what? Only total jerk teachers are still giving homework."

"Thank goodness you're all enterprising young people and can entertain yourselves, then."

The rest of the class trickled back in. I tried to scope LaTasha, but other than deciding that if Merin's "friend" existed it was certainly LaTasha—oh, those lacking-in-subtlety sideways glances, I knew them well—I couldn't tell anything. Her hair was pulled back, as always; her clothes were neat and clean; her books were in order; her backpack not overflowing.

She spent the last few minutes of class scribbling in her black notebook.

I texted Bill after first period to ask what he was doing for lunch. He texted back to ask what I was doing after school. After ribbing him about his apparent hot lunch date (which was, to be fair, probably with a marker and a stack of science exams), I proposed we get coffee.

"'S up?" he asked, in his customary style, sitting down at the outside table I'd snagged for us at the Third and Mooney Sobrantes.

"So. You know Merin at all? She's a junior, but on the slightly older side."

"Merin Beighley, right? With the big black coat?"

"That's her."

"I had her last year for bio, though we didn't necessarily get along. Why?"

I'd already decided to tell him what was going on. No reason not to, and hell, maybe I'd missed something. "She's the reason I asked about LaTasha. They're neighbors, apparently. And I don't know. Something odd's going on there."

"Odd how?"

"I have no idea. I don't think it's a sex thing, though there might be a sort of vague attraction deal on Merin's part. But even that's totally speculation. She's definitely worried about LaTasha, and now I'm worried about both of them."

He raised his eyebrows. "Worried how?"

"You are *terribly* helpful."

"Well, you're not giving me much to go on. And is this worried like it's summer, so we worry about the kids who always slip through the cracks over the summer? Or worried like there might be some kind of acute thing we can fix, or change, that would help?"

"Hell, Bill, I don't fucking know. Merin looks worse every time I see her, and I guess mostly I'm worried that she doesn't have a peer group of any kind that I can see."

He nodded, absently swirling his coffee in the cup. "No, I noticed that last year. She never sat next to anyone, or seemed to chat with them. Mostly she rebuffed anyone's effort to make contact with her."

"And she does the same in the history class she has with me, and the same in Journalism, except with LaTasha."

His eyebrows shot up. "They're friendly?"

"Honest to god, I can't decide if Merin has a creepy stalker thing going and LaTasha's oblivious, or if there's some kind of mutual crush LaTasha hides better. I'd love to know what she's writing in her notebook."

"I actually have a lead on that. Someone asked her about it the other day and she said it was 'research.' Whatever that means."

"Research." That was definitely interesting. "Merin said she was, uh, 'freaked out' by the drag king's murder. You remember that?"

"Really? Why, do you think?"

"Wait." Merin had asked about the GSA. For "a friend." "You think she might be queer?"

He blinked. "No idea. It's never occurred to me before. Then again, I've never seen her hanging off anyone's arm, girl or boy."

"True. Maybe I'm misreading this. Damn." I shook my head and took another hit of my coffee. "Sammy got a job down at the little bistro, whatever-it's-called, three doors over from the San Marcos Grill."

Bill leaned forward. "Oh, in the Harbor District? Bistro El Capitan, right? I've heard good things about it."

"That's the one. I'm glad he has an excuse to be out of his house a lot. Callie's more of a trouble spot, since she just turned fifteen and she hasn't gotten a work permit. She's got three or four little sisters she watches."

"That—" He hesitated. "That doesn't seem like something she'd especially enjoy."

"No. But it's probably better than being stuck at home alone with her mom, who as far as I can tell is never without a prescription to ease her way through life." I probably should have felt at least a little crummy for shitting on Callie's mom . . . but I didn't.

"Ouch, Jaq."

"I used to be nicer about the parents. Not so much anymore."

He nodded. "I guess that means I'm definitely coming to the meetings."

"I'm not going to show up at your house and force you into my truck, but I'd appreciate it, yeah. You want the rest of the rundown?"

He glanced at his cup as if gauging the level of coffee left. "Hit me."

I sketched out the things I looked for in the usual suspects, not all of whom would be able to make it to the summertime meetings. (Merin was right; we should probably stop referring to it as the GSA over the summer, since the GSA was a school club, and therefore suspended when school wasn't in session.) There was something nice about sitting in the sun, sharing my burdens with Bill, who nodded, eyes clear and attentive, occasionally asking a question here or there, but mostly taking it in.

I hadn't realized how heavy it felt to be the only one the kids relied on, until I shared a little of that pressure with someone else.

CHAPTER  11

I set up a punishing routine in the gym on Wednesday, to make up for the fact I'd be missing my Friday workout.

"I don't know . . . why I have . . . to suffer . . . just because . . . you're—" Zane broke off in a fit of wheezing. "Dying . . . dead—"

"Save your breath," I managed. But I dialed it down on the off chance I was really killing us.

We skipped Club Fred's and hit Taco Junction instead. Because who didn't need a little taco bar in their life?

Zane grabbed her tray and followed me to the table. "God. I'm eating at least three. I fucking earned it."

"Quit bein' a baby." I tucked my taco together better. "This is delicious. We should eat here every day. Forever."

"We should have our own Taco Junction. Breakfast tacos, dessert tacos."

"Dessert tacos?"

"Yeah, you know"—Zane waved her taco around dangerously—"like a sugary fried tortilla with ice cream and nuts or something."

"Mmm, okay, that could be good."

In the midst of further taco-based contemplation, apropos of nothing, Zane said, "So when are you going to freak out and dump Hannah?"

She ruined a perfectly good bite of taco. I'd been savoring it, but suddenly everything I tasted was sour. "The hell does that mean?"

"What do you think it means?"

"There's no— We aren't— What the hell, Zane?"

"Listen, honey-pie, I love you. But this is right about the time you usually start to freak out that you're getting too close to someone and, uh, withdraw."

"I do not! I don't freak out!"

"Oh seriously? You really believe that?" She sat back and wiped her hands on a napkin. Since she still had a whole other taco left, that was a very bad sign. "Jaq. Who're you talking to? I'm your best friend. I know every single time you've dodged out of a relationship because you were scared."

"I *do not*—"

"There was sweet Abby in high school."

I shook my head. "Not even! She moved away."

"You dumped her three months before she moved, Jaq. You dumped her like the day after she told you that her dad was looking for work in Texas. He hadn't even found a job yet!"

"Shut up."

She rolled her eyes. "Jess beat you to the punch, but you could have hung on to Dred longer than you did, and you completely broke her heart, didn't you?"

"I did not break anyone's heart. And how do you know, you weren't there!"

"I know." Zane's voice went all *Matlock interrogates a witness on the stand*. "You dumped her a week and a half before I got home from Madagascar. As if you were *scared* of introducing us."

"Shut up. You're wrong. I wasn't scared. I was— She was— It was complicated."

"Uh-huh. Then you and Iris were hot and heavy until you wigged and dumped *her*."

"I did not 'wig and dump her'!" People at other tables looked over. *Oops*. "I did not. But she was planning to, y'know, move, so—"

"She moved to San Francisco. Half an hour away isn't exactly a long-distance relationship."

"Half an hour with, like, no traffic, maybe," I muttered.

Zane rolled her eyes. Again. "Then there was Amanda, and Monique, and oh, I almost forgot Prz—"

"That was totally different. Prz wasn't into relationships. So what would the point have been? She was always with other people."

"Jaq, she's polyamorous, that's not the same as 'not into relationships.' Obviously she was with other people. Were you jealous?"

I pushed my plate away. "Not really. But I might have been. Eventually. If I hadn't, you know, broken it off with her."

"Ah yes," she said, in her *Masterpiece Theatre* voice. "And here, at last, we come around to the actual point. You *might* have gotten hurt. So instead of taking the risk, you ended it. With everyone you've ever been with."

"Shut up," I said. Weakly.

"Listen, babe, you can't even commit to a fucking hobby. Let's see." She held up her hand to tick things off. "There was scuba diving when we first got to college, which you got your certificate for and never actually went anywhere to use. You trained for a marathon, ran it, then promptly never ran again. You started that quilt when you were with Dred, and stopped working on it when you broke up with her. What else? Oh, how could I forget photography! You even signed up for that class at the college, then forgot and stopped going—"

"Enough. I get it." I paused. "Dred's trying to get me into knitting. Um. She said there's a class down at the yarn shop."

Zane laughed. "You should take it! Take the class, learn to knit. You definitely know how to do a lot of different stuff, but it's always been like you're sampling, Jaq. Everything except teaching is just the thing you're doing today, not the thing you want to *do*."

"Teaching's the only thing that keeps my interest." And even then, it kept my interest because I changed it a lot. I tried to find new assignments, new books, new ways to read the old books. Bill thought I was crazy for switching up my lesson plans all the time, but the truth was, I got bored so easily. It made more sense to take time out to plan different lessons than to, you know, quit my job and find a new one because I hated teaching the same old thing.

I rearranged my taco again. "You really think this is a thing?"

"Well, yeah. I mean, it's obviously a thing. Or, like, remember that time you decided you were going to do all your vehicle maintenance yourself? You changed your oil and took your tire off and put it back on, to make sure you could?"

"Ha. Yeah. And bought manuals and watched videos."

"Right. So you did all that, and you thought you were going to change your own oil until you were too old to get under your car."

She raised her eyebrow. "When's the last time you changed your own oil, Jaq?"

"Yeah, that was the first and last time."

"Exactly. I don't know, it's sort of like you've always been looking for the person you needed to be, and all your hobbies and diversions were just ways of testing those things out. Testing them against yourself to see if they stuck."

"Huh."

"And women were the same way. Does this one fit? Or this one? None of them fit. If Hannah doesn't fit either, you'll drop her like a bad habit and move on."

"Hey. Harsh."

"Okay, maybe it is harsh. It's just . . . I watch you. I know there's some psychobabble side of this where your mom died and it's hard to believe things can work out, or be permanent. And I'm not saying Hannah is your one true love. But Jaqs, sometimes we take a chance, even when it feels impossible."

I bit down on my lip and rearranged what was left of my taco.

"And I swear, sometimes it works out."

"That sounds like something I'd say to my kids," I mumbled.

"Yeah, well, it's true for you too." She returned to her taco, thank god.

I tried to eat mine, but it didn't taste nearly as good as it had before.

I didn't really think I tried people on like clothes, or like I was trying to fit them to my image. That would be fucked up. Wouldn't it?

Then again, I was having a hard time refuting Zane's points in my head. Stupid Zane. I fought with her in my head all night, then thankfully had better things to obsess over during the last two days of school.

The last two days of school. Before I'd picked up the electives, the end of the year hadn't been a huge thing to me. But the second I'd had seniors in my classes, I'd realized I'd have to fight the growing energy of graduation pretty much constantly or be swept up into it.

I wasn't the teacher who made everyone work like demons until the final bell on the final day of school. I'd brought in *His Girl Friday* for the Journalism and Creative Writing kids to watch the last few days, and *Sense and Sensibility* for everyone else. (Oh, Emma Thompson. You can write me a screenplay anytime.) My scattered seniors were all kinds of nervous and excited, and everyone else fell somewhere between relief the year was over and dread of either the boredom of summer or the longer work days. I'd never been full-time at any of my jobs as a teenager, not even during school breaks, but I would see a good number of my kids bagging groceries, serving coffee, or shelving random stuff at Walmart for the next few months.

It was fashionable to think the youth of America was apathetic and rude, but most of my students were hard workers, and a good many of them were helping to support their families with that work. And those were just the ones doing legal jobs.

We had a bit of time left at the end of Journalism on Friday after the movie had run its course, and LaTasha had skewered it for seeming to be about a woman who was making her way in a "man's" world but reinforcing a lot of old stereotypes, so I asked who was going to graduation.

Sammy raised his hand. "My cousin See-Saw is graduating."

"Your cousin's name is fucking *See-Saw*?" Merin asked incredulously.

He shrugged. "That's what we always called him. Anyway, he did most of his classes at home, but he's graduating in the ceremony, so I'm going."

"I'll be there, obviously," I said.

"Do you have to, though?" Dana asked. "I mean, what if you didn't care about the seniors? Could you stay home?"

"I actually like graduation." Only partially a lie. I liked the idea of graduation more than the execution, but I didn't hate it or anything. "I love watching everyone in their gowns walk to pick up their diplomas, and I've had enough people in my classes that I don't get too bored."

A few of the kids laughed.

LaTasha looked up from her notebook. "I'll probably be bored. But my mom and dad will be there, so I have to go."

Dana turned in her seat. "You don't want to? But isn't it kind of a big deal?"

"Not really. I took my classes and took my tests, and now I want to go to college."

In the corner of my eye, Merin shifted, as if suddenly uncomfortable in her desk.

"But you're going to Grad Nite, right?"

"Probably." LaTasha went back to her notebook, Merin shifted again, and I wondered what the hell was going on. Before I could come up with appropriate non-nosy questions, the bell rang.

"Have a good last day of school!" I called. "I might see those of you going to graduation later!"

They cleared out, quicker than usual, and I thought Merin might stay for another pointed conversation, but no. She was out the door right behind Sammy.

Second period was English. I checked my little list of where we'd left off on *Sense and Sensibility* yesterday and cued up the video.

CHAPTER 12

I was only lying a little about graduation. Our principal—the remote fortress Mrs. Gravestein, and yes, that was her real name, no nickname required—always gave a very short speech about the value of education and the strengths of the graduating class. It was the same speech every year, but like I said, very short, so we forgave her.

Various community leaders took turns giving the "celebratory invocation." The graduating class of 2016 was treated to an actually pretty amusing speech by the editor in chief of the local paper, a stooped old man called Jeremiah Alder. Instead of trying to bestow wisdom on the kids, he told a couple of stories about being their age trying to make a name for himself in Journalism, pulling foolish stunts, and chasing the story. I judged at least thirty percent of it was entirely fabricated, with another thirty being a greatest-hits collection of other people's stories (I was pretty sure I'd seen at least one of them in Walter Cronkite's autobiography), but it made everyone laugh and wasn't as endless as a few past speakers had been.

The previous year had been notable for hosting a speech by a former graduate who'd started a weirdly successful gift shop. You could tell by the tone of the thing that he'd had visions of going viral and being the next graduation address sensation on YouTube. Unfortunately, he'd come off smarmy instead of wise, and actually attracted a couple of "boos."

No booing this year. The valedictorian and salutatorian were both nervous, but earnest. The droning of the names lulled me into a nice waking nap until Bill elbowed me back to full consciousness because one of my students wanted a hug. I'm not a favorite, so I sit in the second wide row of faculty, but it's pretty common that we give hugs during the ceremony. Frowned upon, but it's the last thing we can do for the kids, so we do it.

"Congratulations," I whispered to a girl called Anna, who I'd had in Creative Writing for two years. "You'll do great out there."

"Thanks, Ms. C." She sounded teary.

I gave her a squeeze before pushing her toward the stairs.

Three other kids wanted hugs. LaTasha shook my hand. A few kids tried mild stunts—rebel yells upon receiving their diploma, or one young man who pulled up his gown and mooned the audience, to the delight of a group of his friends and scattered shouts of "My eyes! My eyes!"

I only covertly checked the time a dozen or two times. And forced myself not to go on Facebook. Because that would be inappropriate, even if it was tempting.

Graduation ended just past seven. Which meant we had about forty-five minutes to eat before heading to the gym for our overnight prison sentence.

"Taco Junction?" Bill said.

"I ate there yesterday. Subway?"

Angel—aka Ms. Fernandez—shook her head. "C'mon. Let's go to the vegan place. I'm buying."

"The vegan place?" Bill glanced at me, clearly looking for an ally. "No offense to the vegan place, but can they get us in and out fast enough?"

"We'll call ahead. Bill, your car?"

"We're definitely not going in Jaq's again."

"Hey, my truck is fine!"

"It looks like you live in it. You have room for you and exactly half of another person."

I hit him, Angel laughed, and we waved good-bye to the fourth in our little cadre, Juniper Symonds, who taught art and metal shop. Juniper had gotten out of Grad Nite obligations by merit of having given birth to twins a few months before, the selfish bitch.

"Kiss the kids for us!" I called.

"We're gonna go talk shit about you!" Angel added.

Juniper blew us kisses. "I'll be thinking of you guys when I climb into my nice warm bed, with my cup of tea, and my book—"

"And your *man*, you mean." Angel threw a discarded tassel at her. "Go away."

"Ta-ta, children!" She waved her fingers and turned away.

"Are you sure the vegan place is going to have enough protein to get us through the night?" I asked.

Bill leaned over to stage-whisper, "We'll pick up burgers too. Just in case."

"No joke."

"We won't need burgers. Plus, the vegan place has kick-ass black bean burgers. You totally won't miss the cow-face you're used to eating."

"Mmm, delicious cow-face," Bill said. "I miss it already."

The vegan place took half of forever getting us our food, though I have to admit, the black bean burgers were delicious. I would have ordered a second one to go, but by then we were late as hell.

Mrs. Gravestein was standing at the door to the gym, giving dour looks to those of us chaperones who arrived late.

"If you were attempting to avoid helping set up, you succeeded." She eyed each of us in turn.

"For future reference, Creatures Great and Small does brisk business on Friday evenings," I said. "Where do you want us?"

"The students will being arriving soon. Why don't you three volunteer to check them in?"

I controlled my reflexive flinch. "Sounds good."

"'Sounds good'?" Angel whispered furiously when we were out of earshot. "In what universe does being tied to a table all night sound *good*?"

"Hey, it's not like you came up with a better idea!"

"At least if all three of us are there, we might have fun," Bill mumbled. "Hello, Cait. We're here to help."

Caitlin Winchester had been running the high school from the front office since I attended it. Which explained why Bill and Angel—from not-La Vista—greeted her with a breezy "Hello, Cait" apiece. I forced myself to mumble it, sounding like a grudging kid thanking Grandma for a terrible Christmas sweater-vest.

"Well." She surveyed us. "And what the hell did you three do wrong?"

"Language, Cait!" Bill waved a hand. "We're late. Though in my and Jaq's defense, it's Angel's fault."

"Because she's the only one who has a watch?"

Angel leaned down. "Have you been to Creatures Great and Small? It's delicious."

"My dear, I do not eat tofu. I don't eat anything that comes in a block and tastes like an old sponge."

"Aw. But it can taste good!"

Mrs. Winchester merely raised an eyebrow. "Tofu aside, how convenient for one of you that we only have three lists. You'll have to draw straws for the pleasure of remaining here at the table in my company tonight."

"Not it!" I said quickly.

"Cait said to draw straws. We don't have straws."

Mrs. Winchester sighed. "I'm thinking of a number."

"Seven," I guessed.

Angel poked me. "Boring. A hundred thirty-one."

"Seventy-nine," Bill said, after an extended pause suggesting he was solving the mystery of life.

"The number was—"

"Wait," I interrupted. "What determines who stays at the table? The two people closest? Or the two people furthest away?"

"Clearly the reward is to sit with me," Mrs. Winchester said. "In which case Angel, I'm afraid you will be forced to wander around the gymnasium tonight, only wishing you were fortunate enough to share our company."

"That, Cait, is a tragedy." Angel kissed my cheek. "See you around. Oh wait. No. I'll see you right here. Don't worry, I'll check in."

"You little—" I bit off my words when Mrs. Winchester gave me a *look*.

"Jealousy is so ugly on you, Jaq." Angel flounced off.

"The least she could have done was offer to bring us punch or something," Bill said. "Now, before anyone gets to it with their illicit substances."

I considered it. "That would be a worse job. We could be stuck guarding the refreshments."

"Are you implying that you are 'stuck' with me, Jaqueline?"

"Um."

Bill laughed. "How about I go get us something? Anything for you, Cait?"

"A sparkling water, please, Bill. Thank you."

He was smirking when he walked away, leaving me with Mrs. Winchester. And in case you wondered: no, no relation to the rifle family. I had asked her once, in the spirit of lighthearted inquiry. She'd replied, totally seriously, "I believe they died off with the mysterious Mrs. Winchester in San Jose. Any other questions?"

That'll teach me.

I took a clipboard and started flipping through, seating myself at the far end of the table and leaving Bill the chair in the middle. The graduating class was two hundred seventy-three students, though historically only about half showed up for Grad Nite. Don't ask me why we misspelled a word for a school event. Was it supposed to be cute? Was there something wrong with the original spelling? Did a printer error the first year cause a ripple effect all down the lines and now we accepted it as if we didn't notice?

My eye hit a name. And stopped.

"Mrs. Winchester? How do we pull this particular list? Is it from the list of graduates?"

"Actually, not that we advertise it, but anyone who has enough credits and isn't on the disciplinary list is eligible for Grad Nite. Even those on academic probation who haven't technically graduated yet."

I wasn't looking at someone on academic probation, though. I was looking at Merin's name. Merin, who wouldn't be a senior until September, though if she'd pushed her classes, she might have had enough credits to count as one now.

"Why do you ask?"

Damn. Mrs. Winchester was looking at me. I definitely didn't want to launch an investigation into Grad Nite attendees. "Oh, just wondering. I don't recognize all of these names, and here I thought I knew everyone."

"Hmm."

Bill returned with drinks (and a folded-up napkin full of pretzels he discreetly placed between us on the table, behind a weirdly Thanksgiving-like centerpiece of fall leaves). The door

Mrs. Gravestein opened the doors. Kids decked in their fanciest clothes started streaming in.

I kept my eyes peeled for Merin.

The key to a good lock-in event is having a whole lot of constant activity. From the registration table, I could pick out a Texas Hold'em area, some kind of arts-and-crafts station that seemed popular, three photo booths that never stopped running all night, and a small staged area for a hypnotist. Someone had set up one of those dance competition video games, and at some point they'd start painting the senior mural, which was made on Grad Nite and hung up the following year in the front hallway of the school in a place of honor. I looked forward to the mural mostly because a few of the cleverer kids always found a way to add inappropriate content and not get caught; Bill and I would spend most of September studying the mural and counting the penises.

I was tethered to the main table for the first two hours as kids trickled in. We didn't lock the doors until ten, which felt roughly like a year and a half after we'd eaten black bean burgers. I really wished I'd brought one with me. Say what you want about food with faces, but at least it sat in your guts long enough to keep you full.

Mrs. Winchester gave me another narrow look. "By the way you've been jittering the last thirty minutes, I assume you have urgent business you have to take care of, Jaqueline. Don't let us stop you."

"Um." Urgent business? I could definitely invent urgent business. "Yeah, well, anyway, I'll be back in a few minutes." Or never. Either way.

I'd opted for white shirt/black slacks as a nod to the formality of the evening, and it was a little disheartening to realize I basically blended in with the high schoolers. Walking across the gym in a sea of kids, also in formal wear, many of whom were taller than me, made me feel abruptly transported back in time to my own Grad Nite. I'd kissed a straight girl named Lula and she'd spent the next hour telling me how she'd expected it to be weird, but it *wasn't*, it wasn't *at all*, and did I know that it wasn't that weird to kiss girls? Did I *know*?

At least tonight would not be a repeat of any personal disasters. I only had to be on guard against other people's disasters.

None so far, though. Some tears. A few minor irritations cropping up here or there. As far as I could tell, the refreshments monitors hadn't let any booze slip into the general punch bowl (you'd think that would be easy; it isn't), so the only intoxication so far was what the kids had managed to do before walking in. There would be more later—they always found a way to sneak it in—but right now everything was basically copacetic.

I slipped out a door, nodding to the guard standing there (my fellow history teacher, Mr. Lanai), and into the cool, deserted hallway beyond.

So quiet. The music/laughter/talking/noise of the gym still rumbled beyond the wall, but my entire body was relieved for a moment of peace. I went to the bathroom, got a drink of water, and when I couldn't think of anything else to do, I returned to the chaos.

No personal disasters. That's what I'd thought. That's what I'd planned for. That's what I'd gotten—until little Annie Potts cornered me in the soda machines alcove.

Her name was Annie Potter, but Juniper kept slipping up and calling her "Annie Potts," and it burned into my brain until I couldn't think of her any other way. Sweet kid, with an edge of needy mixed in with an edge of "old before her time." I'd had her for English last year, and she'd been a decent student, turned in her work. She hadn't had anything especially genius or original to say about *The Handmaid's Tale*, but at least she'd seemed to understand it, which was more than I could say for a good portion of my students.

Annie Potts, in a bright-red, very clingy dress, breathing pot breath in my direction. Not that I judged. Zane and I had never gone to a single school event sober.

"Hi, Annie."

"Mrs. C! Mrs. C, I've been looking everywhere for you!"

I sighed. "It's 'Ms.' And why?"

"Because. Because Mrs. C—" She hiccupped, giggled, and tried again. "*Ms.* C, I have to tell you something!"

Here Annie Potts paused, dramatically, staring me right in the eye, and damn, could you get hotboxed from someone's breath and slinky dress? The dense, trapped scent of marijuana was distracting.

"Yes?"

"Mrs. C, I think . . . that I'm . . ." She leaned even closer to me. "A lesbian!"

I wanted to say, *You really aren't.* But that would be wrong. Even if I was pretty sure it was true.

She was still looking at me.

"Oh," I said. "That's nice, Annie. Will you shift back, some? I'm running out of fresh air over here."

She shifted forward instead, and that's when my early personal-disaster warning alarms began blaring. I straightened up, keeping my arms at my sides, ready to bring them in between us if necessary.

"But . . . I'm a *lesbian.* I just realized it. Because I was watching this music video, with Pink, and she was naked, and she was *so. Beautiful.* I couldn't even stand it, you know? So I must be a *lesbian.*" Every time she said "lesbian," she whispered.

"Okay," I said. "That's real interesting. I'm gonna go back to the registration table now, Annie."

"But . . . don't you think— I mean— Aren't you—" She pouted. "That's it? I thought you'd be happy for me or something."

"I am happy for you. It's always good to know yourself." I moved sideways, trying to make it clear I intended to leave now. "I'm very happy for you, Annie. Now why don't you go hang out with your friends, okay?"

"But . . . I can't tell them. I mean, I *could,* but they'll say I'm making it up." The pout hardened into determined lines. "I'm not, Mrs. C. I'm *not* making it up."

Here's the thing about our new culture of sexual fluidity: maybe she wasn't making it up. I mean, maybe she'd only ever be with boys, and maybe naked-Pink was the only woman she'd ever be attracted to, but that didn't make it invalid, and it didn't make her less queer than me, really, because that's not how it worked.

I patted her arm—carefully, below the elbow. "I know you're not making it up, Annie. I absolutely know that. It's okay. And anyone who gives you shit about it, tell them to go fuck themselves, okay?"

I took advantage of her slight gasp and slipped out of the alcove, making a beeline to Bill at the registration table.

"You look like hell."

"I think Annie Potts just hit on me. And came out to me. And hit on me. Maybe."

"Annie Potter? Really? That's a little surprising."

"This hardly seems like an appropriate topic for discussion," Mrs. Winchester said.

"Sorry," I muttered, wishing I had a jacket or some other form of armor.

Bill patted my shoulder. "You know what you need? Chocolate."

"I really do."

"Be right back."

I nodded, feeling a weird little backwash of misery. Annie Potts, with her crush on Pink (What sexual person could possibly watch Pink and not have a crush on her?), and her friends who'd tell her she was making it up. My heart twisted for her, just a bit.

"These things happen to us all, Jaqueline." Mrs. Winchester didn't look up from inputting her registration list into a battered laptop. "They're awkward, and embarrassing, and we persevere as if they aren't."

God. Had some young stud once hit on Mrs. Winchester? She'd been at the school since she was like twenty-three or something, so it wasn't actually that hard to believe.

"They don't usually happen to me," I said.

"I'm sure they're just usually less overt. No matter. We move on."

"Thanks, Mrs. Winchester."

"Of course."

We move on. Right.

I looked at my phone, but time seemed to have slowed down until it barely moved at all. Apparently it was only seventeen minutes since the last time I'd checked.

"This is the longest night ever."

"Tsk, dear. Surely it's only the longest night since last year's Grad Nite."

I gave that some thought before agreeing. "Fair."

"And chocolate." Bill dropped a handful of mini Hershey bars in front of me.

"Thank you, thank you, thank you." My phone vibrated, giving me an excuse to look at it again.

Hannah. *How're you holding up, soldier? I'm heading off to bed, so I guess this is a "see you in the morning" that is also a "see you at the end of your very long day." I can't believe you're going to be up all night. That sounds dreadful. Maybe I'll lie here and think about you while I—*

I hit a button on my phone and stuffed it into my pocket.

He nudged me. "Who was that?"

"No one."

"No one? Are you blushing?"

"Shut up."

Bill raised both eyebrows. "Next time we go to coffee, I want to hear all about this 'no one,' Jaq."

"Leave the girl alone, Bill. And give me a few of those candies. I think I'll stretch my legs, you two. We should only need to sit here for another few minutes."

"Okay, Cait." He squared off his list of names. "We'll hold down the fort for you."

"Thank you, dear." Mrs. Winchester zipped her computer into a laptop case and slid it under the table. "Please watch my valuables."

"We will," I said.

Bill kicked out his legs and stared at me, like he was waiting for something.

"What?"

"Nothing. But that was a blush, and that"—he indicated my phone—"was a someone, and I'm pretty curious. But I'll be good. And wait until it's a more appropriate time to interrogate you about your someone."

"I don't. Have. A someone."

"I kind of think you do."

"If you had a mustache right now, you'd be twirling it, wouldn't you?"

"I really would. Should I grow a mustache? It'd have to be a serious one, not some kind of noncommittal I-forgot-to-shave kind of thing." He twirled his imaginary mustache. "I think I could pull it off."

"I'm sure you could." Not that I could focus on Bill and his potential facial hair. Where was Hannah right now? Lying in her bed? In the dark, probably, with only the lights of the East Bay shining in through her windows . . .

"That thing your face is doing? That's an 'I have a someone' face, Jaq. I recognize it."

"Shut up. Can we process how one of the students hit on me? I feel like I haven't processed it enough. Also, Mrs. Winchester and I had a moment over being hit on by students, so that was a little shocking."

"Oh man, seriously?" He quit twirling his pretend 'stache. "You think she was a fox when she was younger?"

"A *fox*? What're you, twelve?"

He laughed. "Sometimes. I told Abby I'd take over for a shift at Hold'em. What're you doing next?"

"Staring at my phone and willing time to go faster."

"Oh really? Got a hot date with 'no one' later?" This time he fluttered his eyelashes.

I smacked him. "Bite me, Kent."

"You can take the Hold'em shift after mine. Do you know how to play?"

"Um, it's like poker?"

He sighed. "Yeah, it's poker, with some extra bits. It's no big thing, I'll show you. That's two more hours down, after that, Jaq. We will survive Grad Nite."

"Was it always this awful? I feel like it's worse this year than usual."

"You say that literally every year. It's not midnight yet. You think we should text an update to Juniper so she knows what she's missing?"

That sounded like fun. "Oh, we really should. I just *hate* that she's bored at home right now when she could be here with us."

We texted alternating stories to Juniper until Mrs. Winchester came back and freed us from our bonds. Bill's gleeful *Annie Potts tried to mack on Jaq!* message was the one that finally got a reply: *OH MY GOD I MISS EVERYTHING.* Then Bill went off to deal Hold'em and I resumed wandering around.

A few more hours passed. I'd seen, I thought, all the kids I knew. I dealt Hold'em. I coordinated mural-painting. I grudgingly let a few of my (now former) students paint my hands in rainbow colors and apply them to various T-shirts, then sign my name under them. Mementos, of course, from their high school lives. I wondered how many of them would sentimentally pack those T-shirts into bags for college, then shove them to the back of generic dressers, never to be worn.

Most of the population of Grad Nite were the kids heading to college or LVCC. They'd been the ones who had felt successful at high school, the ones who felt like celebrating their success. A lot of black kids, a lot of white kids, a lot of Asian kids, a smattering of everyone else. We weren't doing a great job reaching our Latino students, especially the recent immigrants, and looking around at the skewed representation at Grad Nite made me a little irritated at our failure.

I was thinking about how the hell we could engage better with the kids who seemed to fall off the map. They weren't the ones with behavioral issues, usually; they were the kids who passed their classes quietly with unremarkable test scores and parents who worked long hours. Many of them were older siblings responsible for caring for younger siblings, who never dreamed of college because no one they knew had that kind of money or could take that kind of time away from wage-earning.

I finally got bored enough to head out to the faculty restroom again.

A nod to the new door guard—Ms. Lowell, from the science department, where she taught . . . something science-y. Another moment of relief when the heavy door shut firmly on the sounds of the gym.

Except. This time I heard voices down the hall.

The gym was big and full of people; presumably it wasn't that strange that more than one chaperone had decided to take this moment to slip outside. Still, I investigated, mostly out of innate nosiness than anything else.

The front hall was clear. One hall branched off at each end, heading back into campus; this was where most of the English, history, and math classes were held, in the main building. We'd been steadily growing too big for the property for years, eating away at the parking lots and open spaces with a succession of grouped portable buildings that housed all the rest of the subjects: foreign languages here, sciences here, arts and other electives here.

I made my way, quietly, to the math hall, which had only a third of its ceiling fluorescents lit. No talking now, but I definitely hadn't made it up.

Carefully edging around the corner (I already cited my hard-earned spy credentials, right?), I managed to see the two people in the hall before they saw me.

Until I gasped, out loud, like a spy who deserved to be found out for terrible fucking spying, and they stopped kissing to look over.

"Hey, Ms. Cummings," LaTasha said.

Merin, leaning up against her, buried her face against LaTasha's neck and said nothing at all.

"Hey." Oh. That was my voice. Right. Okay, then. I straightened up. "What are you two doing back here? Aside from the obvious."

"Just the obvious." LaTasha brushed a stray lock of hair behind Merin's ear. "It's Ms. C. She isn't going to tell anyone."

"I'm definitely not going to tell anyone." Well, except for Bill, probably. And maybe Angel and Juniper. But no one else. Except for Zane. And possibly Hannah.

"Mer, it's okay."

I risked walking closer, though I'm less than totally comfortable seeing any of my students in a kissing-type embrace. "Yeah. You two are supposed to be in the gym, but other than that, you aren't doing anything wrong."

"No one's supposed to know," Merin mumbled.

"Ms. C doesn't count. And anyway, we only have a few more months, do we really have to act like criminals the whole time?"

Merin finally picked her head up. "Pretty much, yeah. You're going away. You get to go live your life. I'm stuck here with all these fucking people, so yeah, we have to act like we're criminals. Because I basically *am*."

"Sorry," LaTasha said, after a moment. "I didn't mean it like that. And I know. I shouldn't have said anything."

I was still experiencing a disorienting sense of vertigo. LaTasha, easily one of the brighter stars in her class, was kissing—in secret—Merin, who was easily one of the problem children of her class. Who cracked homophobic jokes all the time that I let slide because she didn't seem to mean them (and when I asked Sammy if they bothered him, he'd shrugged and said, "I think that's just how she shows affection").

"So." What was the appropriate course of action here? I decided on a question I'd been meaning to ask for a while, which had nothing to do with kissing—because while I was curious about how two apparently disparate people got along, mostly I didn't want to know, at all, any details, because *ohgodno*. "LaTasha, what have you been writing in that black notebook all the time?"

She blinked. "That's not anything like what I expected you to say."

"You aren't anything like who I expected to see over here."

"It's research. I started researching the drag king who died. Then I started researching crimes against trans people. Then I broadened it to all hate crimes. Then I brought it in to hate crimes against queer people, and tried to find reliable statistics for them. Do you know that in some places rape isn't considered a hate crime, even when it's overtly motivated by gendered and homophobic intent?"

"I guess I didn't know that."

"Well, it's screwed up. I mean, say what you want about hate-crimes legislation—and it's a little like affirmative action; I can see the arguments for it, but I'd like it to be a temporary measure instead of a permanent one—if you're going to have hate-crimes legislation, you should apply it in a logical way, shouldn't you?"

I really wished we were having this conversation in a classroom, when I'd gotten a night of sleep, and had fresh coffee to drink. I wanted to engage, but my brain was sluggish. "Yes. Though how often can you prove 'homophobic intent' for anything? Merin makes comments that appear to have homophobic intent behind them all the time."

"Massive overcompensation. Anyway, the black notebook is mostly ranting, but I think someday I might be able to really make something out of it."

"I hope that you do. And when you do, send it to me, LaTasha. I want to read it."

"Sure thing, Ms. Cummings. You were a really good teacher, by the way. I guess this is my last chance to tell you that."

"Well, thanks. You were a really good student."

Merin groaned. "Why don't you two jack each other off a little more, and I'll wait over there?"

LaTasha smacked the back of her head. "You be nice. It wouldn't kill you to express your appreciation for other people every now and then, Mer."

"You don't know that. It's untested. It might literally kill me to express appreciation for anything."

"Mm-hmmm, whatever you say."

They kissed. Again.

I looked away, clearing my throat. "Anyway, you two should really think about coming to the summer GSA meetings. That'd be good."

"I can't do that," Merin said.

LaTasha ducked her head down to catch Merin's eye. "It's the Gay-*Straight* Alliance, Mer. No one would have to know."

"Whatever."

"Sobrantes in the Harbor District, Fridays at five thirty, starting next week," I said. "Now I should probably herd you two back into the gym."

"Can we stay out here a little longer?" LaTasha asked, stroking Merin's hair again. "No drugs or alcohol, I swear. We're just trying to be alone for a minute."

The responsible thing would have been to say no, and make them go back into the gym, since that was the rule.

I couldn't do it. I remembered too well the simultaneous feeling that change couldn't come fast enough, and that it was coming too fast, too much, and all at once. And Merin didn't strike me as a kid who got a lot of soothing physical affection in her daily life.

"I never saw you," I said. "If you cause trouble, I swear to all that is holy—"

"We won't."

"Good. Think about coming to the meeting next week." *Think about doing it for Merin, if not for yourself, because she's going to need other people to stand by her when you leave for college in the fall.*

"I'll try to convince Mer to go with me," LaTasha promised.

"Glad to hear it. Take care of yourselves."

She waved, I waved, Merin hid her face in LaTasha's neck again.

I went to the bathroom, mechanically, without thinking about how fucking strange it was that I'd had the two of them in class together for an entire year and never suspected this. And also, oh my god, seriously, was my gaydar completely fucked? Was this a thing where you couldn't tell with teenagers because not all of them were fully developed into their adult personalities yet? Because Merin and LaTasha? Really?

They were either significantly quieter on my return trip down the hall, or they'd moved into an unlocked classroom. I didn't hear anything and went back into the gym like nothing was amiss.

I didn't tell Bill. Or Angel. Suddenly I actually wanted to keep their secret for them. At least for a little while.

CHAPTER 13

I may have fallen asleep in the diner waiting for Hannah. When I woke up, there was a steaming mug of coffee in front of my eyes, with a bowl of creamers beside it, and Hannah just beyond it, smiling at me.

A real smile.

"Heyyyy," I slurred. Drooling. That was attractive. "Um."

"Hey there. Long night?"

"Oh shut up." I wiped the drool from my face and began methodically dumping creamers in my coffee.

"You don't take it black?"

"I do. But." I sipped, and sighed, and sipped again. *Oh yeah, baby.* "I drank it black all night out of a vat of coffee at the refreshments table, so my digestive system is pretty much over this whole 'black coffee' phenomenon." I took another blissful sip. "God. So good."

"This place is kind of hard to find, by the way. I thought you were joking with the name."

"Nope. The View. I don't know what they were thinking. Who says, 'Want to meet up at The View for bacon and eggs?' Seriously."

"It's a play on 'La Vista'?"

"Right. A translation. But it's a terrible name for a diner, so everyone calls it 'the diner' instead."

"I can't believe I never knew it was here." Hannah leaned a little over the table and lowered her voice. "But the bacon and eggs?"

"Fucking the best thing you've ever tasted in your life. Great hangover food, if you're into that sort of thing. Zane and I have met up here after many a long night." I caught the server's eye and he made his way over. "Hey, I'll have two eggs over medium, bacon, hash browns, wheat toast, no jam, extra butter. Oh, and orange juice, please."

The kid—maybe twenty-two if that, whose little name tag read *Keith*—grinned. "One of those nights?"

"I chaperoned Grad Nite."

His mouth transformed into an O of understanding. "I'm so sorry, on behalf of all LVHS graduates present and past."

I waved. "No worries. Did it myself way too many years ago, and I think we actually got breakfast here after."

Keith nodded. "I think I did too. Though I didn't have company." He turned to Hannah. "For you?"

"Everything she got sounds good. Except no bacon, and no orange juice. What else do you have?"

"Well, coffee—"

"Oh, definitely coffee, hon. Let's say in addition to coffee, I'm going to pretend to get something healthy for my beverage."

"Oh! Grapefruit juice, then."

She wrinkled her nose. "If you say so. Sounds awful."

"The first few gulps are pretty bad," he confided. "But after that your taste buds go numb. Supposed to be really healthy, though."

"All right, then, Keith, I'll bow to your experience. If I spit it out all over my date, though, she's probably going to file a complaint."

Aw. The cutie's whole face opened up and a blush stole across his cheeks. He glanced at me, then back at Hannah. "I'll take the risk. Give me a minute for your coffee."

"I won't time you."

Keith walked away, and I tsked her. "Did you embarrass that nice boy?"

"Kid's gay."

"What? Are you serious? I swear I used to have a functional gaydar."

"Well, you didn't have the advantage of seeing him kiss his boyfriend good-bye."

"Thank god. Because I'm gonna have to return my toaster oven if this keeps up."

She grinned. "Did you just reference the *Ellen* coming-out episode?"

"Laura Dern, baby. If I wasn't gay already, I'd totally be gay for Laura Dern."

"Okay, not that I want to be one of those obnoxious LA people who name drops everyone all the time, but I went to a party once where Laura Dern was supposed to be."

"Liar."

"I'm not! But I didn't actually see her that night. Arnold Schwarzenegger was there, though."

"That doesn't actually sound that awesome."

"It wasn't. He's big, though, in real life. That's no joke."

I sipped my coffee. "So fancy LA parties and movie stars, huh? And now you're back in La Vista."

"I am. I guess I needed something that felt more . . . contained." She smiled her thanks as Keith set her coffee down. One of those hybrid smiles of Hannah's that was mostly generic, but had a little core of something warmer.

I didn't pay *that* much attention to her smiles or anything. Obviously. I didn't file away pictures of Hannah smiling different smiles and what they meant or anything, you know, creepy.

"You're staring at my lips, darling."

Oh god. "Sorry. I was—um—nothing."

"I think my new goal is to make everyone I talk to today blush. That sounds like fun."

"Anyway," I said determinedly. "Things happened tonight. Horrible things. Like one of my students hitting on me."

She grimaced, which was the correct response. "Ugh. That sounds embarrassing all around."

"Thank you. When I told my friend Angel, she acted like I should be flattered."

"Flattered?" Hannah shook her head. "That a high schooler thought you were hot? Ew. I'm grossed out even thinking about that. What did you do?"

"Well, she had me cornered against a soda machine, and she was clearly stoned. And yeah, I didn't want her to remember it later and want to crawl into a hole for the rest of her life, so I tried to be, you know, gentle with her."

"You didn't burst into laughter or call for reinforcements? That was nice of you, Jaq."

I tried to smile. "It was incredibly awkward. I can't even."

"And your friend thought it was cute?"

"Maybe not cute, exactly." Angel had laughed and told me I should take it as a compliment. Gross. "I think it was more that she didn't think it was threatening because the student was a girl."

"What difference does that make? If anything, that could get you in *more* trouble, couldn't it?"

I considered it. "Well, I'm out, officially. It's not like someone could blackmail me about being a dyke. But it's still . . . yeah. Not all danger is physical. I wasn't worried little Annie Potts could overpower me, but I definitely didn't want anyone getting the idea that I liked her attention or in any way invited it."

"Well, that sounds awful."

"It was, kind of. And then she said she couldn't tell her friends she was a lesbian because they'd say she was making it up, which just made me sad."

Hannah stirred sugar into her coffee, a line appearing in the center of her forehead. "Do you see a lot of that? I know it hasn't been that long since we were in high school, but it seems like it's significantly better now."

"I'm not so sure. It still comes down to the families, and the parents, and that's not quite liberating them from expectations yet. Another one of my kids came out to his parents, who told him he could stay in the house as long as he never acted on his feelings."

"So 'pretend you're straight or get out'?"

"They're Catholic. I think they genuinely believe he can be a good Catholic gay boy as long as he never kisses another boy. They made him watch a whole documentary about celibate gays and lesbians who 'maintain a close relationship with God.'"

"Jesus, Jaq. That's horrible."

"He'll graduate next year. I'm going to push him to go to college somewhere else. There are a few scholarships he might be able to get."

Keith arrived at the table with our food and both of us sat back to make room.

"Everything looks delicious," Hannah told him. "Thanks, hon."

"Sure. Let me know if you need anything else. And if you hate the grapefruit juice, Lottie said to add sugar or salt and it might make it taste better."

"Sugar *or* salt?"

He shrugged. "That's what she said. I just drink it straight or with, um, rum, which we don't have."

"I'll add sugar, then, and pretend I'm drinking rum and grapefruit."

"It definitely can't hurt. Enjoy your breakfast."

"Thank you," I said.

There's something about a big breakfast. I like to keep all of my foods separate, but Hannah mashed hers together, demolishing the hash browns, busting up the egg yolks, stirring all of it with a fork in one hand and a slice of bread in the other. I couldn't help watching her make one huge pile of breakfast foods.

"No bacon?" I asked.

"You know, I don't really eat meat."

"Seriously? Not that there's anything wrong with not eating meat, I just didn't, um, know that."

"I'm not a big die-hard about it or anything. But I like being healthy, and I already face a lot of shit from doctors because I'm fatter than their little charts say I should be. If I go in with a cough, they tell me I should lose weight." She gestured to her body with the toast, meeting my eyes, effortlessly sexy. "Mostly on a dare from my ex, I stopped eating meat for a couple of weeks, and I actually felt a lot better for it. I mean, Sandra's a chef. Before that dare we were pretty carnivorous omnivores. I think she only dared me because she didn't believe I could really quit meat. When I realized I felt better, I didn't see any reason to go back to eating it."

"That's really interesting. I tried to be a vegetarian for a minute in high school, mostly to annoy my dad, but I was too lazy to make my own food, so it didn't last. Every time I watch one of those horrible documentaries about how cows are treated or whatever, I vow to quit. I never do, though."

"Sometimes I let people believe I'm that good a person, and that's why I don't eat meat, but it's a lie. Obviously the way animals are treated is terrible, but I knew about that for years before I quit eating meat." One corner of her lips twitched up. "I'm really in it for that moment when a doctor wants to lecture me about my weight and I get to say, 'I'm a vegetarian.' That usually shuts them up, which is ridiculous, because you can be an unhealthy vegetarian like you can be an unhealthy everything else, but doctors seem pretty swayed by it."

"I'd love to see that. I'm the opposite. I don't get shit from doctors because my metabolism is crazy good, but I eat like a frat boy and at least one meal a week is deep-fried appetizers at Club Fred's."

"Skinny bitches," she said, smirking.

"Don't act like you don't love it." *Shit. I said "love." But in context. Not in a personal way.*

"Whatever you're doing, sugar, it works just fine for me. Any other highlights from your night?"

"Actually, yes." I told her about Merin and LaTasha, keeping their names out of it. You never knew who was at the next booth, listening to your every word, and La Vista seemed bigger than it was sometimes. It was easy to think you were anonymous when you weren't. "Basically, we're back to my gaydar is broken. Maybe irrevocably."

"How do you get one of those repaired? Or is it recalibrated?"

"I'd have to go on a gay cruise, don't you think? Enforced contact with queers for a week or two should do the trick."

"I'd jump off the boat. Can you imagine a thousand lesbians floating around in the ocean? Or worse—a thousand lesbians doing activities and coordinated tours." She shuddered. "That's my nightmare."

"But if the ship broke down, at least a few dozen of them would probably be able to fix it."

"See, there's a stereotype I wish applied to me. I can hang a picture, and that's basically it."

"You can hang pictures?"

"Why don't you come over later and find out?" Damn, Hannah going all-out seductive smile at me made my insides turn to jelly.

I took a breath before speaking, so my voice wouldn't be all high-pitched and needy. "Maybe I will. After a long nap. Anyway, I thought I was worried about one of them, but now I'm somewhat more worried about the other one. It's probably nothing. Or normal teenage stuff." I didn't really want her picturing me as a hand-wringing old maid, freaking out about my teenagers being moody.

"I don't know, Jaq. Seems to me if your instincts are telling you something's wrong, you might want to listen to them. Not that I ever do, but there are definitely some moments I look back on and wish I had."

"That's my fear. If I do nothing and something bad happens, could I have prevented it? But I'm sure they'll be fine for the summer. I just feel better when school's in session and I can watch out for them. Anyway." I gestured to our nearly empty plates. "How'd you like your breakfast?"

"Delicious, as promised. I'm trying to work up my nerve for the grapefruit juice."

I pulled the glass toward me and dumped three sugar packets into it, stirring with the handle of my knife. Then I pushed it back. "Give it a shot."

"I will if you will."

I gave the glass another look. "Deal. You first."

She picked up the glass. "I'm holding my breath. I don't think smelling it's going to help matters."

"Good call."

She inhaled, then tossed back half the glass in one go before shoving it across the table while her face contorted. "Oh, that's *vile*. I can't believe I just drank it. Your turn."

"Are your eyes watering?"

"I'm crying tears of disgust."

"Drama queen."

"You try it."

I stirred it again. Whatever sugar was on the bottom would be more concentrated, which meant at least my sip would be sweeter than Hannah's.

"Bottoms up." I picked up the glass.

The first sip tasted like licking a lemon rind, but maybe Keith was onto something; I made myself drink a little more, and it actually wasn't that bad.

I finished the glass, swirling the sugar around on my tongue for a minute before swallowing. "Not bad."

"You're lying."

"It could have been worse." I leaned across the table and coaxed her forward, kissing her. "I got the sugar."

"You *are* the sugar." She deepened it, and I tried not to arch into her lips. Public. The diner. La Vista. But, damn, I might have to start drinking grapefruit juice if it got me kisses like this one, Hannah searching for sweetness on my tongue.

"I'm considering this a promise for later," she said softly, looking me right in the eye.

"Definitely." I may have sounded a bit breathless. Perfectly normal. It was the grapefruit juice. Right. I swear.

She picked up the check. "My treat. When do you want to come by later?"

"Dinner? We could go out."

"We could eat in. I can put dinner together."

"And dessert?"

"If you're a good girl."

"I am *such* a good girl," I said. "I'll come over around six."

"Perfect." She stood up, then leaned in for another kiss. "See you then."

"Thanks for breakfast."

"Anytime."

We walked out together after she paid young Keith, who told us to have a good day. She kissed me chastely and waved.

I wanted to follow her to her place, curl up in her bed, smell her on the sheets. Instead I got in my truck and thought about all the ways everything could go wrong.

Zane might have a point about me dodging out on relationships.

CHAPTER 14

I slept fitfully, like you do when you're used to being awake during the day but you're exhausted. I got a hard three hours or so, but after that I was too tired to get up and too alert to stay asleep, so I tossed and turned and obsessed over things. Like Merin's home life, and how worried I should be about Annie Potts, and if Callie would be okay taking care of her siblings day in and day out while secretly dreaming of a future when she could transition. When I'd exhausted my current batch of student concerns, I moved on to wondering about whether Zane would ever actually get pregnant, and what would happen if she did, because she wouldn't be able to hit the gym three times a week and head to Club Fred's after. It would impact *everything*. Probably there were bigger things to think about, baby-wise, but I was stuck on *What if we can't go to Fred's after the gym?* Which was selfish, but half in and out of sleep was a weirdly twilight time of random thoughts. My brain had no filter.

From thinking about the inevitable future when Zane would be a mother, I became preoccupied with the fact that Dred already *was* a mother, and I hadn't even seen her. Hell, I haven't even called her except once, to congratulate her. I'd left a message, which she hadn't returned, which I took as letting me off the hook. She texted me twice, to tell me about the knitting class she was doing at the yarn shop. Nothing about the kid. Nothing about the dick guy she'd had the kid with, who I heard was out of the picture for good.

That was one of those futures I could have had, and didn't. Not with Mildred, probably, because we'd been too young when we were together. (She'd been . . . embarrassingly young when we were together.) At some point, though, I could have chosen to have a kid with someone.

Hannah could have had a kid with her ex. Seven years was a long time. That would be a lot worse than having a house together. A lot more complicated.

Well, maybe *worse* was the wrong word. Probably if you had a kid, you didn't think to yourself, *It'd be a lot more convenient if we only had a house together.* Right?

Or a dog. Did straight people get as weird about their dogs as queers? The relationship Carlos had before he met Tom had ended ugly with a custody battle over a pug, I swear. One night Zane and I got really drunk and told him to get over it, it was only a dog. He didn't talk to us for a month after that.

I could get a dog. Wait, no. Hannah didn't like pets. Plus, I already had a dog, over at Dad's. I should go visit Ducky. And Dad. And god, I hadn't talked to any of my siblings in weeks. Grades were due Monday. I could call them after Monday. Or something.

God, Monday. What an exhausting thought. And how cruel could the administration be, making Monday the day final grades were due after at least half the faculty chaperoned the lock-in Friday night? Granted, we were supposed to be inputting our grades to the online system every three weeks so students could be held accountable for knowing their current grades. I'd been pretty good about it, so at least there was that. The first two years I taught I used to leave grades for the end of the semester and it made me pretty homicidal. This was better, now that I was used to doing it more frequently.

Summer. It was summer. Or it would be, after I got my grades in. Summer, summer, summer. Summer, and Hannah, and maybe Zane would get preggo, and I should really call Dred and ask her how the kid was, and maybe Hannah would make another coconut cream-based dessert, because damn, those strawberries...

Shit. Wait. Did I—did I just write Hannah into the future? Fantasizing about eating dessert with her was *so* not the right thing to do. Damn it. Sex was one thing. Enjoying sensual desserts she hand-fed me was...was...something else.

A tingling sensation radiated out from some deep place in my body. Not arousal. Something else. A little more like low-level fear, like the prickle you got walking around at night when it might not be totally safe.

I finally woke up for good around three and took a long, hot shower to prove it. I may have shouted, "Good morning, Vietnam!" as loudly as I dared without disturbing my neighbors.

Back in my misspent youth, I could roll out of bed and barely notice I'd missed a night's sleep. These days, I noticed if I missed bedtime by half an hour. Age is cruel.

I discovered leftover Chinese food in my fridge and it didn't smell totally off yet, so I ate it. Which might have been the wrong decision, so I followed it with a dose of Mylanta and read my book sitting very still in my chair until I was pretty sure I wasn't going to puke.

My filled-to-overflowing bag and stacks of grading yet to be done guilt-tripped me from the kitchen table, but I ignored them. I deserved a rest, damn it. I deserved to sit in my chair with a good book until it was time to go to Hannah's.

I didn't puke. I didn't grade. I fell asleep again in my chair and ran late for dinner.

Hannah made some kind of intense salad for dinner, with a side of roasted vegetables. Which reminded me she was a vegetarian, because I kept wondering where the "real" food was, though it had to be mostly psychological; the salad was delicious and filling. I certainly didn't need any more food.

"This is fantastic," I said. "I almost made myself sick off old Chinese food earlier. This is really good."

"Really good when compared to old Chinese food?" She arched a smartass eyebrow at me. "Good to know."

"Oh, shut up. You know what I mean."

"Why on earth did you eat bad Chinese?"

Good question. I sipped my wine, casting about for a logical explanation, until I finally gave up. "I wasn't at my most clever, okay? Anyway, what's for dessert?"

"It's definitely not time for dessert yet. I thought we could watch a movie. Or something."

"Or something?"

"Well. Or we'll save 'something' for later."

"Tease."

We talked about basic things. I mentioned going to knitting on Wednesday, and she asked if she could come with me. I almost said no, except the idea of introducing her to Dred was actually kind of interesting, and the idea of the two of us side by side at the yarn shop, trying to knit was . . . intriguing.

I told my brain to quit being intrigued by shit.

After we'd mostly cleaned the kitchen, we turned on a movie—some comedy I hadn't seen because it looked dumb—but she'd unpacked her books, so I ended up snooping while she handled a flurry of text messages from her ex about the second offer they'd received on their house.

"Isn't it weird that after you break up with someone you notice so many of their flaws? I guess I knew Sandy was pigheaded, but the *depths* of her stubbornness actually keep surprising me."

"She doesn't want to take the offer?" I pulled a book out at random and flipped through.

"She doesn't want to negotiate. Or pay closing. Or do any of the requested maintenance. I mean, we should really replace the back deck. We always meant to and both home inspectors so far have said it needs to be replaced."

I looked over. "Well, but shouldn't the new owner have to do that?"

"That's her argument. That if they want the house badly enough, they won't balk at paying for a new deck. But no one so far has wanted the house enough to even get this far. It seems stupid to say no at the last minute when all we'd have to do is hire someone to go in, fix it, and it would be done."

Which sounded like it made sense. "Hannah—is it that you don't have the money to buy her out? Or that you don't want to?"

"Do you have any idea how much a house in West Hollywood costs?" But she kept glaring down at her phone instead of looking at me.

"Not really. But I don't have any idea how much you have, or how much this condo costs either."

"Well, that's the thing. I could have bought her out before I bought this place. I probably should have. But then I had no idea how long it would take to sell the house, even after we lowered the price, and we still had a lot of money wrapped up in it, so I guess I got scared."

"That it wouldn't sell for as much as you needed?"

"Yeah. And it *will* sell eventually. But in the meantime I have somewhere to live."

"Which is good," I said, letting a question creep into my tone.

"Okay." She grimaced down at her phone and turned it over on her thigh. "The real truth is I didn't want to make it easy for her. If I buy her out, she doesn't have to think about it anymore, it's done, and she makes a pretty penny. She wouldn't have taken less than half of asking minus what we have left on the note. Which is a lot of money, and I probably wouldn't have necessarily made double that in a sale."

"And you didn't want to make it easy for her."

She shot me a look. "Yeah. The thing about Sandy is she's little, and cute, and one of those fireball types of women. Everyone thinks she's darling; she smiles with her dimples and people fall at her feet. 'Can I prep everything for you, Chef?' 'Oh, let me bring you a coffee, Ms. Deostino.' It gets a little exhausting, everyone falling all over themselves to do favors for your wife. And she *loves* that shit. I'm sure it's how she hooked up with her girlfriend. A good dose of hero worship always went a long way with Sandy."

"Is that how you guys got together?" I waggled my eyebrows inappropriately.

She offered a tired smile. "Actually, I think it was the opposite. We got together when she was a lowly prep cook and I was in law school. At the time, it looked like I'd be the one with the promising future and she'd be the kept woman once I got successful. Then she entered one of those cooking contests, not a big cable one, but a local TV station running the same kind of thing. And people loved her. The judges loved her, the viewers voted for her every week, and she won."

"Really? That's kind of amazing."

"It was. I'm bitter about it now, but it was, undoubtedly, at the time. We couldn't believe it. Or she couldn't believe it and I said things like, 'That's because you don't know how hot you are, baby.'"

I hid a snort behind a book. "Did you?"

"Hey, we were in love. And it was thrilling, being caught up in all that. She didn't want to do TV, like that's the dream for a lot of the folks who win those contests. She really just wanted to be a head chef somewhere nearby, design menus, try out new recipes. Which she would have done eventually, probably, but she got a few incredible job offers after the show aired, and took one of them."

"And the rest is history, huh?"

"Yeah. I don't know, maybe I couldn't handle her success. Not that I wanted to be the only one earning a decent living, or that I couldn't take it when she started making a lot of money. It was more that everywhere we went, I was Sandy D's wife. I was Mrs. Sandy D." She shrugged wryly. "Do you think I'm terribly shallow?"

"I think I lucked out. No chance of my success overshadowing you, anyway. I mean, not that we're getting married—" Oh fuck me. I hid behind the book again, pretending to be super interested in the building of the Chicago world's fair.

"Oh really? Dash my hopes, will you?" Just a light tease, but it was enough so I could quit hiding behind my book. She shrugged. "Maybe it's like any relationship you get into young. We both changed so much, and not necessarily in the same direction. And I did stupid things to get her attention when I thought I was losing it. I cheated on her."

"You *didn't*." Whoa. That was freaking intense.

"I cheated on her with one of her employees."

I goggled. "Holy shit, Hannah."

"I know. It was so stupid. *I* was so stupid. But at the time I thought she might notice that something was really wrong between us and, I don't know, somehow go from 'you cheated' to 'we can work it out.'" She shook her head. "So dumb. But I was done and looking for an excuse to get out. I just didn't know it yet."

"I can't believe you cheated. On your *wife*."

"One time." She smiled wryly. "Not that that makes it better. Or more excusable. But one time and I felt so sick about it I literally threw up. Not that *that* makes it better, either." For a second she just played with her phone, one fingernail picking at the case. When she looked up, there was no trace of the smile. "The whole thing was ugly. And I kind of wish I hadn't told you about it now."

"Relationships are messy," I said, because I didn't know what else to say. People cheated all the time, obviously, but I'd never had a straight-up conversation where someone admitted it like that, and definitely not with anyone I was sleeping with. *Damn.*

"That they are." Hannah forced a laugh. "I have the worst desire to defend myself and tell you how horrible she was—and she was—but nothing deserves cheating. Hell even being cheated on doesn't deserve cheating. It's such a fucked-up way to hurt someone."

"Did it work? I mean, obviously it didn't *work*, but did it hurt her as badly as you wanted it to?"

She looked away, blinking a little too fast. "That was the worst part. It hurt me much more than it hurt her. By then she had all of these fans, all these people who'd do anything for her. She had invitations to events all over the city. She didn't need my attention. And after that, she didn't want it."

"This is going to sound kind of wrong," I said, hoping I was striking the right note. "But I'm happy you got a divorce, Hannah."

She uttered a choked, watery laugh. "Me too. You have no idea. Are you completely disgusted by me now? I can't believe I told you all that."

Since Hannah was the last person who acted guilty about anything, it unsettled me that she seemed so disturbed about this. I got up and crossed to sit beside her on the futon. After a second, I took her angrily buzzing phone and set it on the coffee table. Which only made it louder. "Jeez. That thing's insistent."

"I know it. Sorry." She silenced it and left it on the table.

"I'm totally not disgusted. I'm sorry you did things that made you feel awful. I'm sorry that you felt so awful you did awful things. All that's behind you, though, right?"

"That's what's so frustrating about the house. It'll never be behind me until we're done with the house, but at the rate she's willing to work, that feels like never. She's haggling over stupid, small things, things we can afford. It would be one thing if they were demanding we drop a hundred thousand dollars into the house, but this is dumb stuff. I don't know. I'm sorry I keep talking about this." She reached for my hands. "So not sexy."

"You let me whine at you about my students, which is also not sexy."

"No, but that was actually interesting. I admire that you teach. And I don't mean that in a patronizing way. You do something that means a lot to you, and that's admirable."

I wondered if she'd thought the same thing of Sandy when they got together. "What you do doesn't mean a lot to you?"

"I didn't get into it for that kind of fulfillment. I wanted to never worry about the bills. Ironically, I also wanted to be able to maintain a certain quality of life without having to rely on a second income. Then I rushed out and got fucking married."

"My dad used to say he and Mom had everything planned down to his retirement exactly at age sixty-five and how they'd sell the house, get an apartment in senior living somewhere, and spend the rest of their time going on adventures."

Her face crumpled. "Oh god. And she died."

"And she died, so he had to quit the sales job that paid more money to get a job locally so he could raise four kids. I know he's got a little saved up for retirement, but it's nowhere near what they'd hoped to have. The best-laid plans, right?"

"Would your dad go to breakfast with us tomorrow if we asked him?"

I winced. "Shit. He usually picks me up for church. Hold on."

Right, so, texting your dad that you won't be home to ride to mass with him because hot sleepover, that's not awkward at all. He texted back, *I'll see you girls there. Behave yourself, dear. XO*

"He told me to behave myself and he'll see us at mass. So I guess we aren't skipping."

She smiled. "I like his style. I like St. Agnes too. Way less stuffy than St. Pat's."

"I've never—" *dated someone who went to church.* I blushed and froze, unable to think of any less incriminating way to end that sentence.

"You never what?"

Danger, Will Robinson. I had to backtrack. "Most people don't seem to get why I keep going to church."

"Really?"

"Well, Catholic church. There's a lot of great Unitarian places people keep trying to get me to go to, but it's not the same."

Her fingers drifted along mine absently. "I tried to break ties with the church. I was a Buddhist for a while, and a Wiccan, and I couldn't pull off being an atheist, but I wanted to."

"You wanted to be an atheist?"

"Definitely. It seems so simple. Everything that is, is. Everything that isn't, isn't. You know? But ultimately I couldn't figure out how science can still be growing as a field and have all the answers already. Obviously it doesn't, and never will. There will always be questions. And I . . . will always look outside the physical, proven world for at least some of those answers."

I nodded. "I guess I take comfort in it. I'd rather think that some things are unknowable, and God is one of them, than think life is just another standardized test with right answers and wrong answers."

"Exactly." Her fingers traced the bones of my wrist. "But do you get comfort from the church? I want to. I remember being a child and feeling safe, loved. I don't know if I lost that somewhere along the way, or if I'm too broken for it to mean anything."

"I get comfort from it. It's familiar. It feels like home." I swallowed, focusing on the sensation of her fingers. "It feels like my mother, or the closest thing to her. But only to me. My sisters and brother won't even set foot inside a church unless someone's dead or getting married."

"That's how I used to feel. I don't know. It might be all in vain, but I'll keep trying church and see if it reminds me of being whole. I really miss that feeling of sitting there and knowing that everything was going to be okay." She brought my hand to her lips and kissed my knuckles. "Sorry. I didn't mean for this to get so deep."

"It's okay. Did you want to text-yell at Sandy more, or should we finish the movie and make dessert?"

"Other way around. Let's make dessert, finish the movie, forget about Sandy, and use our imaginations for the rest of the evening."

"Sounds delicious."

"Good."

We leaned in at the same time to kiss, still holding hands, and some low, frightened thing in my guts somersaulted, making me dizzy.

"Dessert is going to be fun. Have you ever made chocolate fondue?"

She managed to top the strawberries and cream. We served each other fruits and nuts dipped in chocolate and made a huge mess.

And never stopped laughing.

CHAPTER

We went to mass with Dad in the morning, but he declined breakfast.

"I'll take you up on a quick coffee before I get to work, though."

"Great." Hannah fell in beside him as we walked toward Sobrantes. "What kind of work are you doing today?"

"One of my children, who shall remain nameless, promised to help me build a shed today."

"Oh *shit*," I said. "I forgot all about that. Sorry, Dad."

He waved a hand. "You have better things to do than build sheds. I'll do what I can and leave the rest."

"I have time this week after I turn in my grades on Monday." I pulled up on his other side. "Nothing but time for sheds."

"We should be able to get a few hours in after I get home from work, since it's summer. I'll make hot dogs."

"Sounds good."

"Now, Richard, Jaq led me to believe she wasn't that handy."

"My Jaq? Sure, she's handy. Now, if you were standing in front of something broken or in need of building at the time, she might not have made a big deal out of it—"

"Hey! Don't be rude! And I'm not *handy*. Just because I can screw in a nail and pound in a screw doesn't make me handy."

Dad shook his head. "Unfortunately, handy as she is, she has an inflated notion of how funny she is, so I apologize for that, Hannah."

"I think Jaq's plenty funny. I might make her demonstrate screwing in a nail for me later, though." She winked at me.

I huffed a sigh. "You know, I'm not sure either one of you deserve my company."

Dad hooked his arm through mine. "Tell me all about graduation. And that all-night thing after."

"Bill and I got stuck at a table with Mrs. Winchester for *hours*, Dad. Hours. It was brutal."

"And how is Mrs. Winchester?"

"Exactly the same as always, except apparently she's had students hit on her, which . . . boggles the mind."

"Some folks like a firm hand, dear."

Hannah snorted.

"Let's never ever talk about Mrs. Winchester being a firm hand again, Dad, okay? Because no."

"You're so squeamish, Jaq. Hannah, you aren't as squeamish as Jaq, are you?"

"Oh, I'm not squeamish *at all*."

"So this thing where"—I gestured between them as I opened the door to the shop—"you two are bonding? I'm not okay with it. FYI. And Hannah's buying, Dad, so get whatever you want. Something expensive."

"I'll try to embellish my coffee enough to satisfy you."

Once we moved away from alarming subjects, coffee was kind of fun. Hannah charmed Dad, he charmed her, and we hadn't been sitting down for longer than fifteen minutes before Dad decided "that shed won't build itself" and said good-bye.

"He's a lot of fun." Hannah watched him walk back down the hill to St. Agnes.

"Yeah." Now that I was awake, and alert, and didn't plan to worry about anything responsible until tomorrow, I didn't particularly feel like sitting in public with coffee. I made my voice a bit camp and said, "I can be a lot of fun too, baby."

"Is that right?"

"Why don't you take me back to your place and I'll show you?" I spoiled it by laughing. "Damn."

Hannah's eyes glittered in the late-morning sun. "I think I'd rather take you back to my place and play with you like a toy, which would definitely be fun for me."

I tried to pout, but failed. "If you want me to pretend I'm objecting, I can."

"Oh no. Don't bother. I'll have you begging me in no time, and it won't be acting. Let's go, girlfriend."

Girlfriend. Casual slang for female friend. Likely not meant as a term relating to committed or romantic partnership.

I mumbled something about a refill and hid inside until I was no longer blushing.

Hannah hadn't been joking.

"I really wish I hadn't buried my sex toys in some obscure box, but oh well. We'll have to make do." She pulled my shirt off my shoulders and tossed it over a random dining room chair that was sitting in the corner of her bedroom. "I should seriously make an effort to move in, now that I paid a lot of money for this place."

"Um." Because that was about the height of eloquence I could come up with while she pinched my nipples through my bra.

"How do you feel about strap-ons, sugar? When I find my box of goodies, you'll have to let me convert you to a dick-loving lesbian."

"Um."

"I never got that whole thing where lesbians considered strap-ons tools of the patriarchy. I mean, if I'm wearing it, it's a tool of *me*. And if I'm using it on you, you better believe you're not thinking of men."

One of her hands slid inside the front of my slacks and— Oh damn. I jumped.

She giggled, dragging her fingers lower. "I do have one thing out, though. I'd never put *it* in a box."

I struggled to stand still, loosening my knees a little so she could—oh fuck yes—dip a finger inside. I was incredibly fucking wet already because she'd been working me up on the walk back to the condo, going on and on about screws and holes and finding the sweet spot to drill in. It would have definitely sounded like gibberish if you didn't know she was really talking about sex.

"But I warn you, Jaq, if I show you my lovey, you have to let me do whatever I want to you. I don't show it to just anyone, you know."

"Your—ah—lovey?" I bit back a moan and spread my legs more, but she withdrew.

"My lovey. My postdivorce gift to myself. It loves me but good when no one else does." Her cheek pressed against mine, and she nibbled at my ear before saying, "Do you want to see my lovey, Jaq?"

Hell yes I wanted to see it. Was that a joke?

"I'll show you, and then I'll *really* show you. But you have to say yes to all of it, or no peeks."

I grabbed her hand and tried to get it between my legs again, but she laughed and stepped back. Evil woman. "You fucking tease."

"Say yes. Abandon your will. Let me play with you."

I'm not super adventurous, but I like to think I'm pretty game for anything. I'd never been with someone who seemed to have the imagination Hannah did. I'd never been with anyone who looked at me like she did, as if where sex was concerned all the doors were thrown open and we could walk through any of them, at any time.

"Is this gonna be some kind of kinky thing where you tie me to the bed? Uh, not that that's a deal breaker."

"Put a pin in it. No. No restraints. Just you, me, the bed, and my lovey. But I'm in charge."

"Um." Honestly, five seconds ago I would have let her tie me to the bed, which would have defaulted to her being in charge anyway, so I didn't know why it tripped me up so much to say yes.

She grinned. "I'm gonna make you feel so good. Your head's gonna explode."

"Yeah, okay. Except for the head exploding, I'm in."

"Take off your clothes."

I took off my bra and slacks and folded them, trying to pretend I didn't feel conspicuously naked in the bright sunlight streaming through the three high windows of the bedroom. When I turned, Hannah was standing there in a bra and panties, looking so epically sexy I wanted to fall to my knees and worship her.

"You are fantastically gorgeous," I said, feeling bashful.

"Oh honey. I know. I make it a little hard to concentrate, don't I?"

"And modest. So, so modest."

"Get on the bed."

"And demure. So, so—"

She came in close like she was gonna kiss me, so I waited. Then she smacked my ass. "Get on the bed. On your back."

"Yes, ma'am."

She smacked my ass again as I scampered toward the bed, and the quick there-and-gone sting of it only made me hotter.

I lay down on my back, feeling yeah, a little fucking vulnerable, and a little turned on by it. She waited until I was still before going into her bedside table, and emerging a minute later with a vibrant purple vibrator.

"Oh my god," I said.

"My lovey." She switched it on and my eyes followed it, noting the powerful-sounding buzz. That was no cheap vibe with a single double-A battery. That was at least two D-cells.

I squeezed my legs together and said, "Oh my god." Again.

"Yeah, she's a good girl. She's a good reward for other good girls. Now, Jaq, I want your hands up there holding on to the headboard."

"Um." I couldn't stop watching it, but I obeyed.

"Look at your breasts." She moved closer, taking a seat beside me, and I wasn't paying attention to her free hand because I was too busy watching the purple buzzing blur that was Lovey.

The pinch was a shock. I gasped, nipple tingling, and arched back.

"Good little girls feel very, very good, Jaq, when they do as I say. Plus, that didn't really hurt—did it?"

All my *yeses* and *nos* were jumbled up in my head. My nipple didn't hurt *now*, though, so I guess it must have been okay? I bit down on the inside of my cheek and settled back.

"Such a good girl." Lovey came at me and oh fuck, touched down at the point of my nipple. I couldn't help flinching, but it didn't hurt. It felt wild, unrestrained. And it moved away almost immediately, leaving my body braced for more. With a click, the buzzing cut out and I sighed.

Hannah's fingers trailed down my arm, not quite tickling, curling over to slide up my throat. So fucking sensual. I finally managed to look away from the vibrator and met her eyes, almost wishing a second later that I hadn't.

Whatever we were doing wasn't a game. Not to me, and, judging by the intensity of her gaze, not to her, either.

"Mmm, so pretty." Her fingertips traced my lips, and I allowed them to part, but she didn't come inside. "So very pretty."

I don't think of myself as "pretty." I skew a little too far on the masculine side for "pretty," and it's never bothered me. I'm butch; I don't need to be pretty or sweet or cute. But Hannah taking a tour of my skin while I was stretched out for her, seeing in me some kind of beauty, made me feel more exposed than taking off my clothes had.

"Open your legs, sugar. Let me show you what my lovey's all about."

I wanted to keep it light, crack a joke. But I couldn't. This was too deep all of a sudden, so I did as she asked, letting myself fall open for her, and the small smile—acknowledgment that I'd pleased her—made me warm all over.

"I love your trimmed little bush," she murmured, running her fingers through it. "Trimmed little triangle bush." She hadn't strayed to anywhere especially sensitive, but my whole body was a live wire, and I shivered with the jolt of contact.

Then she powered on her lovey again.

"This is my favorite vibrator that I've ever owned. There are a million attachments for it, but I like it all on its own, as long as it has fresh batteries." Lovey grazed the line of my pubic hair and I trembled. The fucking vibrations were *strong*—I could feel them in my bones, my tissues. It was amazing.

For the first time in my life, I realized that actually powerful vibrating massagers would be good for sore muscles. Who knew?

Lovey dipped lower, off to one side, clearly avoiding, oh, say, my clit, which was already humming from the proximity. I gasped a little when the vibrations shifted, now to my lips, my thighs, oh god.

"Wider now. Open for me. Let me play."

I splayed my legs, and Hannah knelt in between them, which was a little alarming, but hell, I wasn't about to complain. Lovey trailed down to my knee, then back up to my breasts, drawing lines beneath them before dipping back down to my navel. I swore my organs were thrumming along with it, and it was too powerful to be soothing. It kept me a little on edge.

"Good girl, Jaq." Lovey inched back to my bush. "Such a good girl." Lovey grazed lightly down, catching the edges of my somewhat embarrassingly aroused labia, which were basically holding up a sign saying *FUCK HERE!*

If I were cracking jokes, like I should have been, I'd ask her if that thing was waterproof, because I was very wet. Instead I tried to be still and earn another "good girl."

One of Hannah's fingers slipped into my cunt, and she pressed Lovey against her wrist, sending the vibrations in deeper than they could reach from outside, and oh fuck, that was intense, and amazing, and damn, damn, had she said I couldn't come? I didn't know if I could hold back.

"Isn't that nice? Who needs attachments when we have hands. Wider, Jaq." Her finger slid out, and up, parting my lips, dancing over my clit. "I want you so open for me I can see everything. I want to introduce my lovey to all your most vulnerable bits."

Which sounded impossible. Lovey was far too strong for my most vulnerable bits. But I wanted to make her happy, and I wanted to see what she'd do, so I stretched my legs out and pulled them back, giving her everything.

She leaned down to lap at my clit for a second and I bucked up into her, but she only laughed. "Not yet, naughty girl. Don't make me spank you."

Don't make me beg. I couldn't say it.

"Now, let's see what you've got."

She teased, and played, and vibrated, sometimes over the line of too much. I tried to close my legs, but she always nudged them wide again and returned, dialing it down, using her lips or tongue for a few minutes, or two fingers, three fingers, sending Lovey's pulses against my G-spot until I thrashed.

I came. And came. And came again. She didn't stop. She changed course, changed sensation, changed location, but she never let me fully come down.

When my entire body was trembling from exertion and arousal, Hannah stripped, then knelt up, her knees at my ass.

"Now we're gonna ride my lovey all the way to the end of the line, sugar. You ready for this?"

I probably wasn't. In truth, I probably hadn't been ready for any of it. "Oh god yes, please, whatever it is—"

Was that me? Pleading? For whatever she wanted?

She leaned over to kiss me, and I tried to rub against her. She only laughed again.

"Exactly my plan." She braced one arm on the bed. The other held Lovey against me while she pressed against it, clit to clit with a little lovey in between.

Then she powered it on and I came, immediately, thrusting up while the weight of her body held me down. Hannah's orgasm, as far as I could tell, was a fucking tsunami, and I swear her eyes rolled back in her head. She came for what felt like hours, and I subtly shifted just enough so Lovey wasn't right on top of my poor defenseless clit anymore, but it was still more pleasurable than I expected. Because she was beautiful, because she was into me, because she'd devoted all that time and energy to pleasing me. And now pleasing me had pleased her, so much that she had the longest orgasm ever recorded in human history, fucking a purple vibrator on top of me.

When she was done, she collapsed. Lovey rolled off the other way, ending up at my side. I clicked it off and set it on the bedside table.

"That was insane," I whispered, taking the opportunity to pull the clip out of her hair, loosen the braid. "Hannah, I've never done anything like that before."

"Oh, we're only beginning." She curled into me. "Keep playing with my hair. I love it when you do that."

I love it when you do that. The heated thing in my heart that wanted to expand, that I'd been keeping at bay with threats and dire outcomes, finally broke free. I lay in bed with my girlfriend, who'd fucked both of us nearly unconscious, and played with her hair. Because she loved it when I did that.

CHAPTER

I did not spend the night at Hannah's. I forced myself to go home, after cuddling and reading in bed, ignoring the twinges all over my body where I wanted to be having more sex with her, even if Lovey's batteries died permanently.

Damn it.

I went home, ate a frozen dinner, and went to bed at a reasonable hour like a responsible adult.

I woke up on Monday hating the world. Like a responsible adult.

A pot and a half of coffee into my day, I began to feel like maybe, just maybe, I was making progress.

I'd done the Creative Writing class's grades first. Since there was no test and I'd already returned all of their papers, that was a simple matter of basic math and percentages. Done.

Journalism was the same. Done. I vowed to set up one of those clever spreadsheets for next year with all the formulas already in it and stop using my battered old grading notebook.

A ton of coffee and two classes down.

Grading finals, though, was my nightmare. I'd used the little computer-readable bubble tests the first year, but it felt impersonal. So I'd switched to hand-grading. I think maybe the problem was I didn't feel like I suffered enough when I could send the sheets through a reader and be done. Then again, it could also be I got lazy and didn't want to go down to the school and stand at the machine feeding in tests.

So now I did this. In my apartment. In my pajamas. With my coffee.

Page... after page... after page. After a while it was easy to visually assess each test and mark them almost without going line-by-line, but it was still tedious as hell. And the last four years had basically found me cursing and swearing to go back to Scantrons, but so far I hadn't. They really *were* impersonal. And I really didn't want to put on pants, which was probably the bigger issue. Plus, there was a run on the machine on grading day. (I could just hear helpful people mentioning that being better prepared would save me a lot of this whining, but let's pretend I had my fingers in my ears.)

I took a break to get my mail from downstairs. Huh. A fancy envelope from Liz and Marla, both of their names crammed onto the return address as if they were one entity. The bills and credit card offers went in a pile I assigned to some future date when it got too tall to ignore, but I opened the fancy envelope right away.

Hell. It was a picture. The picture. Of Hannah and me at the wedding. Her laughing. Me sort of gazing at her with this big stupid grin on my face. A note slipped out.

Liz's handwriting: *I admit, the two of you make a damn cute couple. Hope you're well, Jaq. Love, Liz.*

It *was* a good picture. I didn't even remember what she'd been laughing at, or how I'd felt at the time, but now I could look at her face and know exactly the kind of laugh it was, how it sounded. How her eyes would tear up a little, and if she was in the sun, they'd kind of gleam.

Shake it off. Go back to work.

My phone vibrated, startling me. Zane, asking about the gym. I'd planned to skive off, even if I had most of the work done, but Zane accepted my *Sry, grading, see you Weds* text as a challenge.

When someone knocked on the door, I foolishly hoped it was Hannah. Which of course was impossible, because she had no idea where I lived.

"What do you want?" I glared blearily at Zane.

"I want the health and happiness that come with having a toned physique and a bitching cardiovascular system!"

"I hate you."

"You wish." She pushed past me. "Oh god, you're full-on grading den today. I thought you said you felt prepared for final grades this semester?"

"I was! But they still have to actually be done, which is annoying."

"Hey, three months off. Quit whining."

"Oh, sorry, Zane, did you want to be a teacher? I had no idea." I flopped back into my armchair, but I'd been sitting in it all day, so the cushion had slid forward and my ass hit a spring. "Ow. Damn it."

I laboriously rearranged the cushion before sitting again, and Zane burst out laughing.

"Man, you're in rough shape. Oh my god, this picture! Is this at the wedding?"

I snatched it back. "Yes, the wedding. Shut up."

"It's so cute!"

"Shut up!"

She grinned. "Ah, you're so sensitive. What, didn't get any sleep last night?"

"I got plenty of sleep last night. But I don't recover as quickly as I used to from all-nighters."

"Is that it?" She leered at me. Well. She tried to leer at me. But Zane was five two, her hair was purple, and she was in gym clothes. And she's just generally not that leer-some. So her leering fell a little flat.

"Shut it, Suzanne."

"Oh-h, so there *is* something more to this story! A little bird told me you spent the day at Hannah's. Though he must not have seen that picture yet or he'd have implied a lot more than he did."

I groaned. "Dad is such a fucking gossip."

"He really is. So? Tell me everything. On the way to work out."

"Fuck your working out, Zane. I gotta finish grading."

"See, if that was true, you'd be looking at me, but you're studying the fascinating upholstery on a chair that's been yours since your dad got rid of it twenty years ago. So I call bullshit on this whole 'I gotta finish grading' thing."

"You think I'm lying about the day final grades are due?"

"I think you're lying about how much work you have left."

"I'm nearly done grading English finals, but I still have to process the grades for all the history classes."

"Fine. You keep grading, I'll do math, then we'll— Actually, fuck the gym. I want to hear about Hannah. Let's get smoothies and hit the pier."

Smoothies on the pier sounded amazing. I had all my fans on, but it was a hot day, and the pier was always windy and cool.

"Deal." I passed over my grading book. "I gotta switch to the computer."

"Why don't you let me set it up for you? Excel is my friend, and this is all simple stuff."

"I don't know. Having a grading book feels so . . . teachery."

She rolled her eyes, reaching for one of my pencils. "Doing things in the absolutely most inefficient way humanly possible feels 'teachery'? Not sure that washes, babe. Plus, it's been six years now, Jaq. You *are* a teacher. When are you gonna start, y'know, feeling it without props?"

"Maybe never. But anyway, I know, I gotta move away from the book, even though hand-writing all the little numbers makes me feel cool."

"Too bad you suck at math. A few of these are wrong."

"What? They are not! I use a calculator."

"Sure you do. Show me which of these are ready?"

I sticky-noted my three history classes. "So all you have to do is total the points earned, divide by—"

"Seriously, I've got this. Grade your finals."

"Bossy ass."

She laughed. "This is fun. Usually it's you being a bossy ass on gym days."

"Shut up."

We settled in to work. I started on the last batch of finals. When Zane was done applying her math skills, I gave her the finals and let her enter them on my sheet and then calculate grades. Even though that was totally the most satisfying part of having a grading book. Next year. Next year I'd go digital. For real.

When everything was done except plugging them into the electronic database, we took a break for smoothies.

"Tell me about Hannah." Zane huddled against the car, tugging her hood over her hair. The wind on the pier was especially intense, and we held on to our straws tightly as we started walking. "*Everything*."

God, the image that brought up: Hannah, hair still back, mostly naked, waving her lovey around like a hypnotist because my eyes couldn't look anywhere else. I blushed and turned my face into the wind, which was strong, but not quite strong enough to swallow Zane's laughter.

"Oh god. Everything. All the things!"

"Shut up!" *Redirect!* "Damn, it's fucking cold out here. Why is it always thirty degrees colder on the pier?"

"Too bad Hannah's not here so you could snuggle up with her—"

My first strike missed, but the second landed on her arm and she yelped. "You're lucky you didn't make me spill my smoothie or I'd've had to throw down."

"Oh, color me scared."

"Shut your face, bitch."

"Make me!"

We laughed, jostling back and forth as we walked.

"I learned something disturbing at Grad Nite," I said.

"Do tell."

"Mrs. Winchester commiserated with me about being hit on by a student."

Zane's jaw literally dropped. "She. Did. *Not.*"

"She really did. It was awkward as hell."

"I guess it would be. God. That is— Ew."

"It was weird. But also, weirdly not that weird after I got over the initial shock."

"I will take your word for it. But seriously. Ew." We went a little bit farther before she spoke again. "So don't tell anyone, but it's day fifteen."

I stopped walking. "Shit."

"Don't get your hopes up. It's day fifteen, and if I was pregnant, I should be testing positive. I'm not. So I'll probably see Aunt Flo in the next day or two. Still." She shrugged, her non-smoothie hand stealing toward her belly. "You never know. I usually have a thirteen day luteal phase, every now and then twelve or fourteen. Fifteen is long."

I wanted to get excited because it *would* be freaking exciting if Zane was pregnant. But we'd gotten excited the first two cycles—she'd thrown "conception parties" back then, when she shot herself up with sperm, before she started going to the midwife to get all spermed up.

These days she didn't even tell me when she was ovulating, like talking about it tempted the fates.

I grabbed her arm. "Okay. I won't get excited. I mean, my last friend who had a baby I haven't even talked to since she gave birth, so maybe it'd be the end of our friendship or something. Maybe I should start rooting against Future Kid."

"Future Kid's gonna love their Auntie Jaq." She tugged me over for a kiss on the cheek. "Thanks. I hate how this takes over my life. Like it's all I can think about today, my emotions are totally wrapped up in it, and when I get my period I'm gonna crash so hard to the ground, you know?"

"If," I said. "If. I mean probably, but it's still an 'if.'"

"If, okay. Anyway, tell me about you. You really spent the night with her?"

"I spent the night with her after the wedding."

She poked my side. "You dog! Everyone said you went home."

"You watched me leave with Hannah."

"Well, yeah. I knew you got laid. I didn't know you made a love connection!"

I made a grab for her smoothie in order to threaten its life, but she was too fast.

We were about halfway out now, where any residual sheltering we had from being close to land disappeared and we were totally at the mercy of the wind on the Bay. The Berkeley Marina was a lot bigger than the pier in La Vista, but they'd been built around the same time, with evidence of other less fortunate structures still littering the coastline. I let Zane tug me over to the railing and focused on a few boards still jutting out of the Bay, eaten away by wind and water and time.

"What's up?" She shouldered into me.

"Nothing. Except I'm stupid."

"Hey, no argument there."

I rolled my eyes.

"Seriously, though. Why'd you go all sad?"

"I'm not sad. It's just, you know, I really like her. I have no idea if she likes me as much as I like her."

"Well. Dad likes her. That's something."

"He does." I leaned against Zane for a minute. "I really like her. I know everyone says she's nuts, and she's drama, but I don't see all that. I mean, sure, she cheated on her ex, and she smokes—"

"Oh my god, she smokes? I can't even believe you had sex with her the first time!"

"She's quitting. I mean, she quit. She's not currently smoking. But she quit before and started up again."

"Ha-ha-ha, wow. I have to reassess everything. She cheated on her ex? I assume not Marla."

"No. The ex-wife."

"Oh man. That's so wild. Damn. Maybe I had her pegged wrong."

"It only happened once," I mumbled.

Zane shook her head. "You have it so bad right now. You don't usually fall for people this hard, so now I gotta think about it. And have an emergency meeting with Carlos and Tom. So we can discuss the threat level of this whole thing."

"Hey." I attempted to glare at her. "What threat level?"

"Well. You kissing someone who smokes makes this a much bigger thing than we realized."

"No, it's— It's not like I— I didn't—" I sighed, hoping she'd pick up the conversation, but she didn't. Which meant I had to . . . try to explain what I meant. "It bugs me. Like how a lot of the time I can't read her bugs me."

"Like she's performing?"

"Kind of. But not for me. It's as if she plays this person, who I like, and then when she drops that she's . . . different. She's a slightly different person."

"Who you really like."

"Yeah. Yeah, true. I don't mean to make it sound like she's— It's not like she's two totally different people."

Zane waved a hand. "No, I get it. I mean, everyone does that to a certain extent. And if she's an attorney, she might have more need for it, presenting herself to clients."

Everyone does that? "You don't do that."

"Sure I do. I don't curse as much, I wear different clothes, I don't fuck with my hair. I smile like this—" She formed her face into an expression I'd seen before, but not in a while.

"Wait, so your 'bullshitting clients' face is the same as your 'bullshitting teachers' face?"

"Ha, yeah, that makes sense. Listen, I want to hang out with her. Is it too soon? I mean, you've never made it to the 'hangs out with friends' relationship level before, so I don't want to put pressure on you. But you did let her meet Dad."

"Did he give you shit?"

"You know he did. I tried to defend myself that I already met her, twice, but he seemed to think the wedding and seeing her for a minute at Club Fred's didn't count. He's competitive for an old man. Anyway, if you feel good about it, then don't worry about drama, or Marla's shit, or any of it."

"I think she's a drinker." My last reasonable objection.

"You've never dated anyone who wasn't."

"I know. I kind of thought maybe that was part of the problem."

She shook her head and sucked down the last of her smoothie. "Listen, not that I'm blaming you for anything, but it's not like you were a shining star of love and commitment, Jaqs. You cut out on every woman you even thought about falling for."

"So what?"

"So I don't think them drinking or not drinking was the root of the thing."

"I didn't want to do this again." I turned back to the water. "I didn't want to be waiting for the 3 a.m. phone calls, or taking a cab because she can't find her car keys in her purse."

"Then don't worry about that. I know some people are drunks, but you know that just because Hannah drinks doesn't mean she's a drunk. This is an excuse to not commit, babe."

"Maybe."

"She sell her house yet?"

"They're in negotiations, I guess."

Zane whistled. "Do you know what the fucking commission is going to be on that? Damn. I mean, I hate doing residential, but that's gonna be a pretty penny for the agents."

"If the ex ever agrees to the terms."

"And that is why I hate residential."

I tossed my empty smoothie cup in the closest trash can. "So tell me exactly how much you hate wedding planning right now."

"So, so much. Hey, is Dred still taking jobs? We are gonna need some serious help."

"I think so. I'm, uh, supposed to do knitting class with her on Wednesday, so I can ask if you want. It's not until winter, right?"

"Right."

I hesitated before adding, "Hannah might come with me. To knitting. She said she always wanted to learn how."

Zane socked me. Hard. "I can't decide if I'm more pissed that Hannah's meeting Dred before I am, or that you're cheating on me with a new hobby buddy."

"It's not that big a deal."

"Oh, it is. I'm definitely pissed. I just have to figure out how much and what about."

I stretched, feeling creaky. "I should get back to drudgery."

"Oh, poor you. Summer vacation sucks so much."

"I have a busy schedule this week. I'm helping Dad with his shed tomorrow, and I have knitting or whatever on Wednesday, and the queer kids on Friday, and Fredi's thing—"

"Very busy, I can tell. It's Come As You Are night at Club Fred's, by the way."

"Yeah, I know, but other than making us feel old, what's the point of that?"

"Knowing Fredi, that *is* the point." She shook her head. "I'll know by then. If I'm pregnant. I'll either be not drinking at all, or I'll be . . . thrashed."

"If it's option two, I got your back."

"I'm sure you'll be busy with Hannah. Hubba-hubba."

"Oh shut it."

"For real, Jaq, this thing with Hannah—even if it's not forever— it's good. I like her."

Even if it's not forever. "What if I kind of . . . want it to be forever?"

She whistled and started walking. "Hell. Way over my head."

I fell in beside her, glancing over. "You could fall in love. Nothing stopping you."

"Except for the part where I'm totally incapable of falling in love, plus the part where I'm trying to have a kid, plus the part where I'm really good at being alone. And it's okay. I'm okay with it."

I tried to study her more closely, but she had her "smiling at teachers" face on now, so there was no hope of me figuring out what she meant. "If you don't want to be alone, you won't be."

"Aw, Jaqs. That's sweet, but that kind of line only works in fairy tales. Let's head back to your place. You input the last of the grades and I'll order in."

"Sounds perfect."

"Because I am, babe."

No one was actually perfect. But Zane was pretty amazing, and really, I hadn't spent much time thinking about how she never had steady girlfriends. Carlos and I usually had someone around when we were younger, until he hooked up with Tom (and the two of them *still* sometimes had another "someone" around). But Zane was always just . . . Zane. She had her lists, and her notes, and her goals. She never seemed to have time for anything else. She never bemoaned her lack of companions.

I followed her back to the car, thinking about how she also hadn't said, "I'm not interested in falling in love." She'd said she couldn't, and she was okay with that.

Such a weird thing, thinking about your best friend as if you hadn't known them so long they called your dad "Dad." I wanted to ask her more, but I knew she wouldn't answer. Zane had moved on in her head, and now she'd change the subject if I tried to push it.

Or maybe I was making it all up. Maybe I wanted to see everything in terms of love because it was on my mind. Not that it mattered.

I got my grades in before midnight, Zane bought dinner, and we marathon-watched *Jessica Jones*. Because nothing beats superheroes.

CHAPTER

The good thing about school was that it kept me focused on external things. The kids, the lessons, the books, the faculty. During the school year, I didn't have time for the kind of intense introspection that landed me in bed all day until Dad called after work to ask where I was, since I was supposed to be helping him with the shed and daylight was burning.

I told him I didn't feel well, still hungover from grading day, and asked if we could do it Thursday instead. He said okay and didn't pry, which had to be some kind of miracle.

All that thinking, and ultimately what I decided was to let whatever happened . . . happen. Which didn't seem like much. But if your friends indicated that your normal inclination was to fight good things, just the act of *not* fighting was kind of revolutionary. Or at least that was what I told myself. I'd accept. Hannah and I were good together. I could accept that. And maybe I could accept that both of us were serious about it. That'd be good.

So good. As if "good" was the best my brain could come up with. Grading was done: good. GSA would meet Friday: good. Hannah would come to knitting and meet Dred: good. We'd maybe go back to her place for dinner: good. Once there, we might do more than eat . . . Okay, that was way better than "good."

I could do this. I could be this person who didn't expect everything to go to hell.

Which was when everything went to hell. Or, more specifically, Los Angeles.

I didn't know what to wear to Wednesday's knitting class, or group, or club, or whatever, but I figured I'd call Hannah to see what she was wearing. Or maybe because I wanted an excuse to call her.

Voice mail.

Okay. We weren't late or anything. And I was going to pick her up at her place. I gave it a few minutes, decided on a black tank top and jeans, and called again.

Voice mail.

Awesome.

I checked that I had money on me, grabbed my keys, and drove over to the condo. I buzzed up. No answer. I buzzed up longer. Still no answer. I called again.

"Your name is a sight for sore eyes, sugar. I've been thinking about you all damn day."

Oh thank god. "Hey, I'm here. Why aren't you answering your buzzer?"

"My buzzer? What 'here'?"

"Here. At your house. To pick you up for knitting."

"Oh hell, Jaq, I forgot all about knitting. I'm not there. I had to fly south again to deal with the house. I'm sorry, it's all happening at once and I didn't even remember we had a thing tonight."

My chest went tight. This. This was why you never committed. This was why you never let yourself hope. Because people were unreliable and would only let you down. I'd *known* this was coming all along, damn it. I had no right to feel this *hurt* about it, like a big whiny baby, when this was the inevitable outcome of me caring about a woman. The second you start hoping for the best, you're just asking to be disappointed.

"Oh," I heard myself say.

"On the up side, I finally convinced Sandy to let *me* pay for the new deck, and we'll split closing, so at least it looks like the deal will go through."

Numbness stole over me.

"Jaq? You still there? Listen, can we go to knitting next month, or whenever it's happening again? Everything will be a lot more calm by then, I think—"

"Sure, okay."

"Thanks, hon. I just need a few more days here and I'll be done, finished, forever."

Done. Finished. Forever. "That's good." My voice sounded mechanical.

"I'm getting out of my car. I'll talk to you later."

"Sure. Okay. Bye." I hung up.

She wasn't here. Of course. She'd flown to LA without even telling me about it, because it was that kind of thing. Because it didn't occur to her that I'd want to know. That I'd planned our whole stupid evening in my head like a fool.

I hit speed dial on my phone and called Zane.

She sounded terrible. "I hate everything on earth."

"Oh shit. You got your period."

She started to cry.

"Aw, honey, I'm so sorry. Put on some decent clothes and wash your face, I'm coming to pick you up. We're going to knitting."

A snort as she blew her nose. "Knitting?"

"Yeah. Hannah's in LA."

"So I'm your second choice?"

"Um. I take the Fifth. Wash your face, okay? I'll be there in ten."

"Okay."

She was crying again as she hung up.

People get pregnant every day accidentally. It's fucking cruel that some of the people who most want to be parents can't get pregnant at all. I went back to my truck and determinedly didn't look at the condos as I drove past them.

Introducing Zane to Dred many years after we broke up was a little weird.

"So, you guys have heard of each other. Dred, Zane. Zane, Dred."

Zane, eyes red and swollen, nevertheless smiled and shook hands. "I can't believe it took her this long to put us in the same room. Nice to meet you."

"You too." Dred shot a raised eyebrow at me before turning back to Zane. "I guess this means she's finally gotten over me being seventeen when we first started seeing each other."

Zane laughed; I looked around to make sure no one had heard her say that.

"Could you please forget that ever happened?" I kissed her cheek. She was wearing her hair natural these days, and it suited her perfectly. Dred was always quick to react, but sweet underneath; post-kid I could see a lot more of the sweetness than I had before. Not in an earth-mother way, more that the tension I was used to seeing in her face had eased off. "You look good, babe."

"I look sleep-deprived and my hair is natty."

"How's the baby?"

She smiled. "Oh, James is good. He's with Obie and Emerson."

"Damn." Zane's face lit up. "Yeah, I forgot about that. I met Obie a couple months ago. They're still together?"

"It's like watching lesbians in slow motion."

Zane laughed.

I left them chatting amiably, which was good, and started poking around the yarn shop. It was the kind of place I'd passed a million times without ever stepping inside. And okay, so I imagined being here with Hannah, but I tried not to think about that now. It didn't matter. And to prove to myself that it didn't matter, I'd silenced my phone so I wouldn't hear her text messages coming in. Or so I wouldn't hear the absence of her text messages coming in.

There were about five or six other people in the place looking like they were ready for knitting, seated on chairs or little sofas. As I was fondling some wool, the door dinged and I looked up in time to catch the eye of the person walking in. Ed was short and a little bit nerdy, the kind of guy who can wear polo shirts without it seeming preppy. Since he'd gotten a job at the local paper sometime last year, I saw his byline more than I saw him.

"Hey, Ed. It's been a while."

Ed gave me a hug and stepped back, surveying the rest of the room quickly. "How'd you get roped into this?"

"Mildred. You?"

"Honey." He gestured to a woman sitting on one of the sofas. "Oh, Zane's here too? I have a hard time picturing Zane knitting."

"I have a hard time picturing *me* knitting." I held up a brightly colored aluminum stick with a little hook on the end. "Seriously."

He rolled his eyes. "Well, that's a crochet hook, so you're already failing."

"Oh. Good to know." I put the thing back. "How's life?" Which was my totally subtle way of saying *How's transitioning treating you? Still getting shit from your family?*

"Life is good. I'm getting slightly better assignments at the paper, so that's been interesting."

"Yeah, I've been following. You get your name on things, now!"

"I know. It's the big leagues when you're more than 'random staff writer.' Hey, are you going to Club Fred's Friday?"

We talked a little bit about Fredi and her theme nights (Ed didn't have any idea what "come as you are" was supposed to mean, and neither did his friend Honey). Honey actually knew how to knit, so that was helpful. She found me a basic scarf pattern and the appropriate needles. I picked out a black-and-gray wool that both of them assured me would look great on me.

Since Dred was busy teaching Zane—the two of them leaning over a deep-purple yarn, Dred's hands occasionally coaching Zane's along—I got all my guidance from Honey and Ed. I couldn't figure out how to cast on, whatever the hell that meant, but once Honey did that part, I was actually okay at the stitches themselves. Back and forth, one needle to the other needle. It was soothing. And since this scarf pattern was easy, I felt like I was making progress on it.

Honey and Ed, beside me, talked in low voices about hormones and doctors and the impossibility of patience.

Ed murmured at one point, "I feel like I've been waiting for this my whole life and it's taking forever."

Honey, who appeared to be many years into her transition, patted his arm. "It's worth every miserable second. I promise."

I slid the yarn on the needles, paying attention to loops and yarn-overs and pull-throughs, thinking about all the things I took for granted. I didn't need to take hormones every day just for the chance at having a body that reflected my gender. I didn't agonize constantly about my cycle and if I'd ever conceive a kid. Or agonize constantly about the kid I had at home, who kept me up all night.

Not that any of it mattered, not that anyone's suffering beat out anyone else's, because that wasn't the way things worked. But still. I sat there and knitted my scarf, wondering how Hannah's momentary forgetfulness could possibly feel so eviscerating. And how knowing that it was a blip on the radar of human suffering didn't make it hurt any less.

CHAPTER  18

D ad wasn't taking chances. He showed up at five thirty, directly from the bank where he worked, and hovered in my doorway until I gave up arguing that I'd be by "later," and put my shoes on.

"So basically you're kidnapping me to help you with your shed?"

"Basically," he agreed. "I plan to feed you too."

"I guess you'd have to, if you wanted to get good work out of me."

"Point." He gestured to my kitchen counter. "Aren't you going to grab your phone? It appears to be blinking."

"Nah. Let's go, old man."

"I'll show you 'old man,' missy."

"Oh yeah?"

The truth is, I didn't mind when Dad demanded I help him with stuff around the house. I was the youngest, and the only one left in town. I liked being useful to him, especially because he'd pretty much given up everything to raise us by himself. It seemed like the least I could do was help him build a shed, or help with the garden, or whatever.

Plus, there was Ducky the Ancient Mutt.

"Boy, you are *ancient*. Sweet old boy." I sat down on the floor to better pet him, since he could no longer haul himself across the house to me without being in pain. His tail still wagged the ground when I walked in, though.

"I'll go change my clothes, sweetie. You might feed your dog, if it's not too much trouble."

"Too much trouble! He's so rude, Ducky."

Ducky's tail thumped in agreement.

I got him a can of food and mashed it up with a fork before setting it down in front of his face and making sure his water was full. "I'll take you out in a few minutes, okay, boy?"

Thump, thump, thump.

I walked outside to see what kind of progress Dad had made on the shed. He'd gotten a nice level pad and covered it with gravel, but when it came to getting the frame up, he'd held off. Definitely a two-person job. I was reading the instructions when he came outside.

"So what's with you and your phone? I haven't seen you voluntarily without it since you first got one when you were seventeen."

"You totally should have bought me a Palm Pilot."

"A three-hundred-dollar toy for a seventeen-year-old? Unlikely, my dear. Who're you dodging?"

"Who says I'm dodging someone?"

"I say you're dodging someone. Is it Hannah?"

I sighed. "I should never go out in public ever, Dad. Everything's so much simpler if I just go to school and go home. And go to the gym with Zane, where I try not to see other people."

"Uh-huh."

"What? It is. People complicate my simple life."

"Uh-huh."

"Stop saying that."

"Uh-huh."

I glared at him as we started fitting bits of the framing into place. "It's nothing. We were going to do something, and then she was busy, so we didn't. It's not a big deal."

"So why are you dodging her?"

"I'm not."

"I can't believe you so cavalierly lie to your father, Jaq. It's shameful, really."

I held the first joint so he could screw it together, then we moved to the next. Assembling the walls would be easy; getting them all to connect at the right places would be when things got challenging.

"It's better to not think things might be good. That's all. It's safer that way."

"Uh-huh."

"Expect the worst, be surprised when everything doesn't totally suck."

"Ah, Jaq."

The front part of the frame, which he'd already laid out, came together more slowly, making space for the door.

"Honey, you have to enjoy things when they're good, even if there's no guarantee they'll last. You only cheat yourself if you choose to be miserable instead."

"I'm not miserable. I just— I don't want to invest in something that's probably transitory, Dad. I don't know how people date, like it's no big deal. I want it to be a big deal, or what's the point?"

"For some people the point is the fun they have while they're with whomever they're with. They don't need a future to ensure against the present." He screwed in the bottom part of the frame and both of us lifted it upright. I waited for him to raise one of the side walls so I could hold it in place.

"Well, I'm not interested in the present unless it has a future," I mumbled, as petulant as any of my students.

"And you know that Hannah isn't part of your future? I don't mean that you get married, but if you like her company, surely she can be part of your future regardless."

"She . . . forgot. About a thing we'd planned to do. Forgot about it as if it meant nothing to her." The argument had seemed a little weak in my head; out loud it sounded ludicrous. "It's not only that. I don't know, Dad. Sometimes I know where I stand, sometimes I have no idea. I know she didn't want a relationship because she just got out of one, so I have no right to expect that to be where we were going. I guess it's more that I . . . kind of wanted it to be."

"There's no harm in wanting something good for yourself, Jaq."

"There is if it always ends like this. If it always ends with me alone."

He passed me the drill and took over bracing. "I miss your mother every day of my life, but I can't regret falling in love with her, even though she's gone now."

"It's different."

"Is it? If she'd left us instead of dying, she'd still be the reason I have you kids. Meeting her would still have led me to this moment, putting up a shed with my daughter, listening to her hopes and fears.

I wouldn't trade any of those nights I wept over your mother for a future without today."

Dad hadn't spoken of her at all right after she'd died. Part of his own grieving process, probably, but it had been hard for us. Hardest for me, at seven, trying to understand what had happened. Trying to make my abstract idea of death into something that applied to real people, to people I loved. After a year or two, though, he'd started mentioning her again. At first with deep sadness, making June cry, sometimes making himself cry. But after a while they all talked about Mom, kept her real, kept her in our memories during the week, when we weren't at church.

I probably didn't remember her all that well on my own. But because of Dad and my siblings, I knew stories about her, about the things she'd loved to do, the food she'd loved to make. Their love infused those memories with color.

"It's scary," he said. "I understand that. And I'm not saying you have to risk everything for every person that you meet. But there are some, and I think you know them when you're with them, who need you to risk a little more than usual. The rewards for that are great, my dear."

"You didn't ever wish you hadn't met Mom? You were so sad, back then." I didn't know how to put it into words, the loss I remembered, and how much I feared feeling it again.

"Oh, there were some dark nights. Nights when I asked God why he had given me such grace and taken it back. Nights when I pled with him to remove this cup from my lips because I could never be the parent you kids needed, I could never be as strong as she was, or as loving, or as good. But that's life, Jaq. Life is pain, life is grace, life is difficult at the same time as it is transcendent."

"It just feels like everything good ends badly."

He patted my arm. "That's the Irish in you, my girl. The Irish in you tells you that everything ends in pain, but what it doesn't tell you is that there's a whole lot of joy wrapped up in that journey too."

I swallowed hard, trying not to see his damp eyes. He'd been through a lot. A lot of shit I'd never have to go through. Even if I married, even if I lost the love of my life, I'd never have to keep it together for children who needed me. I'd never be on my knees praying to God to help me be strong because I was the only person they had.

We finished the initial framing, and I gave him a hug. "Thanks, Dad."

"Sure thing, sweetheart."

I still wasn't sure what I was going to do, but we managed to get everything but the roof up before we lost daylight, and I promised I'd come over on Saturday to finish up.

CHAPTER 19

I planned to put on my big-kid pajamas and text Hannah back. She'd left three messages, just checking in. But then I was tired, and a little sore, and anyway, whatever. Maybe the whole thing was over almost before it started, and if so, there were worse things in the world and I should probably stop obsessing over it.

Alternately, I might be a big fat scaredy-cat. I couldn't find enough evidence to disprove that theory.

I got to Sobrantes early on Friday evening to set up for the club. "Setting up" basically entailed me buying a pot of coffee and snagging a couple of six-ounce cups to share it out.

Sammy showed up first, gratefully took coffee (no cream; that's my boy), and filled me in on the bistro job, which was more table-clearing and dishwashing than tip-infused waiting tables, but he was okay with it for the summer. A few of the other kids trickled in, and I kept my eyes open for Merin or LaTasha, but when we started with our usual round-robin check-in, neither of them had arrived.

Bill slid in the door about five minutes later, throwing me an apologetic look, and Sammy's face lit up, then he blushed. Poor thing.

Check-in came around to me, so I said something generic about being exhausted by grading and Grad Nite, and helping Dad with the shed, before passing to Bill.

"I'm really sorry I'm late, you guys. I'm Mr. Kent, for those of you who haven't met me already. I'm really glad this group exists, and I wish it had existed when I was in high school. Thanks for inviting me."

A few of the kids, who'd been initially wary, shot him a sharper look. *Yes, he's one of us. Yes, he has a right to be here.* In principle, it was a Gay-Straight Alliance; in practice, it was marginalized queer kids aligning with each other.

"I'm really glad you're here, Mr. Kent," Sammy mumbled.

"Me too," I added. "How's the home life, you lot? Everything okay? Have any of you heard of the drop-in center that's supposed to be opening in August?"

We talked a little about the drop-in center (aside from printing a couple of fliers, I hadn't actually done anything to get involved—the best-laid plans, right?), and everyone seemed more or less all right, so I was beginning to think about closing the meeting when the door opened again.

Merin, with LaTasha shoving her from behind.

"Whoa," Sammy said. "What're you guys doing here?"

"We're here for the same reason you are, dummy."

I glanced at Sammy—who grinned—and decided not to start a fight over name-calling. "How pleasant to see you, Merin. A week without your charming company was almost too long."

"Right back at you, Ms. C." She took a chair at the far end of the conference table we'd ignored in favor of making a smaller circle of chairs off to the side.

LaTasha sighed and took one of the chairs in the circle. "Sorry we're late. It took a while to find the right motivation to come here."

"Do we even want to know what that means?" Sammy arched an eyebrow.

She shook her head. "Probably not. Anyway, I really didn't mean to interrupt."

I waved the apology off. "You didn't. You want to check in about anything, LaTasha?"

She looked around at her mostly younger, entirely less well-put-together peers. "I'm not a lesbian. I'm not straight. I like the people I like, and I don't really care what they have between their legs. No one knows about me because I keep my private life to myself, but that doesn't mean I'm in the closet. I'm going to college in the fall, and maybe if there's a group like this there, I'll join it."

Merin made a derisive sound in the back.

"Or maybe I won't. But anyway, I probably would have liked coming to these meetings and I'm sad I never did."

"Don't cry for her, Argentina," Merin muttered.

Sammy turned all the way around to look at her. "So? What's your story, then? Aside from being an asshole all the time."

"That's my whole story."

"Yeah right." His expression hardened. "That's bullshit."

"Oh really, sparkle fairy? You think you know me?"

"I think *you* don't know you, and maybe that's why you're here."

That was more than enough of that. "Quit it, both of you."

"I don't think it's cool that Merin gets to sit in what's supposed to be a safe place and say whatever the hell she wants."

I opened my mouth to say something brilliant and teachery, but Merin was already pushing away from the table.

"This wasn't my stupid idea, anyway. I didn't ask to be part of your 'safe space.' Like I care." She slammed out the door.

"Sorry." LaTasha stood and picked up her bag. "Really. I thought this would work."

"How?" Sammy said. "She's always like that."

LaTasha paused, looking right at him. "You don't know everything about Merin. Sometimes people hide their struggles so well, you look for them in the wrong places. You know?"

She didn't wait for a reply.

When the door shut again, I sat back. "Okay. That was interesting. Sammy, you all right?"

"I guess so. But I don't really get what just happened."

"Me neither. You want me to write Merin up for the 'sparkle fairy' thing when we're back in school?"

He batted his eyelashes at me. "Ms. C, are you trying to say you don't think I'm a sparkle fairy? I'm so insulted!"

"Oh good. We've established that Sammy's a sparkle fairy, Merin's an asshole, and this first-ever meeting of the summer club went very strangely. Anything else?"

The kids dispersed. Bill and I walked out together with our last tiny cups of coffee.

I tapped my paper cup against his. "Cheers to your first meeting."

"Is it always like that?"

"Not so much. I don't even know what 'that' was, really."

"But . . . LaTasha and Merin? Is that for real or am I reading too much into it?"

"No, no. I actually already knew that was going on."

"And you held out on me?"

"Yeah. Actually. I switched to worrying about Merin, by the way. In case you want to play along."

"I'll keep it in mind." He hesitated. "Did you notice anything interesting about the way LaTasha talked about Merin?"

"No. How?"

Bill shook his head, and we both stopped walking at my truck. "She didn't use pronouns. I might be reading too much into that too, but it stood out to me. She didn't at any point refer to Merin as 'she.'"

I tried to comb my memory, but I hadn't noticed or hadn't paid attention. "You think Merin might be trans?"

"I think her girlfriend just went out of her way to make it clear that gender doesn't matter to her."

"Huh. Well, shit, Bill."

"Yeah. Actually, if you were trying to make sure I came back, this worked out well. It's like ending on a cliff-hanger. I want to know what happens next."

"I'd settle for knowing what the hell happened today. Anyway, you coming to Club Fred's later?"

"Um. Probably not."

I sighed. "Jeez, Bill. It's like our local queer dive doesn't charm you *at all.*"

"Look, I'm sorry, but I think you have to grow up here to find Club Fred's charming. It has a *life buoy* on the wall."

"Actually, there are two. But if you haven't seen the secret one, I'm not telling you where it is."

He cleared his throat. "And everything on the walls needs to be dusted. I sneezed all night! Plus, it's fucking dangerous. The last time I was in there I almost got nailed by some kind of wall-mounted trident."

I couldn't help laughing. "Oh man. Fine. You take your highfalutin ways elsewhere. The rest of the queers in La Vista will be at Club Fred's tonight, partying like it's 1995."

"And the theme nights, seriously, what's the deal with those?"

"Get out of my sight, blasphemer! Every business decision Fredi makes is sacrosanct! Begone!"

He waved. "See you next week!"

I checked my phone, just because that's a normal thing people do, not because I was waiting for a specific person to contact me or anything, but there were no messages. Right, okay. That was fine. Everything was going to be fine. Though it was a good thing I quit drinking, or tonight would be ending with me facedown in a toilet, puking my guts out.

Fine. "Everything's fine," I mumbled as I started my truck. "Totally and completely fine."

All I had to do was figure out what to wear to Come As You Are night. Torn jeans and a dirty cardigan? Flannel? God, I probably didn't even own flannel anymore. Then again, the beauty of a vague theme was that no one could decide you'd worn the wrong costume.

I forced myself not to check my phone again until I got home. Still no messages.

CHAPTER 20

I arrived at Fred's fashionably late, and the first person I saw was Carlos.

"My sweet, sweet Jaqueline." He pulled me down to kiss my cheeks.

"My name doesn't rhyme with 'Caroline,' you bastard."

"Oh?"

"Shut it." I shoved my shit onto the stool next to his. "How's the night?"

"So far it's a lot of kids trying to be Kurt Cobain and a lot of old people letting their freak flags fly. Because—"

"Come as you are," I finished for him. "Right. Slight clash of meanings there."

"Definitely generational. For all we know, Fredi's never heard of Nirvana."

Tom leaned over the counter. "You're the fifth person to make that joke. Felipe made it ten minutes ago and she was this close to kicking him out."

"You'd never let that happen to me, though, would you?" Carlos batted his eyelashes, which only made Tom laugh. "Do not mock my seductive face."

"Oh, is *that* what that was?" Tom grinned unrepentantly and moved off to help a guy who'd come in costume as, I think, Eddie Vedder.

"It's 'come as your favorite half-dead nineties rock star' night," I whispered.

"'Come as your favorite over-rated whiny white man' night," he countered.

I clinked my soda to his watered-down scotch. "I can't top that. You seen Zane? I thought for sure she'd beat me here."

"Honey, everyone beat you here. She's somewhere, probably charming some young thing with her fantastic dance moves."

"Don't knock Zane's dancing."

"Because it's *so hot* and I will never understand?"

"Nah. The thing that makes it adorable is that she doesn't care. She just . . . dances."

"That is definitely true." He turned to survey the crowd. "Look, you can locate her by finding the void in the crowd where people have dodged out of the way of her unique blend of flailing and shaking."

I socked him on the arm. "Jerk. You going to be up here for a bit?"

"I came for only a very specific piece of eye candy, yes." He whistled down the bar and when Tom immediately turned, people laughed.

"Got you trained like a *dog*, boy!" someone called.

"Whoo-ee, guess we knows who rules the roost over there!"

Tom bowed low over his hand in Carlos's direction. Carlos blew him a kiss. The folks at the bar broke into cheers and applause.

"You two disgust me," I said.

"Me too," the guy on the other side of Carlos added. "Filthy monogamous types."

Carlos spun to face him. "Oh, we are *not* monogamous. Bite your tongue!"

I laughed this time. Carlos defended their open ways vehemently whenever the opportunity arose, and I could already tell it was time for me to get lost.

I kissed his cheek. "See you later, stud." He didn't even pause in his lecture on the "shackles of the exclusivity system" long enough to say good-bye.

The place was packed. Fredi wasn't messing around with these theme nights; she'd scheduled them not to compete with anything else queer going on in the Bay Area, and she'd advertised them everywhere, as far south as San Jose, and as far north as Sonoma. Normally on a busy night in Club Fred's I still recognized most of the patrons. Tonight I was scraping to find a familiar face. Ed was there, with his friend Honey from knitting. I thought I saw my ex Jess out of the corner of my eye, but when I turned to call hello, she was gone again.

No Hannah. At least not so far. I couldn't decide if I was disappointed or relieved.

Thank god for Zane's purple hair and . . . creative dance moves.

Since she didn't seem to be actually dancing with anyone, I took the opportunity to sidle up next to her. She was giggling before she even turned. "Oh my god! This is hilarious! There are like a thousand people in here!"

"I know!"

The song changed, though I couldn't hear quite what it had turned into over the wild excitement on the floor. Was this Cher?

"Oh my god!" Zane yelled again, grabbing my face.

Both of us yelled, "*Cher*!"

Dancing crazy with my best friend to Cher—which let's be clear, we'd done since we were like seven (if they played Madonna next, we'd freak out)—was incredibly fun. So fun I almost forgot the voice in my head that kept reminding me I was supposed to be here with Hannah. That instead of the sweet joy of memory, we would be here discovering the people we'd both loved as kids, the music that was the different soundtracks to our different lives. None of that mattered, I told myself, even though it did.

I could have a good damn time with my friends and force myself not to think about Hannah, damn it.

We danced through a few more songs before Zane called a time-out and went over to grab a drink, angling herself in beside Carlos and the woman who'd taken my stool. I wouldn't have even noticed, except that Zane swiveled to look at me and the move caught my eye.

Wait. The woman next to Carlos was Hannah.

I backed away, melting into the dance floor, not able to think clearly. What the fuck was she doing here, intruding on my night? Okay, true, I'd invited her, but I hadn't heard from her in a couple of days. What the fuck? Invitations were like Cinderella's fucking carriage; eventually they turned back into pumpkins. Hang on. There was something off about that whole simile. I hid in the middle of the floor, barely even pretending to dance, and tried to sort out how I felt.

She probably wasn't there for me.

If she was, she had a fucking funny way of showing it by cutting off all contact.

Actually, it was possible that I'd been the one who'd stopped texting. But even then. She didn't send a *Hey, I'm at Club Fred's?* Really?

Sitting at the bar. Next to *my friend.* Whom she probably hadn't met, and therefore didn't know was my friend. In point of fact, Carlos said he gets the empty stool sometimes because people feel awkward sitting next to him. Not Hannah, though. Obviously Hannah sat wherever the fuck she wanted and didn't give a shit who she was next to.

"Jaq! Why aren't you dancing?"

Prz. Prz was my lifeline. My life buoy. I clung on to her for everything I was worth. "Prz! I was dancing! Or like . . . swaying at least."

She laughed warmly into my ear, still tall, but not towering over me like she did in her skates. "Why don't you sway this way, baby?"

"That was the worst line *ever!*"

"Oh, I've definitely said worse." She hooked an arm around my waist. "School's out, huh? Maybe we'll be seeing more of you around here, huh?"

"I'm around!"

"Sure you are, but you always leave by seven o'clock, before the party even starts."

Man, the girl danced dirty. My entire body was tuned in to her like a fucking dowsing rod seeking moisture. "You don't want to go to teach high schoolers looking hungover, Prz, believe me!"

She did some kind of hot sinuous thing against me. "You don't even drink, baby."

"That doesn't stop the mockery. I'm trying to be a good example!" *Oh yeah, do that again.* I blushed, grateful for the dancing, the solid excuse to sweat and stammer and flush bright red.

"Well, we miss you during the school year! You'll have to make it up to me!" Her hands slid down to my ass, pulling me harder against her, and yeah, that was good. I wanted more of it. I wanted to fuck Prz on the dance floor, because come as you fucking are, right? Maybe this was how I was.

Except the next time I picked my head up, I saw Hannah. Watching us. Standing still in the middle of the floor, a perfectly put-together professional woman surrounded by the writhing queers of La Vista.

Everything in my body withdrew from Prz. I felt cheap, and sick, and desperate.

Hannah turned and walked away, side-stepping couples, evading bodies.

"Baby? What the hell?" Prz pulled me back and I, stupidly, leaned into her. "What just happened?"

"I'm so stupid," I said. "I'm such a fucking fool."

"Oh, honey, I'm sure it's not that bad—"

I tilted my head so she could see that I was crying.

"Oooo-kay, maybe it is. Let's get you something to drink. Maybe you could use a Cherry Coke, right? And some food?"

I sniffled and let her lead me back to the bar, where Carlos still held court at his end. There weren't any open stools there, so we sat at the other. Or I sat, and Prz stood next to me.

"Fredi, can we get a Cherry Coke and . . . whatever's gonna make Jaq smile again?"

"Onion strings and a Cherry Coke," Fredi said. "What about you, Priscilla?"

"Bourbon. Thank you, ma'am."

I blinked up at Prz. "Are you *flirting* with Fredi?"

"Don't judge. I love a woman with a firm hand, you know that."

Lovelorn and foolish, I said, "Me too."

Prz's eyes widened. "No way. But I thought you—" She didn't finish the sentence, but she didn't need to. I knew what she thought. She thought wearing men's clothes and opening doors for my dates made me dominant.

I tipped forward and leaned my head on the bar. Which was sticky. Gross.

"Oh, honey, what's wrong?" Her hands rubbed my back. "You were fine a few minutes ago."

"Girl trouble," Fredi said. *Thump.* "The onion strings will help. But whoever she is, Jaqueline, she's probably not worth your moping."

"But she *is*." I lifted my head.

Fredi shoved the plate into the sticky spot previously occupied by my face. "Then what the hell are you doing here? Go get her."

"Fredi's right, babe. If she means that much to you, this isn't where you should be."

I took an onion string, swiped it through ranch, and shoved it in my mouth. In protest. This was the only place I could possibly be, didn't they get that? What else could I do? Call her crying? Apologize? But I didn't even know what I'd done. Unless it was give her the silent treatment over something stupid, then show up to a place where I'd told her to be on the night I told her to be there and practically have sex with someone else.

I moaned. "I am so stupid."

"I'm sure it's not that bad." Prz abandoned the comforting back-pat to eat onion strings. "Oh my god, I forgot how much I love these things. They're so good."

They were, though I hardly tasted them. I alternated salty, fried onion strings with sticky, sweet Coke, and didn't stop when my stomach started gurgling angrily at me.

Zane found us, towing other people (Dred's Obie, and his boyfriend, and another boy I didn't recognize). When the onion strings ran out, we ordered chili cheese fries, and I ate until the pain in my gut took over, so I couldn't think so hard about Hannah. About that moment I'd seen her at the bar, before she saw me. How I could have just walked up to her, smiled, kissed her. How she'd been probably hoping I would. Instead of backing away like a jackass and dry humping a friend who would never be more than a friend and occasional lay.

"Another Coke for Jaq!" Zane called down to Fredi. "And a drink for the new recruit—what's your name, kid?"

I didn't hear the kid's name. I didn't care. I sucked on my soda until my stomach twisted, then stumbled back to the bathrooms so I could puke up all those fries and beans and onions, all that black tar-like soda. I was disgusting. I was that asshole puking in the back of the club, and I didn't even have the decency to be drunk. I'd made myself sick on misery and fried food, like a damn fool.

At least I was keeping with the theme of the night.

CHAPTER 21

I've survived a lot of hangovers. Hating hangovers was one of the reasons I'd stopped drinking. Not the main reason, but a supporting reason. *I should quit because all day long I'm salivating thinking about that first beer, and the fifth, and the twelfth, and that's no good. Also, fewer hangovers.* For the most part, a hangover from bar food and soda was better than a hangover from booze, though the greasy sweat of having puked chili cheese fries for a couple of hours wasn't exactly pleasant.

Ugh. I felt like hell. Puking made my whole body sore. Knowing I did it to myself made me feel even worse.

I forced myself to sit very still and drink a bottle of water. As a reward, I was allowed to make coffee.

The coffee settled my stomach, which was reeling a little from too much water.

Suck it up, I told my body. *That's a pun. Suck it up. Literally. The water. The faster we absorb it, the sooner we'll feel less like fried death.*

My body insisted I sit back down and not move. Possibly forever.

Not moving was a good plan. Recovery from hangover-by-food was a lot quicker for me than recovery from drinking all night, and within an hour of getting up, I was already feeling like someone who could conceivably shower. Like a grown-up. Which I did. Slowly. So as not to overtax myself.

My phone started ringing when I was blinking blearily at my reflection in a quickly fogging hand-swipe across my mirror. I thought about letting it shoot to voice mail, but that was just more hiding, and I didn't want to do that again. It was dumb. Please see above "grown-up" functioning. I could answer my phone. Naked. My hair still dripping down my neck.

The call wasn't Hannah. It was a local number I didn't recognize. I answered with genuine curiosity, like I hardly ever did in the time of caller ID. "Hello?"

"Is this Jaq?"

"Yessss."

"Hey, Jaq, it's Kim down at Sobrantes. I have a couple of your kids here, and one of them's looking pretty rough."

"What?" I shook my head. "Sorry, I'm here. Are they okay?"

Her voice dropped a register. "I . . . think so? But I'm not sure. And I definitely didn't tell them I was calling you. I offered free coffee and almost lost a hand."

Merin. The only person I know who'd respond to "free coffee" with aggression is Merin.

"I'll get down there as soon as I can. Thanks for calling, Kim."

"Sure thing. I'll try to keep them here with pastries or something."

"Thanks," I said again.

Well damn. I shivered, even though the day already felt warm on the dry parts of my skin.

A couple of my kids? It would have to be Merin and LaTasha, right? But why were they at Sobrantes? And what did Kim mean when she said one of them looked "rough"?

I didn't know, and it didn't matter. I pulled on clothes and grabbed my keys.

Sammy was a surprise.

They were arguing at one of the outside tables when I walked up. Sammy appeared to be dressed for work. Merin looked like someone had gotten a few good licks in at her face. I kept my expression neutral.

"Don't be so fucking stupid, it's not a big deal." Sammy leaned halfway across the table. "Merin—"

"I don't need your fucking charity, you dick—"

"Really? Looks like you probably *do*, and did anyone ever tell you that it wouldn't kill you to fucking relax once in a while and not be totally offensive to like *everyone*—"

"Good morning," I said.

It was a good thing no one's neck snapped, with the sharp way both of them looked over.

Merin's expression hardened. "It's fucking two in the afternoon, Ms. C. Late night?"

"Yep. You?" I didn't gesture to the black eye, but I didn't need to. She looked away.

"Ms. C, if you could talk some sense into Merin, that'd be great."

"Shut up. We aren't even fucking *friends*, okay? Just because I came to your stupid little club, doesn't mean I'm one of you, or that you and I are fucking buddies now."

"Wow, you are insufferable." Sammy stood up. "Listen, I don't think we're friends. I don't even want to be friends with you. I don't know why you showed up yesterday, and I don't care. But we know each other, and you obviously can't go home, and my family's douchey, but they're safe. So if you need a place to crash, you can come over. Hell, they'd probably be thrilled I had a girl over."

Merin hunched more in her chair.

"So whatever. My phone number's on the Journalism intranet site, okay? If you need a place, maybe swallow your pride for half a second, Merin, Jesus. I'm late for work."

"I don't need your help," Merin muttered.

Sammy, with some grace I don't think I had at his age, said, "It's not a big deal to need someone's help. I'll see you around. Bye, Ms. C."

"Bye, Sammy. Have a good one."

His eyes darted to Merin, then back. "Yeah, you too."

I took his seat without asking and started picking at one of the two cinnamon rolls sitting on the table.

"I don't need anyone's help."

"Okay."

She glared at me from under her hood. "I'm serious. Don't fucking humor me like a little kid."

"I get that you're serious."

"You can't stop me if I leave, you know. I have a right to do whatever the fuck I want."

"You have the right to get up right now and walk away from this table, true." But I didn't think that's what she really wanted to do. She hadn't moved, hadn't even unhunched.

"Why did you come here? Did he text you or something?"

"No, Merin. Sammy doesn't know my number."

"So why are you here, then?"

"I know the manager. She gave me a call, said you looked pretty rough."

"She can go fuck herself. I'm fine."

Seventeen. If someone had actually hit her, I needed to report it. If she refused to tell me that someone had hit her, I should probably still report it, but it wasn't like social services had all the time in the world to go around investigating allegations of abuse denied on all sides when the kid in question was almost eighteen.

"What happened to your eye?"

She snorted. "You wouldn't believe me if I told you."

"It might make for an interesting story, though."

"It's not that interesting. Got in a fight with my parents, my dad got all pissy about how I never apply myself to anything, my mom got all pissy about how I dress, Dad did his usual big shouting ultimatum about how I'm supposed to act when I live under his roof and—" She stopped.

For a long moment I just watched her blink, while I waited for the rest.

"I don't know. This time I just didn't care. He means it. He's completely serious when he gets like that, shouting like any minute now he's gonna haul off and crack me. I can feel how much he wants to. But this time I didn't give a shit, so I told him he could go fuck himself and I was leaving." The spacey look didn't leave her eyes. "He kept yelling, and Mom was yelling, both of them so angry I could feel it on my skin. And I walked out. And then I literally fell down my own front steps, and banged my face on the railing."

I didn't know if I believed her or not, but now she met my eyes.

"They always say that, right? Battered women? Abused kids? 'I fell down the stairs.' 'I walked into the wall.' But this time I really did fall down stairs. I guess because I'd never walked out before. We've had that fight a hundred times, and it always ends with me going to my room, putting my headphones in, trying to forget about them. But not last night."

"What was different?" I asked.

"Me. I was different. I'm sick of their shit, and sick of pretending. Sick of them acting like these whiny little brats every time they don't get their way, every time I don't live up to their ridiculous little fantasies of how I was supposed to be. 'You try to act black,' my mom's always saying. 'You try to be all ghetto and it makes me *sick*, it makes me *so sick* when I see my beautiful daughter acting like a n—'" She cut herself off, visibly clenching her jaw and looking away. A minute later her gaze returned to mine, all defiance and challenge. "They're horrible people, Ms. C. I've dreamed about killing them."

I nodded. Couldn't really argue the logic there. "So where did you go when you left your house?"

"Walked. All the way down to Steerage. Tried to get into that club with the stupid name, thinking there were enough people that I'd be able to sneak in, but they caught me and kicked me out."

"My best friend and I snuck in once," I said. "Same thing. We lasted maybe three minutes before Fredi, who owns the place, booted us."

"This was some big, tall blond guy." She shrugged. "He was nice about it, I guess."

Tom, probably. I wondered how she made it past the bouncer. Also, at some point in the near future I'd be seeing former students at Club Fred's. It had happened a few times so far, and was awkward, but the more my students aged up, the more frequently I'd see them out in the world, in the spaces I'd considered "mine" since I was old enough to get into them. I pushed away the knowledge of how old I was and focused on Merin. "What'd you do after you got booted?"

She adopted another deep contemplation of the middle distance. "Nothing. Wandered. Walked out on the pier. Stood there for a long time, until I was so cold I couldn't feel anything at all. Couldn't get warm again after that, and I tried to keep walking, but I was tired. So I found a good place to sit, and tried to sleep a little until morning. Then I don't know. I just kind of wandered, until stupid Sammy saw me and went all 'save the world.'"

I sent a prayer of thanks. "I'm glad you're okay."

"Whatever."

The door to the shop opened, and I looked up. "Hey, Kim."

"Hi there. Coffee?"

"Please. Merin, you want anything?"

"Coffee's disgusting."

"Hot chocolate?" Kim suggested.

Merin grunted, so I nodded at Kim. She smiled and disappeared back into the shop.

"You gonna go home tonight?" I asked.

"Fuck them, Ms. C. I'm not gonna go back there, and apologize, and beg them to let me in. Fuck them."

Impossible choices. I couldn't tell her that I thought she should grovel for the right to stay in a house where she could never really take a deep breath. But where else could she go? "I think Sammy's is actually a good back-up plan."

She grunted again, but didn't argue.

"I know he's got his own problems, but I don't think they'd turn you away. And I don't think anyone would hit you there."

"I *told* you—"

I held up my hand. "I know. But you said you think your dad wants to blow up at you. Sammy's would probably at least be safer than that."

Kim delivered my coffee and Merin's hot chocolate, and both of us thanked her. She told us to let her know if we needed anything.

How often did people say that, every day? And what I really needed was a safe place for this almost-adult to go to where she could wear whatever the hell clothes she wanted and not cower in front of people who were supposed to provide for her even when she was difficult.

Then again, wasn't this what Carlos had been talking about?

I pulled out my phone and called Zane.

"Whaaaaaat? It's too early for phone calls."

"It's two."

"It is *not*."

I laughed. "It really is. I just need a quick favor, then you can go back to bed."

"Damn right. Not that I'm leaving the bed. For anything. Maybe forever."

"Ha-ha. Text me that business card you picked up from Carlos that night. Remember?"

"Oh. The handsome boy with the plan to save the children."

"Exactly. You tagged it under 'queer youth,' I think."

Merin looked up enough to sneer, but I ignored her.

"Hold on." Her vague mumbling grew more distant as she poked through her phone. "Right, got it. Okay, sending now. Good night, Jaqs."

"Good night, kid. Talk to you later."

We hung up.

The attachment came through my email and I recited the numbers on the card to myself until I could remember them long enough to page away from the picture to the dial pad.

I dialed, and waited.

"Hello?"

"Hi there. Is this Josh? I got your business card from a friend of mine, Carlos. He said you were on an interview panel together."

"Sure, I remember Carlos. What can I do for you?" His voice was smooth, and he sounded incredibly self-assured for someone as young as Carlos had said he was.

"Carlos talked up a project he said you were working on. A drop-in center. I was wondering how that was going, and if it's really going to open soon."

"Not soon enough, and yes. We're looking at August. I can answer any questions you have about it. It's called the Queer Youth Project."

I took a breath. Yeah. The Queer Youth Project. That had a good ring to it.

Merin was watching me from under her hood as she sipped hot cocoa, like she was trying to pretend she wasn't.

"I'm a high school teacher. I facilitate the Gay-Straight Alliance, and I occasionally have kids who need resources that are beyond what I can provide them professionally."

"That's exactly what we're hoping to do. Provide additional resources."

"But you aren't open yet. Any advice on resources that exist right now?"

"It depends on the resource. Is this hypothetical, or is someone in a position today where they could use some help?"

"Hold on one minute." I covered the mouthpiece. "Merin, you'll stay with Sammy, right? Before you spend another night on the street?"

She shrugged. "Kind of thinking maybe I can stay with LaTasha. At least for a little while."

She'd said they were neighbors, so maybe that was a realistic plan. I nodded and went back to my phone call. "I've got a couch-surfing seventeen-year-old who could use some guidance."

Merin rolled her eyes.

"Damn. I really wish we were open. This is exactly why we exist." He conferred quietly with someone in the background. "Does your couch-surfer need a job? We have a lot of work to do and a limited time in which to do it."

"I think she already has one, but I'm sure she'd be willing to do another through the summer, if you're paying her."

Now she perked up. "Who is that?"

"Some random guy I've never met who just offered you a job."

"Ew, Ms. C. Don't be a pimp, that's gross."

I threw my napkin at her. "What kind of job?" I asked, because, actually, good point.

"It's definitely *not* sex work." Josh sounded amused. "We have a thousand postcards printed to go out next week proclaiming our open house in the middle of August, and we only picked up the keys to the place on Wednesday. There's a lot to do in the next month and a half."

"I bet there is." Still, now that I was thinking about it, I kind of wanted to be there when they met. "How about we plan a meeting at your location and you can talk to Merin about what you need?"

"That sounds perfect. Can they do Tuesday morning? I think we can get most of the trash hauled out by then."

I kicked her leg. "You free Tuesday morning?"

She stared back at me, and I could almost read her mind. She didn't even know where she'd be tonight, let alone Tuesday. But she wasn't saying she had work, so I decided that was good enough. "We'll be there. Thanks a lot, Josh."

"You're welcome. And give me a call if you need anything between now and then. Pretty much everything La Vista currently has to offer couch-surfing seventeen-year-olds is stored in my brain. Or in my partner's."

"Thank you. I will."

I hung up my phone and set it on the table. Time for more cinnamon roll. And coffee.

Merin shifted in her chair. "Thank you," she mumbled, a little gruffly, like she couldn't believe she was saying it.

"Welcome. What're you doing the rest of the day?"

"Sitting here. I'm supposed to go to work, but I called out. I gotta wait until I know no one's home to pick up my clothes."

I nodded. "Good, then. I could use a hand helping my dad build a shed. Plus, he'll feed us."

"No way, Ms. C. I told you, I don't want fucking charity."

"Who said anything about charity? You're helping build a shed and getting food in trade. That's not charity, Merin, that's working for your bread."

"Whatever." But behind the cup, and beneath the eye-rolling, she seemed relieved.

Good.

Dad, of course, was delighted to have an extra pair of hands.

"I'm glad you're young," he told Merin. "Jaq and I are getting too old to build like this."

I supplied the obvious reply. "Bite your tongue, old man. I'm fine."

He patted Merin's arm. "Listen to that denial. We all do it. When you're in your thirties you'll tell yourself you're still young too."

Merin accepted the banter and didn't talk much, doing whatever Dad asked her to do. She clumsily helped make lunch, and took off the parka, which she'd never done in front of me before.

Bill might have been right. She was binding, though by the lumpiness, it was probably ACE bandages, and the black T-shirt was definitely for men. There was probably no way I could bring it up, at least not right now, but I made a mental note to ask Ed at some point about the progression of the FTM teenager and how best to approach it. Or *if* I should approach it.

Bless Dad, who treated Merin like he treated me, or Zane, or one of my siblings. Just another kid.

The only moment of awkwardness came when he touched a fraying seam on her parka, which she'd thrown over a chair. She snatched it back and immediately put it on.

He held up both hands. "Sorry. If you leave it like that, though, it'll fall apart. Do you want me to mend that bit? It wouldn't take but ten minutes, and I could make it strong enough to last a while longer for you."

I thought she'd say no. She clearly didn't want anyone touching the thing. But, after a second, she relented. "My brother gave it to me. It was pretty messed up already. I tried to, like . . . keep it together, but."

Dad accepted it with reverence and spread it out again on the chair. "I can see that." He traced the duct tape with his fingers. The fraying seam was at the top of one sleeve. Probably not a great place for tape. "Well, I don't think I can make it pretty, but give me a few minutes and I might be able to make it leak less. I bet your entire arm gets wet when it rains, doesn't it?"

She nodded, eyes never leaving her parka.

I backed out of the room when they started working. Dad busting out his tackle box full of sewing stuff, Merin occasionally grunting a response to something he'd said. It felt good, knowing she was safe. Knowing Dad had helped with that.

I pulled out my phone and opened a message to Hannah.

Last night sucked. I'm sorry. She's a friend, not anything else. I saw you, I freaked out, I don't know wtf I was thinking. I'm sorry.

I hit Send before I could lose my nerve, then resolutely put my phone away, vowing not to check it every five seconds. Then I took it out again and set it to ding *and* vibrate on an incoming message. This time I was really not going to check it again until I had reason to. Seriously.

A vow I held to pretty well for the first thirty seconds. After that I only checked like twice every five minutes until Dad gave me a frown, and a significant glance at my phone.

Right. Disapproving dad-face got me every time. I put my phone away completely and went back out to rearrange the last of the shed hardware we'd somewhat disorganized in our roofing frenzy. Only the door was left, which I could do mostly on my own, as long as I didn't mind holding it in place with my foot and screwing it in with my left hand.

I checked my phone after I'd finished with the door. Nothing.

LaTasha called Merin at 5:05. I could tell it was her by the way Merin's voice changed when she answered. "Hey. Fine. No. Uh, Ms. C's dad's. No. You don't have to take care of me."

After that, silence. Dad stuck his head in from the kitchen.

"Always have room for one more," he said quietly.

I nodded, keeping my eyes on Merin.

"Yeah," she said finally, looking up. "Uh, I don't know. Can you drop me somewhere? I'm meeting up with LaTasha."

"Does she want dinner? It's almost ready, and Dad likes having a full table."

Oh man. I fucking *watched* her struggle with that one. Dad had tried to make her feel comfortable, but it probably just made accepting his help more difficult. I recognized how much she wanted to believe that today, at least, was okay. And how much she wanted to burn it down anyway, because the only alternative was frantically grasping at any scrap of feeling good, because she knew it could be stolen away from her at any second. She wanted to stay for dinner, but she didn't want it to be complicated, and she definitely didn't want to feel like she owed us.

She put the phone to her mouth again. "Mr. C wants to know if you want to eat dinner. Uh-uh. Yeah. Yeah? Okay. I'll ask. Uh, she needs to know where we are."

"Is she driving or on the bus?"

"Bus."

"From where? If she's anywhere near the 671, that goes straight up Mooney, and it'll let her off a block over."

"She said get on the 671 and take it up. To where, Ms. C?"

"Spruce. We're on Cedar. You can text her the number."

"You hear all that? Yeah, Spruce. Uh-huh. Okay. Yeah. No, it's cool. Bye." She texted the house number when I gave it to her and slid the phone back into her pocket.

Zane used to eat almost all of her meals at my house when we were younger. Her parents weren't mean or anything, just sort of vaguely neglectful. I thought about telling Merin that, but figured she'd see it as me trying to relate to her and decided against it. "Is she coming right now?"

She nodded, touching the place on her parka where Dad had trimmed away the frayed threads. "It's real nice of your dad to feed us."

"Merin, I have two sisters and a brother. Believe me, Dad misses the days when the house was always full of people."

"Yeah, okay. That's cool."

I wanted to ask her again how she got that black eye. It might have happened the way she said. She'd been upset. She might have tripped. If she hadn't, though, I wanted to do something about it.

But if I asked, she might walk out. Ultimately, it was probably more important that she eat a solid dinner than that I find out if her parents had hit her.

I didn't ask.

CHAPTER 22

I spent the rest of the night morose and self-pitying, at least after I dropped the girls off at LaTasha's.

"You're coming home with me," she'd said to Merin in a voice I wouldn't have bothered trying to argue with. "My folks know your parents are assholes. They aren't going to be surprised if you don't go home for a few days." I could see that Merin wanted to argue that "a few days" wasn't going to cut it, but she didn't.

What she said was, "I should text Sammy. He said I could stay with him if I needed to."

"Sammy's a good guy. I have his number if you want it."

My budding adults looked out for themselves. I should probably follow their lead, if I knew what was the adult thing to do in my particular circumstance.

I checked my phone again. Nothing. Fuck it. I went to the gym.

I didn't usually gym alone. It was always me and Zane, walking in at basically the same time, getting changed in the locker room, waiting for each other before going out to claim machines. Apparently having a gym buddy was a good thing for me; without Zane I felt naked and exposed, like anyone could just . . . walk up to me. And talk. Or demand I talk.

The gym was a bubble. It was my bubble place. I didn't have my headphones, and not for the first time I wished there were some way to indicate what kind of gym person you were so those of us who preferred to pretend no one else was there would be spared the inevitable awkwardness of running into someone who saw the gym as an extension of their social life.

Like the woman on the next elliptical who wanted to tell me all about her boss. Why? Why would you whine to a stranger about your boss? Who does that? Who wants to hear it? Who cares? I tried to keep my face in the range of *bored*, not *totally fucking rude*.

A stray thought floated through my head. Hannah would engage with this woman. Engage with her, and then tell me the story like, *Can you believe people do that? Yammer on at strangers?* She'd be as confounded as I was, but it would amuse her instead of annoying her.

Tuning out my chatty workout neighbor took energy, but I still had enough left over to obsess. Why the fuck had I been dancing like that with Prz? Was I trying to make Hannah jealous? Not really. It hadn't even occurred to me she'd see us. I just wanted to take my mind off Hannah, and Prz was the first person I'd seen, which actually kind of sucked, but that's how it was.

It had been stupid. Like me being pissed at Hannah for missing knitting, which was more about me being pissed at Hannah for going to LA without even telling me and completely forgetting we had plans, as if her life there was more important than her life here. Even though I knew she was trying to wrap things up. Even though I knew it had nothing to do with me.

But maybe that was what hurt more than anything else. She'd been so casually apologetic, her head in her other life, as if it really hadn't registered for her that I was waiting, that I'd planned something. That, okay, I was actually somewhat committed to this thing.

Basically: I'd felt too good, got scared, and overreacted to something dumb. And when she hadn't fallen all over herself trying to convince me I mattered, I'd decided that was as good as a brush-off. Because I was a fucking fool.

Merin stood to lose her parents because she wasn't who they expected, and she'd lose LaTasha in the fall when college started. Her life was full of genuine uncertainties, the kind that meant she accepted spending the occasional night on the street as a matter of course. My uncertainties were either things I'd invented or things I risked without danger, without fear for my safety.

I couldn't justify writing off everything I'd enjoyed with Hannah because I got scared. That was ridiculous.

Chatty Cathy finally trailed off because something on one of the eight or nine nearby televisions caught her eye, and I took the opportunity to escape. I had a plan. It might not be a great plan, and it definitely might crash and burn, but it was a hell of a lot better than doing nothing and checking my phone a thousand times an hour hoping that she'd text.

The grocery store at ten on Saturday night was pretty low-key. I wandered around, in no rush, picking things out almost at random. I wanted strawberries. And heavy cream. And chocolate, though I didn't know what kind to get, so I picked something kind of expensive, figuring that would do. Pasta. A creamy sauce that looked delicious. French bread and butter and garlic. I hesitated over the garlic. But garlic bread was delicious. And this wasn't our first date; if everything went balls-up, it wasn't going to be because of the garlic bread.

I grabbed a sweet potato. A lemon. A fancy brick of cheese and totally not-fancy crackers that I happened to think went well with cheese because the fancy crackers were always too dry. Pimento-stuffed olives. I walked through the aisles without any clear destination, grabbing things that looked good.

At the last second I threw in one of those really pretty, fruity pints of gelato. My single meal of groceries cost more than I usually spent in a week, but even if the whole thing failed, I'd be eating like a fucking queen tonight.

As I walked up to her building, arms overflowing with stuffed cloth grocery bags like a jackass, I told myself that this would be the hardest part. This moment. Waiting to see if she'd let me in. If we could do this thing with one another. If we could be irritated and break bread and forgive.

I told myself that hitting the buzzer was the hardest part. I just needed to hit the buzzer.

And wait.

And contemplate that, in fact, she might not be home.

Or worse: she might be entertaining someone.

She might not even be in La Vista, though obviously that didn't make a whole lot of sense.

She might be—

The speaker crackled to life. "Hello?"

"Uh, it's me. Jaq." My heart was pounding as if this were some kind of potentially fatal interaction. Sweat broke out all down my back.

A full minute passed. "Hey."

"I went shopping. For food. There's cream, but I didn't, uh, whip it yet."

Another endless stretch before I heard the telltale clicking as the door unlatched. "Come in."

Thank god.

The hardest part is walking up the stairs. The hardest part is approaching the door. The hardest part is knocking.

She opened the door and stepped to the side, not speaking. Deep blue again, like her bridesmaid dress. The perfect blue for her, even in a soft cotton shirt over sweats.

I carried everything through to the kitchen.

The hardest part is unpacking groceries in her kitchen when she hasn't even really said hello.

"I got a lot of random shit. I don't know. We can eat, or not eat, or whatever. Unless you've eaten. I ate a few hours ago at my dad's—"

"What are you doing here?"

Shit. I gave up unpacking and turned. "I'm sorry. I was kind of a jerk about the knitting thing, and then last night— Hell, I don't even know."

"Last night, when I thought we were meeting up at a thing you invited me to, then you were macking all over some woman on the dance floor?"

I winced. "Yeah. That."

"What the hell, Jaq? Why did you do that? Why did you come here?"

All good questions. I wanted to find an excuse not to look at her. "I bought gelato. Raspberry. Can I put it in the freezer and then . . . can we sit down?"

"We can sit down. Bring the gelato and a couple of spoons."

The hardest part is not doing a happy dance because she's accepting gelato as a peace offering.

"Okay," I said, totally cool.

She took the pint out of my hand and curled up on one side of the futon, warily surveying me. "What did I do that you were trying so hard to hurt me?"

"I wasn't. I truly wasn't. I wasn't trying to hurt you as much as I was trying to get over you. Which was a douche move in so many ways."

"Ya think, Jaq?"

The casual slang sounded strange from her mouth, slurred "you" becoming a perfectly enunciated "ya."

I leaned forward, hoping I could come clean and that would count for something. "I'm sorry. I didn't mean to hurt you. It's just, I have these issues—"

"If you're about to explain about your abandonment issues, spare me. You're a grown-up. I'm not interested in why your childhood made you dance with some other woman."

"Thanks a lot for your concern, Hannah."

She leveled the spoon at my face. "Fuck you. I thought about you all week. I looked forward to last night. I dressed up. I did my goddamn hair. I sat there thinking you were showing me up, then I finally found you and—" The spoon returned to the gelato. She took one more bite, then put it on the cushion between us. "Did you forget you asked me to come with you?"

"Did you forget how to use your phone?"

"Did you? I texted to ask you how knitting was, to ask how your ex was doing. I figured you must have been tired or something, but then nothing on Thursday, either. So you were pissed at me. Good for you. Sorry if me trying to sell my house made *knitting class* slip my mind."

"It wasn't like that," I muttered.

"It was, actually. It was exactly like that."

"You didn't even tell me you were going to LA! I had no idea. I stood here, buzzing your apartment like an idiot, and you were eight hours away."

"Six hours, please. You'd have to drive like a little old lady to take eight."

I sat back. "It felt like you took off, like it was nothing. Sunday . . . meant something to me, okay? I started thinking maybe it meant something to you too. That this was more than we hooked up at a wedding and didn't know when to quit."

"So why did you act like a bitchy little baby?" She started to reach for the gelato again, then stopped. "I don't get you, Jaq. Sunday meant something to me too. I don't introduce just anyone to my lovey, you know. I don't go out to coffee with people's fathers for the hell of it. It has to mean something. And it did. Then I committed the apparently cardinal sin of forgetting about knitting class—"

"Stop fucking saying it like that. It had nothing to do with knitting. You forgot *me*." God, it sounded so bald and needy when I said it like that, but I forced myself to keep going. "It didn't occur to you to call, to send me a text? When you were waiting for your flight, maybe? When you were making reservations? On Sunday you were here, with me, and everything was good. Then somehow, poof. You disappeared without a word."

"I went to LA. To sell my house. I've been down there almost every week since I moved, Jaq. It's not out of the ordinary. And no, I was on my phone straight through the cab ride to the airport, checking in, and I barely took a break to get through security. I had to hit it onto airplane mode while Sandy was still talking because I couldn't get her to shut up."

I bit down on a smile. "Don't lie. You liked doing that."

"Maybe a little. She just . . . *processes*. She had some kind of breakthrough in therapy about holding on to the past, symbolized by the house, blah blah blah. God, who cares? But you have to let her yammer all the way through or she'll call again tomorrow and start at the beginning."

"Seriously? I can't believe you were together so long."

"I guess I used to find it kind of fascinating, the way her mind worked, the way her entire thought process was revealed by her constant talking. Then I tuned it out for a long time." She shook her head. "And if I'm being exceptionally honest, it's kind of a relief, that we can do that again. That I can be the person who listens to her endless blabbering again. After seven years, and breaking up horribly, and hating each other for a little while—I actually missed it. Can you imagine? One of the things that most made me want to kill her when we were together, and I missed it."

"I think I get that. I mean, especially if it was constant. If it was a hallmark of your relationship, of being with her. Makes sense that you'd miss something like that. I don't think I've ever been with anyone long enough to get used to them, really. Except Zane and Carlos, who don't count."

She sighed and stretched her legs until her toes brushed my thigh. "I can't do more drama. I did nothing but drama for a long time, Jaq. We had ridiculous shouting matches, usually at home, but every now and then we'd have them at the restaurant where she was working, or on the street. Stupid stuff would blow up and then we'd be in each other's faces again. And I told myself that was relationships. That people have to be able to fight, to disagree. But it was as if the only way we could disagree was to make everything into some kind of global conference on nuclear proliferation. Every stupid thing potentially caused the end of the world. I think that's why I cheated on her. I had to see if something finally *would* end the world. The most extreme thing I could think of."

"I guess it worked," I offered, feeling a little naive. We were the same age, but that kind of commitment took practice I'd never had and wasn't sure I was ready for.

"Not really. But it did end the marriage, and until then I didn't realize they weren't the same thing. We meant it, you know. Our vows. We thought we'd be together until we died." She glanced out the window. "I can't do more drama. I can't do more 'till death do we part,' Jaq. Maybe someday, down the line, I'll be able to go there in my head again. But right now? I want simple pleasures. Strawberries. Sex. Coffee. Looking out at the view from this window. Possibly while having sex and brewing coffee."

"Couldn't fit the strawberries in, huh?"

"Oh, there are a lot of places I could fit strawberries in that picture."

I flushed, a phantom berry dragging along my inner thigh, my belly.

Hannah smiled, like she knew. "I was having fun at the club last night, talking to people, buying drinks for randoms. It was good. I could get used to hanging out there, with you. No drama. No big declarations. Just us, enjoying each other's company without needing it to be the most important thing in the world."

"I want to be your girlfriend," I said, and held my breath.

She raised her eyebrows at me. "Shit, sugar, I thought you already were."

"I thought you were looking for casual. Isn't that what you're saying?"

"Casual? I don't know. I don't think that's what I want. I think it's more—" Her toes began to massage my leg. "There must be a line between casual and marriage. I want something in the middle of all that. I want to know I can fuck you with my lovey whenever we want, and no one's getting in the way."

I shivered, because yeah. "I want to know when you're getting on an airplane before it happens. I want to give you a ride to the airport and kiss you good-bye, okay?"

"In my defense, everything happened fast."

"Next time at least call me."

"I will. And I'm still intrigued by knitting. Mostly because I'm all for any excuse to buy those knitting needles. I can think of some fun alternative uses for them. But Jaq, if you're pissed at me, tell me. Don't go off and make out with a woman at a bar to get back at me, okay?"

"I wasn't making out with Prz. I'll introduce you to her when you let me drag you to roller derby. I just . . . I thought I'd gone to fantasyland and made up the whole idea you might be interested in me for more than sex. I was punishing myself, if anyone."

"So you didn't know I was there?"

I considered lying. For a second. "I saw you at the bar."

"Jesus, Jaq. Why the hell didn't you say something?"

"Because I was stupid. Because— I don't know. Because I thought if I walked up to you I'd see how I'd made it all up, that I'd take one look at your face and see I meant nothing to you. I didn't want to see that."

"I was there to see you. Of course you mean something to me." She shook her head. "Listen, I can't deal with stunts. I did that before, and I'm not doing it again."

"Me neither. That's not what I want."

"What do you want?"

The hardest part is telling her what you want when there's nowhere to hide.

"I want you. I like that you don't expect me to have hard edges for you. You don't expect me to take charge. I can be softer. I can—I can yield with you, and it's effortless. I've never had that with anyone, and it's exhilarating, but it scares me too. That you'll get tired of me. That you'll decide I'm not enough for you."

"Why would I do that? Honey, I love that you yield. There's nothing as gorgeous as a beautiful woman giving herself up to my hands, my mouth. And I'm not a one-trick pony, you know. I can yield too."

I knew that. I'd seen it here and there, in flashes; I'd heard it in the spaces between her words. "I want more time with you. I want us to get to know each other slowly, without pressure. Not move in together tomorrow and learn one another all at once."

"You want to ease into it," she said. "I can do that, Jaq. That sounds wonderful."

"Good."

Her toes dug in to my thigh more insistently. "Yes. Good. If you aren't going to eat that gelato, we should put it in the freezer."

I picked it up. "Is it all right? I got it because it looked fancy."

"It tastes plenty fancy. I already ate dinner, you know. It's like eleven o'clock at night."

"Yeah. I think I just needed an excuse. To come over."

"Or you could have called and professed your deepest apologies and your willingness to do whatever it takes to make it up to me." Her eyes glittered with challenge.

"Whatever it takes, huh?"

"I think it's important we're both clear on the terms of abject apology."

"Which are what?"

"I get to do whatever I want to you."

"For how long?"

She smiled, slowly, not one of her glowing all-for-me smiles, but a more subtle, serpentine twist of her lips. "Well. Obviously I'd have to let you get *some* sleep, since we have church in the morning."

What else could I do?

"I apologize abjectly, Hannah." I slid to my knees. "Your wish is my command."

"Exactly what I want to hear. Give me the melting gelato. I have some ideas for it."

It was warm enough to be naked in the condo, but the gelato was still cold. I shivered as she laid down ribbons of it over my skin, and I moaned when she licked them up.

If every apology felt like this, I might have to be bad more often.

CHAPTER 23

Friday's meeting of the summer GSA started with an entirely different kind of apology.

"Anyway, sorry for being a dick. It's kind of my personality." Merin, who'd managed to take a seat in the circle this time, waved a hand. "Like, I'll be a dick again, so this isn't so much me saying I'll stop, as it is me saying you shouldn't take it personally."

Sammy rolled his eyes. "I can't imagine what she sees in you."

"Shut it, sparkle fairy."

The insult—or maybe it was a nickname now?—made him smile.

I cleared my throat. "We can get to check-in in a minute, but I thought you guys might be interested in the new drop-in center Merin's going to tell you about."

To my surprise, she didn't fight me on it. "Yeah, it's gonna be pretty cool once they clean the place up and get fans in there so it smells less like piss and homeless guys."

"What drop-in center?" Callie asked. "For kids?"

"Huh-uh." Merin kicked her legs out in front of her. "For teenagers up through like twenty-five. Listen, these two dudes—who are *totally* fucking—are starting this whole thing up down on the east side. They got this huge warehouse that they're gonna clean up and make into the kind of place you can go during the day, you know, if you have nowhere else, or even if you're just hungry or something."

Sometime in the middle of Merin's impassioned description (LaTasha was at work; was it possible she spoke more in LaTasha's absence, without the safety net of her excuses?), Bill elbowed me, gently, in the side.

I glanced over and he nodded, not taking his eyes off Merin, who was now talking about plans for a self-serve kitchen at the drop-in center, where people could cook their own food and maybe even have cooking classes.

Yeah. This was good. It wasn't a solution to the world's problems. It wasn't a solution to Merin's screwed-up relationship with her parents, or her potentially screwed-up relationship with herself, but it was definitely something. She'd taken a job with the two young men, Josh and Keith, almost immediately, bashfully accepting their offer of "low wages, not enough hours, but lots of pizza." As luck, or La Vista, would have it, I'd already met Keith, who'd served Hannah and me at the diner. He blushed when I said, "Oh, we've met," and Josh's heated look in his direction definitely confirmed Carlos's theory that they were more than business partners.

Merin had been interested in all of it. The more they'd shown her around, explained their ideas, the more she'd lit up, until she actually pushed her hood back so she could see everything.

For months she'd hidden how afraid she was under the guise of being afraid for someone else. Only now, after seeing her so engaged, did I realize that it had probably been years since she'd allowed herself to be this interested in, or excited about, something.

I'm right there with you, kid.

The meeting moved on. I tried to stay focused and not think too hard about seeing Hannah later. My girlfriend. Who was taking me to dinner but promised dessert back at her place.

I halfway hoped *I* would be dessert. Which I definitely had to stop thinking about in front of the kids, who'd mock me forever if I started blushing.

CHAPTER 24

She took me to the San Marcos Grill, and I bought us a nightcap at their bar after dinner, where we sat in the window, overlooking the Bay, all black and inky with San Francisco in the distance.

"So," she said.

"Uh-huh?"

I swiveled on my stool, the better to see the low cut of her top, the swell of her breasts. And she crossed her ankles, which turned me on even when she was wearing slacks.

She snapped in my face. "Up here, hot stuff."

"Er. Yes. Sorry. I was . . . getting ahead of us."

"Can't have that." Hannah leaned in, close enough to kiss, one eyebrow raised. "I have a proposition for you."

I tried valiantly not to tremble. "Yes?"

"Are you acquiescing to my request without even hearing it? My, Jaq, you *do* trust me."

"Shut up. I meant . . . yes? What? What proposition?"

She pouted. "I have the power to reward you handsomely for going along with it, Jaq." One hand tugged my tie. "I can make it worth your while. I promise." The word dragged just enough at the end, a sibilant undercurrent of sex.

"Uhh, what—what am I agreeing to?"

"I'm so glad you're feeling positively." She reeled me in me closer, but she still didn't kiss me.

"Did you have something to ask me? A proposition?"

She smiled. "Yes. Are you ready? Practice your response first. Say 'Yes, Hannah, whatever you want, I'll do.'"

"See, that feels like you're leading the witness there, counselor."

"'Yes, Hannah, whatever you want, I'll do.'"

I pretended a put-upon sigh. "Yes, Hannah, whatever you want, I'll do. That's not legally binding, right?"

"I'm so glad you said yes. I'm buying you a new suit, by the way."

"I like my old suit. Wait, what do you mean? For what? What did I just agree to?"

Now she kissed me, hard. "You're officially my date to Sandy's wedding."

I blinked. "Wait, *what*?"

"I'm serious. Her wedding. She texted me last night."

"Her wedding to the twenty-year-old?"

Hannah shrugged. "They're in love."

"So wait—she had a breakthrough in therapy last week, sold the house, let go of the past, and now she's getting married?"

"Well, next month. Wouldn't want to be uncouth."

I shook my head. "That's crazy. Are you okay with it? And, like, I kind of can't believe she invited you."

"Oh, that's entirely Sandy. She probably expects me to show up stag, looking like I'm putting a brave face on heartbreak. She doesn't know about you, yet."

"You know what this means, don't you?"

Her fist tightened, drawing my lips to hers. We kissed until we were breathless, and it felt like a celebration, even though I didn't know exactly why.

"What does it mean, Jaq? Tell me what it all means."

I ran my fingertips into the hair at the nape of her neck. "It means we'll have to dance all night. Inappropriately. Scandalously. To make sure it's clear you aren't putting a brave face on anything."

"I'm trying to leave my dramatic days behind me, though."

I kissed her, nipping at her lower lip. "One more time. With me. Show me all the drama at your ex's wedding."

"You are a dirty, dirty girl. So rude. I may have to give you a stern talking-to later, missy."

"I look forward to it. As long as it doesn't get in the way of dessert."

"Oh, it won't."

Another wedding. Hannah on my arm—or maybe it would be me on hers, in a shiny new suit. We drew out our drinks, kissing, pushing the limits of how far a couple should go in public. But it didn't matter.

Nothing mattered except this moment, her hand on my arm, the scent of her skin in my nostrils, the taste of her on my lips. I kissed her again.

She whispered, "Pay our tab, sugar. I have plans for you."

I paid our tab and let her lead me home.

Explore more of the *Queers of La Vista* series:
riptidepublishing.com/titles/universe/queers-la-vista

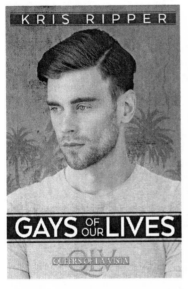

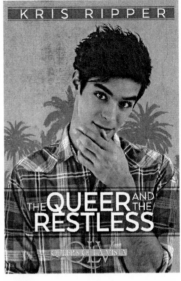

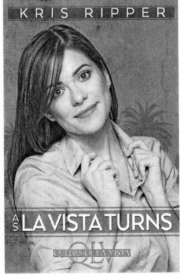

Dear Reader,

Thank you for reading Kris Ripper's *The Butch and the Beautiful*!

We know your time is precious and you have many, many entertainment options, so it means a lot that you've chosen to spend your time reading. We really hope you enjoyed it.

We'd be honored if you'd consider posting a review—good or bad—on sites like **Amazon, Barnes & Noble, Kobo, Goodreads, Twitter, Facebook, Tumblr,** and your blog or website. We'd also be honored if you told your friends and family about this book. Word of mouth is a book's lifeblood!

For more information on upcoming releases, author interviews, blog tours, contests, giveaways, and more, please sign up for our weekly, spam-free newsletter and visit us around the web:

Newsletter: tinyurl.com/RiptideSignup
Twitter: twitter.com/RiptideBooks
Facebook: facebook.com/RiptidePublishing
Goodreads: tinyurl.com/RiptideOnGoodreads
Tumblr: riptidepublishing.tumblr.com

Thank you so much for Reading the Rainbow!

RiptidePublishing.com

ACKNOWLEDGMENTS

My grateful thanks, as always, to General Wendy, who delightedly referred to this book as a "hot mess romp"—exactly what I was going for!

Anna Main took a spin through this puppy after a panicked shout-out on Twitter, and gets a gold star for finding an inconsistency I'd missed.

And a special shout-out to all the teachers out there trying to support their kids in any way they can while still holding boundaries and navigating the incredibly difficult relationship between "offering reasonable assistance" and "becoming overinvolved." Teachers were often my lifeline as a kid who didn't have a hell of a lot of support at home, and I will be forever thankful for the steady, trustworthy adults who gently nudged in the right direction.

ALSO BY
KRIS RIPPER

For a complete book list, visit: krisripper.com

ABOUT THE

AUTHOR

Kris Ripper lives in the great state of California and hails from the San Francisco Bay Area. Kris shares a converted garage with a toddler, can do two pull-ups in a row, and can write backwards. (No, really.) Kris is genderqueer and prefers the z-based pronouns because they're freaking sweet. Ze has been writing fiction since ze learned how to write, and boring zir stuffed animals with stories long before that.

Website: krisripper.com
Newsletter: krisripper.com/about/subscribe-what
Facebook: facebook.com/kris.ripper
Twitter: twitter.com/SmutTasticKris
YouTube: youtube.com/user/KrisRipper

Enjoy more stories like
The Butch and the Beautiful
at RiptidePublishing.com!

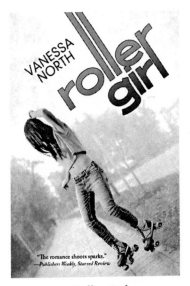

Roller Girl
ISBN: 978-1-62649-418-3

Stuck Landing
ISBN: 978-1-62649-329-2

Earn Bonus Bucks!

Earn 1 Bonus Buck for each dollar you spend. Find out how at
RiptidePublishing.com/news/bonus-bucks.

Win Free Ebooks for a Year!

Pre-order coming soon titles directly through our site and you'll
receive one entry into a drawing for a chance to win free books for
a year! Get the details at RiptidePublishing.com/contests.

CPSIA information can be obtained at www.ICGtesting.com
Printed in the USA
LVOW11s1817101016

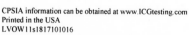

9 781626 494367